THE DEVIL WHO LOVES ME

A Grendel Press Anthology

Edited by Susan Russell

GRENDEL PRESS

ISBN: 978-1-960534-01-9 (Paperback)

Cover art by Susan Russell
Story art by Dany Rivera
Edited and typeset by Susan Russell
Proofread by Rachael Swanson & Kasey Kubica

Contributors:
"Long Black Veil" by January Bain
"Dorian" by Johnathon Heart
"Soul of My Soul" by Antony Paschos
"First I Was Afraid, I Was Petrified" by Rajiv Moté
"Move Fast and Break Things" by Kit Walker
"Old Awakenings" by Alex Fox
"Weight" by Brett Venter
"Just Desserts" by Charlotte H. Lee
"What Lies Under the Candlelight" by Mia Ram
"Changing of the Guard" by Liam Hogan
"The Golden Locket" by Roger Landes
"Shades of Dorian" by Kevin Folliard
"The Promise" by E.J Dawson
"Death in the Highlands" by Melrose Dowdy

CONTENTS

About This Anthology

The Devil Who Loves Me

Within these pages, we unearth stories that challenge conventional notions of good and evil. This anthology delves into the haunting beauty of forbidden unions, improbable affections, and unconventional desires. It invites us to question the boundaries of our own hearts and the nature of love itself... sometimes in ways unexpected.

OLD AWAKENINGS

BY ALEX FOX

I enter the musty stone tower to greet the poor sinner. The poor sinner I will kill three days hence. The chained witch sits within the iron cell of the tower, the sun from the thin-slatted windows falling across his face. The witch does not look like a witch. Nay, for he is a young man, lithe and fine-boned with hair dark as a raven's wing.

He doesn't speak, just looks at me with those amber eyes, lighter than gold they are, and always watching.

"Why do you look at me so, witch?" I say.

He says naught. He just smiles and shrugs.

"I said, why do you look at me so."

The small folk of our hamlet would rather be caught dead than making eyes at a headsman, but this witch, he smirks and watches me, happy as a hen in shite. "I've not had much company over the last few weeks."

I snort. "Aye, most folk wouldn't bandy words with a witch, that's so."

"I'm no witch," he says, the smirk gone from his face. He shifts so he is half-hid in the shadows, the chains about his wrists clinking as he moves.

"You've been tried by ten God-fearing men." Though truth be told, I've never seen a man-witch before, and he bears little resemblance to the crones I've burned in my day.

He shakes his head. "They don't know their arses from their heads."

"They say you were taken by an illness, sputtering water from the murk, white as a ghost, and talking to the wind."

"Aye, ill I was. I helped another, a young wanderer, and fell ill. But I'm not now."

"And what of the wind?"

When he smirks, it's like the fear leaves his face, and he is a man anew. A stranger. "The wind speaks to all who listen. To all who respect the old ones. The ones who were here before Christ came unto this land."

I snort. "Heathenry, then."

He shakes his head. "Nay, sir. To *all* who listen. I can see it in your face—you are of old Saxon stock. Tell me, do you ever hear the lilt of the crow and wonder why it's calling to you? The murmur of the wind through the rushes?"

Suddenly, the dank of the cells and the smell of slops and sweat is gone, and I'm standing amidst the rushes out in the fens, where the cold, briny wind blows in off the coast and the crows circle high overhead. A place from my childhood. And the witch, he's standing with me like there are no bars between us.

"Devilry," I say, but I linger all the same. I close my eyes and breathe deeply. When I open them, I am back in the cells. The witch's arms dangle 'twixt the bars, and he grins at me. It is dark beyond the thin-slatted windows, and I wonder where the time has gone.

I step away. "I'll not be burned alongside you, I won't now. The Lord is my shepherd; I shall not want. And you." I pause, looking him over. "You will burn."

When I leave, I can still feel his eyes on me, even as I follow the muddied streets to the town's outskirts where I live. An old woman averts her gaze as I pass. She spits at my feet and hurries on.

The small townsfolk treat us headsmen like vermin, like things unclean, yet it is we who must contend with the filth of the streets. It is we who drive the sword through the arsonists, through the highwaymen. It is we who burn the witches. Without us, the good law would be run amok, for men are animals, untamed as wolves.

Only when I stand upon that platform do the small folk see me for what I truly am. It is then when I have the power. It is then when I wield the blade, torch, or rope. It is then when I deliver God's will.

And this witch, he will be burned clean.

I can't get the witch out of my head; that proud lad smirking at me, his eyes catching the light. He's a witch all right, he's a devil that one, and glad I will be when the fire catches. I sharpen my blade though I won't be needing her; I sharpen her to clear my thoughts, but my thoughts, they do not clear.

I must see him. I've not slept a wink, my eyes heavy and haggard, and brewing within me is a rage not to be quelled. This damned witch has me by the haunch. If I had an ounce of fire in my blood, I'd be cutting his tongue out today, but I am a man of the law.

I burst into the tower. Empty save for he and I. He stares at the floor, his face half-turned.

"You're putting thoughts in my head," I say. I seize the bars of the cell. "Stop this devilry at once."

Still, he does not look my way. Is he punishing me, I wonder? Where are those eyes, those eyes that haunt my dreams, those eyes I saw in the crow that followed me this morning?

"Look at me."

The witch looks up. 'Tis the first time I've seen him without that devilish glint in his eye, and he does not look like a witch, but a man. "I cannot do such things, headsman."

"Then why do I think of you so?" My grip tightens on the bar, trying to kindle the fire within, but when his eyes meet mine, 'tis like my will leaves me, and there are none in this world but he and I.

"Perhaps it's something more wholly made." He rises, and his chains clink. "And you mean to burn me on the morrow."

"If you've made your peace w' God, you should not be afeared."

"I do not wish to burn."

'Tis something a witch would say, all right. "A witch *must* burn. 'Tis the only way to cleanse the land of their spirit."

"But I am no witch," he says. He leans against the bars. Shadows pool along his face. "You must believe me, headsman. I'd not ask you to break me from these chains. But do not burn me."

I can smell him, the smell of the fens after the rain. In his eyes I see the sunlight as it winks upon the water, dazzling and cold. "You're a witch." Though I say those words, it does not fill me with the hatred of the old book.

"Nay. Just a man who can speak to the land, who knows what makes it so. What makes you." His voice grows softer, and I crane my head toward him to listen. We are so close, I can nearly feel his warm breath on my face, and it smells like the briny wind. "That don't make me a witch." His voice pitches. "Do not burn me."

My voice is softer now, as though the thing between us is a rabbit I mustn't startle. "Why do you do it, then? Knowing well what folk'll think."

"Every day, the world grows more forgotten. The fens, the birds, what rides your blood same as my own." He sighs. He runs a hand through his lank hair. His eyes look troubled, and it troubles me. "Is it wrong to have an ear to listen? To awaken others to the magic of the land?"

I grow quiet. Long have I believed the land to be speaking to me, in tongues I cannot form with my own lips, and is he so different from I? And if God made this land, then is it not He who is speaking to me, to us all?

His gaze holds that fell gleam once more. A small smile plays upon his lips. "You hear it too, do you not?"

The crows squabble above me on the long walk home. They call to me as did the witch himself. O, why do I not fear the fire? Why do I not fear him? Ought a man be afeared of what he cannot understand, is that all a witch is? I feel soft as a snail without its shell when he looks upon me. Can I truly let the fire take him?

My father and I sit at the stained oak table. He's an older man now, yet still with enough strength to wrangle swine. Law books are spread before us, though I've not read a line all night.

"Is there ever a reason not to burn a witch?" I ask.

He looks up sharply. "Why do you ask such a thing?"

"The witch, there's something about him. I don't know. He's from the fens, same as I."

My father's eyes narrow. He never did spend much time in the fens. Nay, he was out on appointment most of my young life, until eventually, he moved me and my mother and my sisters to this sorry hovel. "There's a great deal of witchcraft in the fens."

"Aye. And there's something strange about him, this man. Though I know not if he's a witch proper or something else."

"He is a witch." My father is standing now. He places one hand on the table, his jaw working, staring at me like I'm a two-headed idiot.

"Yes, he is a witch," I say softly.

"And you ask to change his sentence?"

I shake my head. Since my sixteenth summer, I've been taller than my father by a head, but before him, I am a boy again, ready for the lash. "No, Father. I was just—"

"You were just what?" The wrath of God Himself rises in his humble breast, and I know this, for he seems to swell in size. His chest puffs, his eyes go dark, and the fire in the hearth seems to shrink back into itself. "You pity a witch!" My father slams his fist on the table, his dark expression never changing. "What's gotten in you, fool? Are you having second thoughts about tomorrow?"

"No, Father," I plead. "I will be ready, as I always am." I've burned countless witches. Their names and faces I can no longer conjure. Though none of them had eyes like the witch in the cells.

My father backhands me so hard blood spews from my mouth and patterns the wall.

"You better be ready. For if not him, then you will burn, Egon."

As I sit in bed, I read from the Bible, but I don't really read. It's open on my lap, and I trace its pages in the candlelight. I try to conjure the fire in my head, I try to see the witch burn, but he does not burn, he wafts through the air light as a feather. My father will see him burn, the villagers will run me through with stave and spear if he does not. No, I must burn him. I must. I slam the Bible closed.

The day to burn the witch has come. Out in the small town center, the platform is ready, the alder boughs tall and framed against the cross. I pace nervously at its base, and my father watches at the fringe of the growing crowd.

Three men lead the witch up the platform stairs and tether him to the cross. He wears fresh linen from the church, his dark hair falling across his face. He does not strain nor struggle. Just stands there, watching me, as he always does.

I inhale slowly. I know the words, but still, my voice shakes: "This man, Alaric Bentham, has been found guilty of witchcraft. The punishment is death by fire." I look out at the crowd hanging on my every word. It's when they come alive, you see. It's when I come alive. I am the hawk and these folk are the fledglings, and the witch before me, he is the mouse... and these folk are restless and waiting to feed.

"Have you made peace with God?" I turn towards the witch, my eyes checking his for a lie.

He stares at me through his dark, lank hair. "I've none to make."

I lean closer. His arms are splayed against the cross, bound there. If only a little closer and I might feel his breath, I might...

"Have you truly made your peace, now?"

His gaze remains unbroken with mine. "Thou shalt not burn me, Egon." A wind stirs his hair, and it smells like his breath, or does his breath smell of the wind?

I draw myself away, composing myself. Never before was I a man in need of composing. I nod at the men below the platform. They light the base of the boughs. Roosting crows stream from the rooftops and circle overhead. I can hear them, I can hear my name amongst their garbled calls, I can hear their pleas.

The witch's gaze is bright as pinesap through the growing smoke. He strains against his bonds. The flames lick across his feet. His mouth contorts.

"I knoweth what is in your heart, headsman. Spare me the fire. Mercy, please. Mercy." His voice is barely a whisper above the crackling of wood. He's whimpering now, his handsome face sheened in sweat. This man is no witch, or perhaps I am not afeared of him if so, I know not. In that moment, all I know is I cannot bear to see him burn. I draw my blade and with a flourish, I leap and sweep it forward. It's a dangerous cut, not a proper cut; no man alive would want to make a cut like that on a standing man, but I did it for him, and I did it well.

The crowd gasps. Blood spurts from the stump of his neck, and Alaric's head rolls to my feet. Even in death, his eyes still watch me.

I stumble back just as the rest of the body catches with the boughs. The people are angered, they're afeared, and why wouldn't they be? If a witch is not burned, they will linger, and maybe I wanted that. Maybe I wanted what was right for me, not for God, not for these people who treat me like shite beneath their shoes. They're throwing things now. My father, he's redder than a beet, spittle flying. I leap from the platform.

"Egon!" he thunders. "Thou hath shamed me, boy. Shamed us all."

I hurry through the closing crowd, my hood pulled up, holding the smell of burnt flesh and wood near, but I can still smell him as he lived; the smell of the fens after a rain. He must be a witch, for even in death he has me beneath a spell, and I wonder what that makes me.

That night I bed down beneath some stranger's hay, for my father will surely arrest me if he sees my face again. I realize I haven't slept since I've become acquainted with Alaric, the witch who is now headless and dead. I think of him, of what he might've felt like, and if ever it could have been any different. It's hot in the barn and I'm stripped down to my breeches, and I rise and look out into the night. The moon squats huge at the edge of the lane, and I am compelled to follow. I move into the tall grasses and follow the game trail. The moon is risen now, filtering silver through the stunted glade. I can smell the fens. I can smell him, and I can sense his closeness.

I should be afeared, but I am not. The child within my breast is coming alive as I walk through the rushes.

Alaric stands naked in the reeds, his head atop his neck, as he always was. I pause just before the water's edge.

"You did not burn me," he says, and there's a smile in his eyes. O, those eyes that made me forget Sunday's sermons, my father's lash and his fists of fury.

"No," I say. "I did not wish to see you burn."

He watches me. He extends his hand, his eyes flashing even though 'tis dark and shadowed here and how I wish to touch him, to feel him. His hand finds mine, and he leans in. Our lips meet, and for a moment, I am both joyed and shamed. And then I am choking, sputtering, and his grip slackens, but within my throat is a thing pulsing, alive, wriggling like an eel. I fall to my knees, clawing at my neck, the murky waters soaking my breeches. I retch, eyes straining for a glimpse of the man who has haunted me so. Where has he gone, this witch of mine? Was he all a thing imagined? I try to rise but fall back to my knees.

"You must use fire to kill a witch," his voice escapes my lips. Upon the waters stirs my broken reflection. My eyes widen, and though 'tis only beneath the light of the moon, I can see their golden hue. No, no, my eyes are blue, blue as cornflower my mother did say, but here they look like honey. They look like his.

I can hear him laughing. Down past the reeds is something floating, barbed and bristling in the moonlight. I rise and stagger towards it. A bloated head, *his* head, and a cluster of crows riding it like driftwood. Fear taints my mouth, and I wish to run, but I have naught to run to.

"Do not fight it, Egon," his voice again, coming from my mouth. *"We are together."*

"I do not want this," I cry. "I do not!"

"I care not for your wants," he says, his voice now my own. I try to speak, to fight him, but with each struggle, his grip grows tighter about me until I can no longer find *me* amidst *him*.

I—*we*—rise. I do not know who I am, what I am. I am not a witch, I am not. But I can hear the wind, and it calls to me, whispering through the rushes, and it tells me I must find another. I must waken another to the wind, to the old ways of the land.

About the Author

Alex Fox hails from the wintry Northeast, USA. She has words in Podcastle, Hungry Shadow Press, Martian Magazine, Apex's Strange Libations, and Grendel Press. You can find her on Twitter @afoxwrites and maybe one day atafoxwrites.com.

DANY COMICS

WEIGHT

BY BRETT VENTER

*I*rwin.

Decades-old fragments of memory, dusty with misuse, peppered the front of the soldier's mind. *How many years since Irwin?*

The warrior's ragged outline dragged a lengthening shadow, his sword hand clenched on the ancient hilt. A silvered edge droned through afternoon's premature end, as flat and grey as its wielder's unfocused eyes.

A lifetime, perhaps two, since Irwin's end, pinned to the wall of his cottage. His passage devastated the village. Irwin's betrothed died by her own hand. Irwin's parents retired, broken, to a place without memories. He no longer remembered the stranger's appearance. The mage who struck the killing blow. Only the peculiar rasp of the mage's voice. That he remembered. That recollected inflection still summoned the anger of his gods.

The blade ate his anger. Endlessly. As greedy as it was in the first days. When he'd had an inexhaustible supply. Now, his reserves dwindled. All that remained was the sword, weighing heavier with each life. Only death and his thankless quest. Greying lashes brushed seamed cheeks, his eyes fluttering as he cast back in search of answers. Did he ever... avenge Irwin? Was that still his purpose? Was that why so many died at his hand?

He shrugged a tortured shoulder socket, hefting his weapon. What if he'd been the one to pour Irwin's life out on the ground? Did the mage even exist?

Rumination carried him blindly within sight of a crenelated tower in silhouette, vertical shadow stark against faded red that blended to vibrant orange. Sleep threatened him. The venerable fighter occupied his body once more and sought shelter.

A clump of bushes near the side of the road concealed a shallow cave. The crevice beckoned. He hollowed a space in the dust. Then, rising with a creaking sigh, the nameless man gathered enough twigs and branches for warmth. Soon a stack of fuel waited, the flame provided by a stick of flint sparked off the weapon's thirsty edge.

Later, the old warrior reclined against the cold cave wall, fading embers reflecting off the pitted sword half-buried in the sand. The worn pommel and hilt vibrated. The shining strip of steel dislodged grains of sand in a slow, repeating pattern.

Tired eyes regarded the sword's burial in the darkness with hope, hatred, and worry. The aged fighter's hand hovered around the sweat-stained leather grip. Still-healing cuts crisscrossed his sword hand, a deeper gash in his left palm weeping clear fluid from a makeshift bandage. His chest quivered, misting the air with apprentice frost. The wind howled, rattling naked branches in a drumbeat of death.

Warmth spread through the confines of the cave, the sunken hollow sheltered by rubbery bushes that cut off most of the gale. Heat reached into his tired chest, shuttering his red-rimmed eyes closed. His breath deepened. Blood broke over the knuckles in his right hand, convulsed in a death grip on the sword. The front third of the blade sank into the earth. The warrior edged his way into sleep, called by slain voices from the past.

His slumber was coated in the poison of sweat and terror. His turmoil, unlike that first night, was confined to his mind. His body remained where it lay, breathing steadily. The maelstrom raged inside.

Breath hit his chest like an ocean wave. The rise and fall of his ribs brought no pain. His limbs were unmarked by decades of battle. Marvelling at his hands, free from knots and arthritic spasms, he was jolted from his reverie by the thud of running feet. Whirling, his hand travelling reflexively to a sword that wasn't there, he was slammed into the ground by a warm, soft body.

"Come on, Irwin is almost here!" she called.

Attempting to recover the breath liberated by his impact against the turf, he thought,

Irwin...?

The young woman squirmed in his arms. His mind tried to place her name, but it flitted out of reach. His hands mindlessly coiled and linked around her waist, cradling living warmth on his chest. Still, the name avoided his attention.

The pale woman turned, eyes closed. He was blessed with the barest touch of her lips before the world revolved into noise and darkness, a realm filled with rain, blood, and violence. The warrior stood in a field surrounded by trees, eyesight blurred by moisture. The skies fell, but what clouded his vision was warmer and stickier than rainwater.

He attempted to clear the muck, but only his left hand remained free. Smearing clotted waste from his brow, the warrior jerked his trapped arm.

A face hung close to his own, a despairing grin carved across the chalky features. Black blood dripped from the familiar visage's lower lip. His hand was buried inside the apparition's viscera. His blade was so deep that only the pommel remained free from gore. The cross-guard wedged into the stricken man's organs. A quick pull would seal his fate.

Feeling nothing but emptiness, he dragged backwards, staring into the grimace. The eyes flickered and dulled. The drawn-out word cascaded from a groan to a dying gurgle.

"Irrrrwiinnnn..."

The warrior stared at the corpse propped up by the sword buried in its guts, trying to recall Irwin's face, who he really was. His brain searched while he extricated the weapon, ignoring the cooling coils trapping his questing fingers. A dagger in his left hand made short work of the tangled bile-spitting tubes. By the time his red-caked forearm and the sword it held was free, he stood no closer to revelation.

A few steps from the leaking body, the warrior's stomach groaned and his eyes snapped open, gasping in the darkness of his cave sanctuary. His wits scattered, and minutes passed before he gathered enough of them to recall his surroundings. Miniature flames danced along a depleted log. His chest laboured, an old man's again.

His sword, during the night, had buried itself until almost vertical. The grip and the hand that gripped it was half submerged in grainy sand. The mercenary levered his aching bones and took a two-handed grip on the buried weapon. He heaved. The land relinquished its hold, and silvered metal emerged, clean and sharper than ever.

He stared at the implement with longing and loathing, already plodding onward to the tower. An impulse to cast the steel into a swamp and watch it sink gripped his frame. But another piece of his heart, battered and bruised but still violently undying, refused to heave the burden into the wastes. That piece of himself would survive the ending of the world as long as it gripped blood-soaked leather.

The sword began to dance. Greying eyes fixed on a space beyond. Unconscious muscles and tendons flipped and spun the sword in a rhythmic pattern built to strengthen wrists and forearms. A twist of a shoulder socket brought the weapon behind the old man's back to within an inch of shaving skin from his shoulder blades. Unsatisfied, the sword thunked into the ground with jarring finality, splitting limestone like sand. The warrior jerked out of his reverie and took stock of his surroundings. The storm outside had scythed the world clean of foulness. The tracking party would mark his new progress and close the distance. He accepted their deaths. The heavy blade acted as his guide, pushing ever onward in search of... someone. It was an age since he'd remembered who he must end. Since he'd had a home. Since he'd had a name.

All that existed was blood. Blood of the betrayer, blood of the killer. Blood that forced him to become those things in search of vengeance. Still, the sword pulled like a hook in his gut, towards the life that would permit his own to conclude. Nobody would mourn his death. None would welcome it more than he. But not until the bloodthirsty tool had its fill of... of...

His shamble towards destiny was interrupted by baying hounds joyous at the chance to bring their quarry to ground. Bushes crashed, branches snapped. The muscled canines were not graceful. Useful for companionship, a weapon, or as food, if the occasion demanded it. On this occasion, they would serve as a warm-up.

His ears shut to the shouts of the dogs' owners. The warrior's hands disengaged from his mind. His world became a series of breaths.

Inhale.

A dog jumped at his chest. Its jaws anticipated a torn throat and geyser of blood. It hit the ground, oversized skull split. A growl drowned in its throat.

Exhale.

The fighter pivoted. A circling animal died at his heels. A twist of the blade torqued its heart, rupturing vital muscle.

Inhale.

Twin cuts dismembered the remaining pair, frozen in the act of charging. The squeals of their dying companions held them immobile for eternity.

Exhale.

The sword swung to a halt, explosive energy spent. Seconds later, the first of the hunters parted red-stained foliage. His foe's haggard beard, drenched in vital fluid, steamed in the mid-morning air, striking the mercenary into awed silence. The old man's cheeks channelled runnels of blood. A second and third, paid men all, crashed through the brush behind the first. Jocularity fled, replaced by the ancient death-dealer, frozen in time with an aging blade point-first between his feet.

The trio collectively recoiled from the carnage. Vibrant reds rapidly deepening to brown, layered over green, held their terrified gaze. Around the small clearing, scuff marks terminated in cleaved animal bodies.

The old man breathed again. His fresh opponents lacked even animal cunning, tenacity, or thoughtless bravery.

Several hours later, the warrior sought shelter against an uprooted tree, using the trunk to block the wind and burrowing into the softer sand along its length. Fleeing grubs made a quick meal, fingers darting at scampering protein before it could make its own shelter in the burgeoning darkness. Still, his hand clutched his weapon, cradling the talisman. His thinking brain stole away like a thief. The luxury of a sleepless night was denied him. He always slept. With sleep came dreams.

A teacher reared out of the darkness, whacking a rod over the unwilling student's hands. His arm twitched. His hand, unmarked by gnarled knuckles, jumped to a cheek and stroked. The cane caressed his bare fingers again, lovingly enough to bruise.

"Attend, boy. Today we learn of Irwin and the things that were lost."

The teacher's words drowned in a storm that whipped still-brown hair in front of the soldier's eyes. The creaking of a deck replaced the scratching of the classroom. Armour's heft settled on growing muscles.

Waves careened across the deck of the longboat, sweeping horses and unwary men into a vengeful ocean.

The longboat angled as the gods twisted its hull. Gleaming, barnacled rock hurled itself at the boat. The crew scattered to the mercies of the ocean. Sinking, the soldier tore at his armour. Fingers wrenched at buckles and plate. His breastplate tangled in the woollen undershirt of another sailor as it fell, dragging the hapless man deeper into the black. As he sank, the stricken sailor mouthed the word "Irwin."

The warrior was snatched backwards, leaving his breath in a violent bubble of blood and fear. His breath returned. He expected to find himself drenched, his mail beginning to rust. Instead he occupied a lavish court populated by fawning sycophants draped in finery. An outlandish figure admonished the mercenary. A disgusted, amused finger wagged in his face like the tail on a dog. It was the work of a moment to reach out and snap the offending digit.

The regal buffoon's inbred face contorted, first at the audacity and then with pain. A surprised titter raced around the perimeter of the court. The monarch's picked bodyguard moved to intervene. They fell in quick succession, followed by the courtiers and, finally, the king. The fool died blubbering Irwin's name.

The wanderer jerked awake, hand clamping around the blade. The edge sipped the smallest taste of his blood, adding its mark to thousands of others. His mouth was dry. Still, the old man made his inevitable start. Delay only put off the pain throbbing through his knees, elbows, and fingers. Agony was an old friend.

A brief meal, harvested from his trackers the previous day, brought his ageing form to a stream. His thirst slain, he recalled the foolish boy-king. His eyes closed in contemplation, a hand suspended midway between water and lips. His other stole to the sword, the hand wrap soaking blood from fresh cuts as he clutched and released the pommel. A last snatch of memory, pulled from the ravenous maw of a fast-fading dream. The dying gurgle from the king's lungs as blood drowned the idiot ruler, seemed to call Irwin's name like a corpse screaming through mud and shit.

Levering himself upright, the accursed blade's tip a temporary trail in the sand, the ancient warrior left the stream and continued on. Whether annihilation or redemption waited at the tower, the outcome was welcome. The memory of Irwin was a twisted gift, lost for decades and thrown back to him at the close. His fingers tightened. Having a reason, even one he couldn't fully recall, was better than facing an end with none. He climbed, thinking, steady pace carrying him up the slope to the jutting temple. Would he have invented a reason, had one not been provided?

His final trek up the pillar-lined pathway passed bracketing fires that burned in defiance of sense. The sword screamed with a high-pitched vibration. At every moment, the fighter expected the most ferocious of foes. Every step brought his heartbeat thumping in his ears. Time slowed. Long-cultivated battle senses brought his surroundings into sharp relief. Each breath took minutes, rasping like a file over a knot. Every sight was catalogued and dismissed. Each pit and crack in each decrepit pillar sharpened.

No threat greeted his approach. His screaming intuition insisted that an enemy would lunge into view. Still, nothing happened. The temple complex at the base of the tower grew larger. Missing chunks of marble and mortar were joined by webs of cracks cultivating moss. Besides the lichen, only desolation grew. Flames in their glass vessels flickered as though last tended that evening.

The lack of activity continued. The fighter passed the opulent archway, gilded frames embracing rotting wood. A prod with his finger disintegrated lumber in drifts. Even insects had abandoned the barriers as a poor prospect.

Velvet gone to slime draped the walls, the remains of gold and silver stitching marking whatever this crypt's worshippers believed important. At intervals, untouched by time, burning lanterns punctuated the way to the circular room ringed by thin columns along the circumference. Inside, surrounded by a shallow moat of water, was an altar. The rear of the room lay in shadow, concealing what he had come to find.

Grit scraped, the sound all but covered by the slight trickle of water surrounding the nexus. The worn man's eyes adjusted slowly. His heart bumped in his temples and in his throat. Darkness gave way to half-light. His pupils expanded, and his vision absorbed the room's contours.

The sanctum was divided into twelve segments. Mystic, meaningless symbols were carved into the ceiling. The weathered stone altar, channels cut into the anvil-shaped rock to speed away blood, stood on a carved triangular base. The front-facing surface bore representations of the sun and moon.

Beyond the central, rough-hewn sacrificial stone lay his target. The stranger's cloak and shoes were pristine. Remembrance flushed through the venerable fighter. Those were the garments the sorcerer wore the night Irwin had died. Patches of blood stained a sleeve. The discolourations appeared wet.

The mage slumped on the ground, as if he'd died without preamble. His legs extended towards the rear of the room, shoes splayed. His right hand lay palm up at his side, his left out of sight. A desiccated face worshipped the altar, lack of moisture barely altering its gaunt visage. Lips lifted from the stranger's teeth, pasting a grin on the dead face. Tendons, leathered skin, and bone were draped in bloody finery.

Still, the sword screamed, insisting a colossal threat was near. The old man ignored it. His thoughts were soaked in crimson fury. Innumerable dead in service to his pursuit. He'd crossed oceans and kings to arrive and discover that the appointed time had passed. Shrieking, he kicked the mage's remains at the wall. The mortal bundle wafted and splashed into the shallow, decorative moat. The universe behind his eyes went white and then black.

"It took you long enough to get here, old man."

The rasping cadence brought bile to his throat.

"It took you too long to get here, old man."

Its mocking inflection was unmistakable.

The dripping figure levered itself from the water, droplets spilling on thirsty stone. Atrophied, dehydrated muscles pulled the corpse upright. Its dried lips remained still. The fallen eyes had not returned to their sockets. A grating vocalisation emitted from the dead man's throat. An inescapable grin loomed in front of the warrior like a sickly moon.

"My weapon. How considerate."

Empty hollows pierced the warrior's skull. The sword's anger was a wasp in his forehead.

"Take it back."

Trembling muscles flicked the immeasurable weight in the traveller's hand up, years of agonising practise behind the strike. Driven by right-eous fury, the horizontal cut, taken at chest level, should have sheared through bone, cloth, and the pillar behind. Instead it bounced, jolting the decrepit corpse with the force of the blow. Without slowing, the warrior wrenched the sword around, aiming at the skin-covered skull. The blow connected, spiking the lich down as though struck with a hammer. The unholy figure chuckled, unmarked, and made to rise again. Frustrated, the warrior spun into a downswing, intending to split the stranger in two. The sword screamed against a fleshless collarbone and smashed the undead foe to the floor. The shock of the impact sent the weapon flashing up like a fish, torquing its wielder's shoulder in an agonised circle.

The mocking rasp returned. The ancient mage clambered upright.

"The sun will burn out before that edge harms me," the corpse rattled.

He heaved, nearly broken by having regained his vengeance only to lose it again. The sword was loosely held in his left hand. Its point vibrated against marble, white fragments scattering beneath the weight of innumerable dead souls. Aged, beaten eyes tracked the immortal body of his enemy, flitting closer.

A decision was made.

Inhale.

The old man fell to a knee. The sword lay horizontally, lightly suspended between his palms. An offering to the undead stranger. The lich grasped the hilt with a greedy hand.

Exhale.

The fighter dropped all claim on the weapon for the first time in an eternity. All claim, save for a final, calculated cut. His palm. An offering to the dead. The dead mage's grasp tightened. The weight of Irwin's life, of all the lives destroyed in pursuit of the stranger, this burden carried across continents, dropped like a falling star.

Inhale.

Alarmed and off-balance, the immortal entity released its hold. The venerable fighter's experienced grip caught the weapon. Its fall turned into a scything blow with the flat of the blade.

Exhale.

Equilibrium destroyed, the animate corpse crashed to the ground. Its legs sprawled outward. Its skull thumped off a flagstone with a noise like a split coconut. Sightless sockets flared up at the warrior. A semblance of the old man's youth glowed behind faded eyes, the sword poised above the creature's chest.

"You cannot cut me. You cannot kill me."

Inhale.

"I don't intend to."

Exhale.

Almost lovingly, the ancient warrior lowered the sword to his prone opponent's chest. Almost casually brushing aside questing sticks of tendon and bone, he released his burden for the last time. Its hilt lay against the creaking sternum, the point hovered over the thing's ravaged pelvis. A low grinding, like a mill wheel chewing pebbles, filled the air. Even with its fine cloak and clothing scuffed by the battle, the mage appeared to be a knight laid out for burial.

Frantic digits grasped and scrabbled at the weapon. The lich raged and cursed. Each word seemed to lift another weight from the old man's shoulders. Foiled, the creature took to thrashing back and forth under the weight, trying to dislodge it from its chest. It only succeeded in flailing. The soldier's bemused gaze held steady as the mage twitched like a bug under a pin.

The immortal roared its frustration, rattling gemstones out of the sanctuary's mystic sigils.

"What do you want from me?!"

"Tell me," the crouching warrior said, his voice quiet. "Tell me why you killed him. Why did you kill Irwin?"

Prominent teeth clicked together, the ragged jaw flapping. What remained of the stranger's forehead creased in a parody of thought. Stars wheeled overhead in the time it took for it to answer. Its voice was low, rasping like a file against an iron bar. Its tone was incredulous.

"I... I don't remember."

Light bloomed in the old warrior's face as he stood and stretched. He flexed his fingers, laced them behind his neck. With a last glance at the struggling creature, marble dust collecting beneath its impervious shoulder blades, he strode towards the path. The unnatural lanterns faded and sputtered out, one at a time. Behind their artificial glow, the night skies crept back overhead.

"I think that's an answer I can live with," he said.

He walked, weightless, into the deepening night.

About the Author

Brett Venter is a South African writer and magazine editor with an interest in horror, fantasy, and science fiction. He writes cyberpunk when he thinks no one is looking, because everything is awful and writing it makes him happy. Brett has previously published horror and science fiction in the South African anthology magazine Something Wicked. His previous short fantasy story, Protector of the Realm, appeared in an anthology called Visions of Darkness. A new short horror story, The Outrage Machine, appears in an anthology called Strange Aeon: 2022: Hopeful Monsters. You can find him posting about surfing, technology, and metal on Twitter at @DrakonisZA.

SOUL OF MY SOUL

BY ANTONY PASCHOS

She's not flesh of my flesh but soul of my soul: a fragment of my essence which escaped me at her birth. Still, I'll do anything to get her through this night alive. As I unsheathe my Luger pistol, I recollect tonight's events that started with three knocks on a door—and with three knocks, I hope they will end.

I'm perched on Stamatina's bed, waiting for her heartbeat to slow. The smell of her sweat is glued on the stone walls. It dribbles down from the rafters, evaporates through the rags, and fills the dark room like mist, and I know she's dreamt my dreams again. But I can't admit that, can I? I rest my gaze on the blanket shrouding her legs.

"Want to tell me the dream, child?"

"What difference does it make, Aunt Yana?" None. A drop of sweat crosses her chinbone. She sighs, and it trickles down her neck. "It was a battlefield. Again. Only this time, the warriors had some kind of short-swords. And they... they were huddling up against each other. Their shields..."

"Were forming a wall?"

"Yes! How..." Her brows furrow. "How do you know?"

"History books," I lie. The battle she's seen, I must've fought a thousand years ago. Not sure which one it was, though. There were so many.

Her blue gaze sobers. She curls her shoulders in and rubs her arms with crossed hands. I lift her blanket to cover her chest. This cold autumn will resolve into a cold winter.

"Sleep, child."

Is that sound footsteps on the gravel road outside the mansion? A triple knock on the front door.

"Who's that, Aunt Yana?" she whispers.

I grab her wrist and yank her to her feet. "Get up." Last time someone visited us was months ago, when the Nazis gave the valley to the Bulgarians. My fame must have kept most of their grisly lot away until now. "You have to hide."

She jerks away from me, yet she follows me in the darkness; out of the room, down the creaking staircase, and into the kitchen where I pull the rag and open up the secret hatch. An exhalation of stale soil hits me as if the crypt just puffed out her rotten breath in my face.

Knock-knock-knock.

"Get in, child."

I help her down into the crypt. I could've hidden her in the cellar, but it's outside the house and it'd be the first spot someone would look in.

"Auntie?"

I kneel with my hand on the hatch.

"I know those dreams have something to do with you. I just know. Promise me that you'll tell me." A proper time for blackmailing me to tell her. She must've taken after me more than I thought.

"Shush, child." I shut the hatch and pull back the rag on top of it. Someone might notice the lines of dirt on the rag's skirt. I should've cleaned up more often, I guess.

More sharp knocks.

I light up a gas lamp with a match and hurry to the hallway, pausing before the door. When the Bulgarians had come, they confiscated my Mannlicher rifle and Browning pistol. So, I place the lamp on the floor and pluck one of the two crossed-hand axes from the wall. I run a thumb along its edge. I might not clean up often, but every decorative weapon is whetted. I hang its heel hook from my belt and its toe hook pokes my side in a familiar way—how many lives ago I've felt this, though, I cannot tell.

Knock-knock-knock. A muffled hiss in Greek behind my door, "Open up, witch. I know who you are."

You don't know shit. I hang the second axe from my belt as well, grab a cloak from the hanger, throw it on my back to shroud the weapons, and open the door.

At the halo of my lamp, the man's fat nose and loose cheeks blaze red. He's plump, and only two kinds of men are plump in the valley of Serres these days. Bulgarians and those who submitted to them. Under a sheepskin coat with a plush fleece collar, he's wearing silk pajama pants, torn on his knees. Expensive clothes; and only two kinds of men can afford them these days. Bulgarian officers and the snakes who serve them. And of those reptiles, he's the worst: Kinotarchis. The son of a priest the Bulgarians appointed as the mayor in the village of Kotsaki.

"Help me. They're coming." His weasel eyes glance back into the darkness.

"Who's they?"

He wipes a spaghetti of snot from his mustache. "Greeks... Commies... They're trying to make the people revolt. They're killing all Bulgarians. They came to my house and..." The breath of the night wind—pine resin, fir, cedar—carries a waft of voices and rustle. His eyes bulge. "They're here."

"You shouldn't've come here. I want no part in the petty ploys of your kind."

I push the door against his face, but he places his brogue shoe in the gap—it's full of mud. I fondle the edge of one of my axes. It's sharp and reassuring. I look at his sausage fingers on my door as he tries to force his way in. This old woman's body I'm in is feeble, so I retreat in order to put some space between me and him. I reach for my axes under my cloak, but he notices and hisses, "Ashihastar!"

I stand frozen, listening to the faint ticking of a pocket watch. The word is a knife stabbed inside my head. It fires up a numbness spreading throughout my body, shackling my will to his command. I don't ask him how he knows; it makes no difference.

The hinges screech as the door swings open, yet he's not moving in. His weasel eyes glint as he realizes what has just happened.

"Jesus Christ, Dad was right," he mumbles to himself. My cold gaze makes him speak again, "Ashihastar! Ishtar! Astarte!"

The words wedge inside my mind and I can barely make out the voices getting louder, closer.

"My father had told me, but I never believed! You did take over my cousin, didn't you? And when he threw you out of him, you jumped in that pregnant girl at the house next door. But she died when she gave birth, so you ended up in her sister..."

His father; a priest, an exorcist. One of the few people who managed to throw me out of a body. I should've left this valley after murdering him, but Stamatina was too young. "Quit your babble, mortal. And name your wish."

"Save me. Get me in."

I turn the lamp off, nudge him aside, and take two steps out. I try to grab his arm, but a headache pumps against my temples as I try to trick him into an unsafe place.

"You think I'm an idiot? They'll search in the cellar first! No, Ashihastar, you'll hide me in the best spot that you've got. Now."

The voices are nearer. This body's hearing is weak and his commands are making me dizzy. I get him inside the house and my headache dwindles. I shut the door, clasp its latch, and tug him to the kitchen. Breathe in, breathe out. I pull the rag and open the hatch again.

"Stamatina?" I whisper.

"Aunt Yana?"

"Yes, child. Stay put." I turn to Kinotarchis. "Get in."

A smile ripples on his face. "She knows nothing, doesn't she?"

"If you dare touch her..." The pain I've tasted is slight and could tempt me to ignore his command; even try to hurt him. But ages ago, I had the chance to disobey an order from someone who spelled my name. I recall the pain.

He sticks his mouth to my ear—he stinks of Pombena cigars, garlic, and bad teeth. "I know your name, Ashihastar. *I* rule over you, not otherwise."

I nod, and he finally hurries down into the crypt.

"Wha-what's wrong, Auntie? Who's..."

"Patience, child. I'll come for you, soon. I promise."

"Hello, Stamatina. Haven't seen you for..." I cut short his sentence by shutting the hatch.

Knocks on the door again.

A short woman is on my doorstep. She's sporting a large green coat, tailored down to her size and tightened around her waist with a bandolier. Her beret has the iron badge of the guerillas. Her eyes are black, her nose is broken, and she's missing a front tooth. Two lanky oafs stand behind her. The youngest would've been handsome if he wasn't so skinny. The older one has the same fawn eyes, though his ears are so large he looks like a donkey. The rest of his features are a warped version of his brother, as if his mother was still practicing during his birth.

The woman's fingers open and close around the magazine of a battered stockless MP-40 submachine gun—stolen from the Nazis, obviously. She's not aiming at me.

Yet. Not that I care for this frail body. I just don't want to reveal my nature to Stamatina.

"Sorry to bother you, Kyra-Yana." She speaks Greek. "We bring good news. We're throwing the Bulgarians out."

I don't reply. Both oafs switch weight from one leg to the other. The woman coughs. "We're after that bastard, Koulouris. He escaped."

She means Kinotarchis. "We know he's here," says the older of the two oafs, the one with the donkey's ears.

I don't reply with a lie I might regret later. "So?"

"Revolution is on, witch! We're throwing the Bulgarians back to the forests that spawned 'em!"

If I cared, I'd ask if the people are supporting them or if they're trying to force the population into an uprising as Kinotarchis said. But I don't.

The woman nudges Donkey-Ears to silence. "We saw him come here, Kyra-Yana. Please..."

I still have my two axes under my cloak and the pain inside my head. I step back, letting them in.

The guerillas search in the kitchen first, then the rest of the rooms, then back in the kitchen. As the two oafs pretend to check every drawer and rack, they pilfer a vase of molasses, a chunk of dried-up pork, a small sack of flour. Donkey-Ears grabs a piece of bobota bread and chews. I wait, trying my best not to stand above the hatch. The silence of Paggaio mountain is shattered by gunfire and explosions instead of wolf cries and owl hoots.

"He's not here, lieutenant," says Donkey-Ears. "Let's go join the others. We'll miss the hangings."

"Sure," says the woman. "Kyra-Yana, would you be so kind as to give us a bit of corn flour? For the cause, you know."

She glances at the rag. Did she notice the trails of dirt before the two oafs smudged them off? "Sure, child. I've got them outside, in the cellar."

"All right, thanks." She turns to leave but stands under the kitchen's doorcase. "By the way, where's my old classmate, Stamatina?"

She's young but not as young as Stamatina. "She's sick, child. I sent her to the doctor."

She nails her gaze upon me. "To the doctor, huh?"

"Yes. Doctor Thodoros. He's her uncle. His wife is my cousin."

Donkey-Ears chews his bread loudly, sprinkling crumbs on the floor. The younger one's brow twinkles with sweat in the faint lamplight.

"That's strange," says the lieutenant. "Because we just came from the doctor."

"Wha-what?" says Donkey-Ears, and his brother elbows him so hard his piece of bobota falls on the floor. He picks it up and resumes chomping.

I stay silent. Perhaps I should try to nod toward the hatch—these guerillas probably won't hurt Stamatina—but a headache bursts even at the thought.

The lieutenant casts a scowling look at Donkey-Ears. "Anyway, let's go. Sorry to bother you, Kyra-Yana. And I wish you—"

A muffled scream under the planks. I shoot a glance at the rag instinctively, and the thought that this could betray Kinotarchis shoots a pang of pain inside my brain. I pull my gaze away, but it's too late; they saw me.

The lieutenant nods at the two oafs. "Open up the hatch, comrades."

I'm too numb to do anything else than wait as the two oafs pull the rag and clank open the hatch. I grit my teeth to resist the pain; it's still bearable, so there's no need to attack them.

Silence. A distant string of gunfire from outside. A faint *tic-tac* from the crypt, then a gasp, a moan, a hiss. "Shut up, bitch or..."

Donkey-Ears grins. "He's there."

The lieutenant sighs as if tired. "Get out, Koulouris. Don't force me to throw a grenade in there."

Donkey-Ears rummages in the sack where he's stuffed my stolen food and plucks out a grenade. The lieutenant gives him an open palm—a silent Greek gesture to tell him that he's an idiot. Then she meets my gaze.

"We're not hurting your niece," she lips.

"I've got the witch's daughter!" Kinotarchis's voice is trembling.

"We don't care!" says Donkey-Ears.

"It's done, Koulouris," says the lieutenant. "Get out now."

Stamatina comes out first, her hair tangled in a bush. Her gown hangs loose, letting her left shoulder bare as Kinotarchis twists her elbow behind her back. Worms of sweat crawl over his baldness, but his gaze is wild.

Donkey-Ears raises his Mauser rifle, and his little brother aims at him with a pistol that should be a Beretta.

"You commies are fools, you know that?" grunts Kinotarchis. "I had news of your stupid revolution weeks ago. I didn't believe them; said you couldn't possibly be such morons."

I can smell Stamatina's sweat in the brew of stagnant odors brimming the room. Her gown hem is full of dust, and she squints as her blue eyes turn red.

"But you *are* morons after all. It's a setup, you know? They let you fuckers revolt so they'll have an excuse to slaughter the Greeks at will. Come tomorrow, your stupid revolution will be over!"

The oafs' eyes meet. The lieutenant coughs before she speaks. "Tomorrow's another day, Koulouris. A day you won't live to see dawn."

"Don't be stupid, Eleni. Spare me, run back to your mountains, and I'll make sure they won't hurt your family. You know I keep my word, don't you?" He shoots a glance at her breasts.

That does it. Eleni raises her MP-40. "Let Stamatina go, pig."

He twists Stamatina's arm. She groans.

"You'll regret this, Eleni." He looks at me. "Ashihastar! Kill them! Kill them all!"

Tic-tac, tic-tac, every ticking second of Kinotarchis' watch flattens his grin.

"Ki-kill them! It's an order, Ashihastar!"

The guerillas look at each other, at me, at Kinotarchis, at Stamatina. Confusion sinks in the room like smoke after a grenade. Their gazes attach themselves to me, as if I'm a maypole.

"It doesn't work this way, you fool," I say. "You might bar me from slaughtering your sorry ass, even force me to help you. But to kill someone? You need a lot more than my name."

His jaw drops. Stamatina jolts as he twists harder. "Then help me—they'll kill me if you won't! Ashihastar! Protect me!"

I'm not into explaining to him how his command feels like a nail piercing my skull.

"What's wrong, Kyra-Yana? What the fuck is this snake talking about?" asks Eleni.

If only I could tell her that the faster someone puts a bullet in his head, the better for all of us—I'd probably attack or get in the way, but perhaps I won't be able to save him. But two hammers are hitting against my temples, and my body is numb. My only hope is that they'll figure it out themselves.

"I won't say it again, pig," says Eleni. "Let Stamatina go and follow us. Now."

His eyes dart from her to me; a caged sparrow, panicked. I stand there, frozen from the pain building up inside my brain and the numbness diffusing in my body like poison. I have no courage left to think; my hands reach under my cloak while none notices. I don't mind the guerillas, but I don't give a shit about their lives. I need to escape this torment as fast as possible.

Then Donkey-Ears's Mauser aims at Kinotarchis.

And I let all hell break loose.

My muscles are frail, but my moves are flawless. I chop Donkey-Ears's hand with one axe and shatter his skull with the other. The pain ebbs away and a spatter of blood warms my cheeks; a welcome sensation. Everyone's stunned except Eleni; she shoots a burst at me, and my chest and belly explode, my knees give in to pain, and I stumble down; a second burst—"No!" cries Stamatina—blasts my head and suddenly, I'm not bound by the limits of this aged body. I spill out of it, an ethereal essence consisting of a million memories held together by something unknown, hovering as Yana's body crumbles lifelessly on the floor. The air in the room feels thick and viscous. Every sound is muffled in a buzzing sea; the living bodies are throbbing red against a gray mist. They jolt, they move, and I'm drawn to the closest one as I sense whatever's holding me together disintegrate; memories falling away from me like leaves and I dash into a soul and wrap myself around it. It fights back, but my essence has been housed in Yana's body for long enough to become strong. I engulf the young soul, smothering it fast, destroying it with a spark and then darkness.

"Christos, you okay?"

A woman's face is in front of me; it's Eleni, the guerilla chasing Kinotarchis who had caught Stamatina—and the remembrance of her unfolds a string of recent memories that make me push her away and jump to my feet. My weight feels strange. My spine is so straight it's hard not to fall back. I lean on a wall and take a look around. I'm in a kitchen littered with corpses; an old woman's—Yana—a man's with a chopped hand and an axe wedged in his ruined face, another one shot—it's Kinotarchis, the pig is dead!—and a girl's: Stamatina.

A dark stain blooms on her gown over her belly. Her eyes are shut, and her brow is scratched. I don't need to sift through memories dissolving fast into my new brain to recall my love for her; her sight drops me to my knees, and I grab her by the nape—it's clammy. Her eyelids flicker. She's got a pulse.

"What the fuck, Christos?"

I fumble her torn gown. Blood is flowing from her wound; I need to take the bullet out of her. Seeds from my previous lives flourish in my mind in flashes of visions; I've been a warrior and I've been a farmer;

I've been a blacksmith, a carpenter, a doctor—but I've been a doctor so long ago, the humans hadn't figured out how to make gunpowder. And even if I was a doctor as Yana, I'm still too numb to figure out how to operate safely. It might take months for my previous life to set in my new mind—and if I jump to another body meanwhile, it might take years.

"Christos!"

I look at Eleni, and my voice is a beast's growl. "Shut the fuck up, mortal, or I'll kill you."

I have to recall how to use my new vocal cords in a human way, 'cause terror makes her step back as if slapped. As I turn to Stamatina, I hear Eleni fall down, her MP-40 dinging. I grab Stamatina and lift her up—this body's strong. She's breathing, but she's limp in my embrace.

Eleni is up, leaning on the wall and gawking at me. Her jaw's sagged, her lips following along in its trembling dance, unable to utter a word. She's trying to steady the MP's barrel that's dancing in circles around my chest.

"Not a wise choice." I try to sound human—it's hard, damnit. Every first time it's hard. She's already seen what could happen if she kills this body, so I just wait till she figures out to whom I'm going to jump next. It probably works, 'cause she gulps down and lowers her barrel. She tries to speak, but stutters. Then she does it.

"Ashihastar!"

Two kinds of numbness spread throughout my new body; one kindled by her command, the other from understanding my recklessness. That snake, Kinotarchis, had spoken my name, and that bitch heard it.

"Jesus fucking Christ," mumbles Eleni, hiding behind her barrel. "What the fuck are you?"

Truth is, I do not know. After spending years in Yana's body, the memories of past lives that returned reached back four thousand years; but still, the beginning of my existence in this world escaped me.

I don't try to sound human. "Time is short, mortal, and my daughter's dying. Either help me or get out of my way."

"No! Get out of Christos's body! Now! I command you! Ashi—" *Gulp.* "Ashihastar!"

I stumble as her words penetrate my skull; I perch my ass on the table while laying Stamatina's body on it. "Your friend's gone forever."

A lie. An experienced exorcist like Kinotarchis's father could've forced me out, but she doesn't need to know this. Her wrinkles tremble as if her face is a pool disturbed by thrown shingles.

"Don't try to use me, mortal. I'm slave to none, and you lack the knowledge to leash me. Help me save my daughter, or go back to your petty revolution."

"Who? Oh... Where... Where do you wanna go?"

"She needs a doctor."

The sky is a moth-eaten fabric shrouding a blazing light; its shine spilling through a million holes in glowing dots and a scimitar-shaped tearing. The wheels crunch on the gravel as I tug Yana's tumbrel with Eleni. On its bed lies Stamatina under blankets, beside the oaf's Mauser.

I focus on solidifying as many memories as I can from my last life; listening to Stamatina's dreams of my past lives, teaching her how to read and write, reading fairy tales to her before her eyelids flicker and shut, lulling baby Stamatina to sleep in my embrace, falling asleep myself.

The unlucky lad's body is different, but I'm getting used to it. My empty stomach's growling, and a piece of meat rubs against the root of my thigh; I've forgotten how awkward it feels to have a penis. But my muscles are strong and I pull the cart with ease.

"Why do you care?" asks Eleni amid panting breaths. In the expanse of the plains we're heading to, stars explode every now and then; the sound of bombs and gunfire traveling in wafts.

I know what she's asking, but I try to recall the memory as a whole.

"Just asking. You're not obliged to answer."

I'm not, but spelling out a past event solidifies it—I found out that human memory works in the same way when I was teaching Stamatina how to memorize things from books. "It was an accident. Jumped in a pregnant girl."

"Your sister, right? I mean Yana's sister…"

"I was in another body." I refrain from mentioning the exorcism. I hope she hasn't heard of it. "After he died, I jumped into her body. I gave birth and died soon after. So then, I jumped to the closest body I found. Her sister's."

She bobs her head. "Still, why did you raise her? Stamatina, I mean. Do you bond with mortals? Or… or did you think of it as a duty?"

Fragments of kept oaths and broken promises light up inside my brain. Friendships, loves, betrayals. I do bond with mortals, but she doesn't need to know that either.

"No." It's true that I didn't raise Stamatina bound by any duty. It was much more than that. "Seems that Stamatina took a part of me." I glance at her. "Got children?"

She shakes her head.

"Guess it should feel the same."

"So… She's a…" *Coughs.* She doesn't want to say demon.

"I don't know if she can jump bodies too. And I don't want to find out. Not before her body dies of old age." My voice is still a growl.

A distant blast and a flash of light on Paggaio's mountainside.

"Christos was a nice lad. His brother was an ox, but Christos was sharp. And he was very young. We were cousins, you know."

She wants me to apologize, but I don't. I don't care about her cousins. I'm still numb from jumping bodies and my human feelings are limited to Stamatina.

A pause filled with wood creaking, wheel crackling, and distant gunfire.

"I want you to help our cause. I won't try to command you…"

"Sooner or later, you'd fail if you did."

"I guess I would. But I'm helping you. And I'd like you to join us in return."

Before I answer that I'm not into helping anyone, I notice the sharp angles of the doctor's house against the starry sky. The building's perched on top of a small hill. Beside it rise the rectangular shapes of trucks.

Bulgarians. It makes sense; the doctor might be Greek, but he's considered the best in the valley. I didn't plan to join Eleni's band of dreamers, but it looks like I'm going to need her help if Stamatina is to survive.

"Fuck," mumbles Eleni. "Guess we're gonna have to leave. I think that in Kotsaki village there's another doctor who could help your niece… Or daughter."

It's daughter. "No." My voice is a growl. "And yes."

"Huh?"

I take the Mauser rifle from the cart's bed and hang it on my back, then turn to Eleni. "Your gun."

"What? Why?"

"If Stamatina makes it tonight, I'll help your gang." If Stamatina lives, I'd either have to tell her of my nature or sell her on a new tale. And this body I'm in was a commie, so it makes sense to join the guerillas and protect her while we're with them.

She hands me her MP-40. "What are you thinking?"

"Stay here. You'll know it when it's done."

I barge into the doctor's house, knocking the door with my shoulder. The noise makes the commotion of muffled voices cease. The smell of shit drills itself into my nostrils as I cross the hallway; doors on my right, a staircase at its end. Out of the last room a young man in soldier's attire crops up; I shoot him down with Eleni's MP-40. A second, I stitch a burst of bullets in him too. Before I reach the first door, two more soldiers come out, all guns blazing; I shoot them to silence, but—a flare in my stomach—not before one of them hits me.

I throw the MP-40, take the Mauser, and get in the first room; the doctor is standing beside a wounded man on a bed. A lamp is on the nightstand, and the doctor's wife is behind the central table holding another lamp, throwing light on gauzes, a basin filled with water, knives, and tools. Two other Bulgarians are laying on mattresses on the floor, and one is standing in a corner; an explosion and my soul is unleashed again. I dash immediately to the man that shot me and entangle his soul; the first jump weakened me, but I'm still strong enough to choke it violently and take over his body.

I open my new eyes. I'm facing the door I entered and the prone corpse of the commie lad; his head is sunk in a pool of blood. I stumble up, dizzy. The doctor is knitting the wounded's stomach; the stench of shit is unbearable. The doctor's wife is close to him.

"Ivo! What the fuck happened in here?" The language is Bulgarian; two soldiers are standing on the doorstep. I shake my head. They're talking to me. I crouch, and pick up the Luger pistol with which Ivo killed my previous body, while one of the two Bulgarians sags and turns it over.

"Who the fuck's this guy?"

I blast his head, then, his friend's. The doctor's wife screeches. The doctor throws me a glance. Is his hand knitting the Bulgarian shaking? I'll need it to be steady to save... Stamatina, that was her name, wasn't it?

Yes. I throw up on my jacket as a stream of memories flow back into my brain. I spit, then go to the wounded Bulgarians and plant a bullet in their skulls. The doctor has stopped knitting and stares as I near him, Luger in hand. His wife is frantically making the sign of the cross. The wounded guy's eyes bulge out. His chest is swelling like a blacksmith's blower. I shoot him in the forehead—another screech from the doctor's wife.

Then I turn to the doctor; his face is contorted from terror. "How many more Bulgarians?" I ask—fuck, my voice comes out a growl, otherworldly. His frown turns into a grimace of horrid comprehension.

"What the fuck?"

"How... many... Bulgarians?"

"Two. Two in the kitchen."

His wife's screams turn into howls. I peek out of the room. More corpses. I'm not sure how many enemies I've slaughtered before and if the doctor means those ones lying on the hallway's floor, so I quickly check in the rest of the rooms. There's a hatch in the kitchen as well—someone could be hiding in there—does he have any children? I don't remember. I return to the hallway and stumble upon him and his wife; they're huddled in a shaking embrace.

"What do you want from us?" says his wife. The doctor's seizing his chest. He leans back on the wall, his wife holding him. His mouth is a frozen "O." A string of startled faces appears in my memory; he's dying of a heart attack.

Fuck my lives.

"Don't let him die," I tell his wife, who eases him down, sniffing. As I pass across them, I snatch her lamp. I open the destroyed door and wave with the light outside. Out of the shadows materializes the shape of a cart moving slowly toward me. A scream from inside the house, "Thodoros!"

It should be the doctor's name. His wife is weeping, mumbling his name over and over again.

I get there and shut his eyelids. She's not sparing me a glance. Soon, Eleni stands on the doorstep, carrying Stamatina by the shoulder, her eyelids flickering between conscious and coma.

As I dart to help her, Eleni steps back. "It's me," I growl, and she gulps down her unease.

"Stamatina?" It's the doctor's wife. She's still holding her husband but she's turned to us. "What happened to her?"

I struggle to remember if Stamatina or Yana had any relationships with the doctor's wife, but it seems impossible. Either way, we carry Stamatina past the hallway and into the room, throw the dead Bulgarian out of the bed, and lay her on it.

"What are we gonna do?" says Eleni.

If I hadn't jumped bodies twice, I might be able to pluck a bullet out. But I'm still groggy, and my past is a churning soup inside my mind. "Can you do it?"

"It's... it's been a couple of months since I volunteered..." Fucking rookies, isn't she a lieutenant? As if to answer my thought, she says, "I'm a poet. I came from Paris to fight and..."

"I'll do it," says the doctor's wife. She's standing on the doorstep beside her husband's clog. Tears are flowing down her cheeks. "For Stamatina. I'm a midwife."

I gesture her in.

The doctor's wife rummages through his tools on the table, her hands steady despite the slaughter and the loss of her husband. She takes a handful of blades, scissors, and pinchers, orders Eleni to bring the basin, and comes to the bed where I'm perched.

Before she starts operating, Stamatina jolts, her blue eyes open and bulge out as she looks at me.

"Where's my Auntie? What happened to Aunt Yana?"

"She's…" My voice's still a growl. "She's…"

"Silence, niece," says the doctor's wife—so she's her aunt too. "Your Aunt…"

But I cut her off. I'm too dizzy to think clearly, so I just spill out what I withheld for her whole life with a voice that's inhuman. "Remember those dreams of yours, child? The battles? The shield wall?"

She pushes her back against the bed's headboard and moans. Her breaths are short and rapid, and her chest follows along.

"You were right. They had to do with me. They were memories of my past lives."

"How… What… Who are you?"

"Right question is why I raised you, child. I accidentally jumped into your mother while she was giving birth. You took something from me. That's why you see those dreams. Then, when she died, I jumped into your aunt Yana."

"I-I…"

"Say what you will, child, but you are daughter to me. And now we have to get you right."

I turn to the doctor's wife and nod at her to start.

Stamatina has fallen to sleep when a distant rumble of engines is heard, getting louder fast.

Eleni wakes up and gets to the window. She pulls the drapes and peeks outside. "Oh, fuck. Bulgarians. A lot of them."

The doctor's wife comes back from the kitchen.

"The revolution…" mumbles Eleni. "What the fuck happened?"

I shrug. "Kinotarchis could be right." My voice sounds almost human by now.

"Can-can you?"

"I can help you, yes. But I can't protect you against so many enemies."

It takes a couple of held breaths to take that in. "I have to go. Good… good luck."

She nudges the doctor's wife as she darts out of the room. Her footsteps knock on the hallway and dwindle outside. I wish I could leave with Stamatina, but it's too late now.

"You brought this upon my house," says the doctor's wife. She stands still in front of the doorstep. "Now they'll kill… they'll kill me too." I guess the pause was because of an accidental "us" she withheld. She's probably hiding a child—or more—somewhere.

I could tell her I'm sorry for her husband. But I'm not. "You have a hideout. And you have your children in there."

Her face doesn't give away anything.

"Go hide. And take my daughter with you. I'll make sure you make it through the night."

She nods.

"When this is over, go to my mansion with Stamatina and your children. I'll make sure no one hurts you." My plan is simple: after the upcoming confrontation, I'll probably end up in a Bulgarian's body. Hopefully, I'll leave no witnesses behind.

She opens her mouth to reply—a shot, a woman's cry from outside. Eleni, probably. The doctor's wife nods again.

She helps me lift Stamatina. She's light—or this body I stole is strong. She does have a hatch. It's below the basin in her kitchen, under piles of pots and pans.

"Mom?" says a voice when we open it. It should be a boy.

"Shh."

The opening is smaller, and it takes a while to get Stamatina in. I shut the hatch and put the pots back into place when I hear three knocks on the door.

How many bodies will I have to waste to save her? I do not know. She might not be flesh of my flesh, but she's soul of my soul: a fragment of my essence which escaped me at her birth. Still, I'll do anything to get her through this night alive. As I unsheathe my Luger pistol, I recollect tonight's events that started with three knocks on a door—and with three knocks, I hope they will end.

"I'm coming."

About the Author

Antony Paschos is a Greek author with short stories in *Galaxy's Edge, ZNB Presents, James Gunn's Ad Astra, Metaphorosis,* and other magazines. He has also published three books and several short stories in Greek. He is a member of the Athens Club of Science Fiction, and lives in Athens.

DANY
COMIC

THE GOLDEN LOCKET

BY ROGER LANDES

The knight climbed the inner stairs of an ancient castle built long ago by his king's ancestors and carefully wiped his blade clean of the blood from the monstrosities he had slain to reach this point. Six had been sent to reclaim the southern garrison after years of occupation by the forces of evil.

Only he remained.

Exhaustion crept through his body as he made his way from the stairs to the doors of the once-grand hall. As he caught his breath, the knight imagined the feasts, the merriment, the titans of leadership that sat in the room beyond these doors. He imagined the bards singing songs of pretty women and the powerful men who defended them from the horrors that had found their way to the castle. Instead, the only sound was of the friction from his gloves on the hilt of his sword. He kicked open the heavy wooden doors and rushed through the entryway.

It was horror that he expected, but not like what he had found. It was indeed a feast, but one interrupted decades before. Men and women, or at least the skeletons of such, lay slaughtered in their seats. Food so rotten not even the bugs would not touch it spread across the tables. The ward of this castle, skin torn from his face, sat motionless on his throne, head resting against a curled and bony fist. The knight's eyes rapidly searched for some beast responsible for such mayhem.

"So, you are the man making all that noise," said the being on the throne. His jawbone cracked when he spoke. "Come to take back your castle, did you?"

The knight raised his sword forward. "Fiend! It is you who lead these abominations? Then yes, it is I who will rip you from this mortal coil."

He barreled down the hall toward his foe.

The dead man slowly rose from his throne, raising both hands toward the sky. As his hands lifted, so did the bodies of the partygoers. The knight slid to a stop as the skeletons reformed before his eyes. A dead woman in a pink dress swiped at him with a steak knife. He swung through her neck, leaving the rotting head to plop onto the floor. Undeterred by her decapitation, she continued her assault.

"This—this is necromancy!" He kicked over the skeleton, keenly aware that the dead were surrounding him. His grip on his sword waned as he thought of what would happen after he succumbed to the horde. As the dead encircled the valiant knight, he closed his eyes and prayed for a quick death.

Suddenly, he heard a collective thud from around the hall. He opened his eyes to find that his tormentors had collapsed. On the throne, the dead king returned to his position of malaise. The knight confusedly raised his weapon, this time with more caution of the powers of the dead wizard before him.

"What game is this, fiend? I have slain every monster in this castle on my way to you. And now, you refuse to face me?"

"Is that the case? A proper king never fights his own battles."

"Is it a king you are?"

"Do you not know? A pity. I do so long to be 'ripped from this mortal coil' as you so aptly put it. Alas, you are not the one to do it."

The knight let his sword drop to his waist. "And how do you know that?"

The dead wizard leaned forward from his throne. If he had eyes, he would have squinted at the knight. "Do you know what I am?"

The knight spun his sword in his hand. There were many legends of good knights falling into traps from the minds of creatures like this. He had read them all in hopes of avoiding this very situation.

"You are Drugghod the Deceptor. I will not be led astray by your wickedness."

"That is who I am. Answer the question that was asked."

The knight thought hard and grew frustrated. "You are an abomination who has too long claimed these halls from those that belong here."

"You will need to be more specific if you are to claim what you insist is not mine."

The knight was unaccustomed to this position of ignorance. The discomfort made him shuffle his feet. "I do not know what you are."

His inquisitor leaned back on his throne. "Too bad. It would appear I must go on living then." He clapped his hands twice. The skeletons rose around the knight, this time with more vigor.

The knight scrambled to a defensive position. His mind raced through exit scenarios that did not end with him losing any limbs or turning into one of the creatures. Through the crowd of undead, he noticed that the thing on the throne was sitting low. Without muscles in his face, it was difficult for the knight to infer too much of his enemy's emotions, though he couldn't help but think that the undead wizard seemed melancholy.

"Wait! I have a proposition for you! If you would lower your horde, I believe I have a solution to both of our problems."

Drugghod's empty gaze lowered to the knight. The skeletons staggered forward, then came to an abrupt halt. "I am listening, human."

The knight bobbled his sword, trying desperately not to be distracted by the desecrated dead around him. "You say you wish to no longer live. As it would happen, I also have the same wish." He slowly nudged his way past two skeletons toward Drugghod's throne. "Perhaps you could help me in relieving you from whatever burden you carry."

Drugghod slowly came to his feet. He sauntered down the short staircase to stand over the armored man. He dwarfed the knight by several feet and carried himself even taller. "I am intrigued. What is your name?"

"Sir Lewis of the Hills."

"Well, Sir Lewis of the Hills. If you will have it, I will tell you a story. At the end of the story, I hope you will have found some detail that can bring about the end of my reign. If not, I will kill you."

Sir Lewis nodded, more encouraged than fearful. "These are terms I can live with."

"We shall see about that." Drugghod snapped his fingers, and the skeletons began clearing a space at a table. Sir Lewis slowly sheathed his longsword and made his way to the table. Drugghod sat across from him, removing his tall steel crown and setting it between them.

"I have worn this crown for longer than I was alive. It is unimportant to our story how I became what I am today. I accept that you yourself would never understand why I would choose this life. What I do need you to understand is why I took these castles. Why I once controlled the entire southern continent. And why I gave most of it away.

"When I awoke in the darkness in this hideous form, it amazed me at how quickly I lost all sense of humanity, of earthly desires. As your legends would undoubtedly tell, I came down from the Burmasen Mountains with a horde never before seen by the likes of men. I took my first castle nearly a century ago, happy to hold the land and grow my army. I had no ambition to stretch my territory. But, alas, your kind couldn't stomach having wickedness so close to home. And it was because of this that my armies continued to march south.

"When I say that I no longer had earthly desires that included such a brazen emotion as ambition. Ambition is a disease that controls men like you. You will never find happiness because you must always work toward the next success. After I sacked this castle in the coastal city of Windsburgh, I sat heavily upon its throne. My army was vast, my territories wide and heavily protected. I had finally found contentment. This lasted for exactly twenty-two minutes.

"It is not in my nature to hold prisoners for any reason. I have sacked many cities, sat on many thrones. The first act of my armies after taking a city is to empty the prisons. These people are not my enemy, so they are free to leave. When my horde unshackles these people, they spread word of my generosity. They speak of my mercy. It helps quell rebuke; it is a simple tactical decision. I do not have mercy, as I do not have a heart.

"It had been very successful until Windsburgh. After my twenty-two minutes of contentment, a captain approached and told me there was trouble in the castle dungeon. 'A feral woman will not leave,' he said. 'She won't let us loosen her bounds.' I took myself to the wretches of that city, deep in her bosom, to where it kept those they wished to never see again. It was there that I met Eoned for the first time.

"They had chained her to the wall, naked as the day she came into this world, covered in her own filth. I ordered a soldier to break her chains. As he reached over her, she bit his clavicle off. She stared up at my wickedness and chewed on the bone. 'More dog than woman, sire,' said my captain. 'Might as well put her out of her misery.' Her eyes darted to the captain, her jaws drifting the bone in his direction.

'So you understand, don't you?' I stooped to enter her cell. She stood abruptly; she knew I was no mere undead. The bone dropped to the floor. 'Well then, maybe they taught you to speak. What is it, woman, that you desire if not freedom.' Her bottom lip shook like a leaf in the wind. I reached my bony hand to her chin and lifted it to meet where my eyes once lay. I could feel her jaw strengthen.

'Vengeance.'

"I felt something in that moment that I had not felt in centuries: surprise.

"I reached over her head and broke her chains, draping this very cloak I wear today over her nakedness. I brought her to the Queen's chambers, where her majesty lay dead in a bronze tub. As I ordered my men to bring hot water, she had already thrown the monarch into a closet. She strolled across the carpeted room, sliding my cloak to the floor. She stepped into the pool of regal blood in the tub's bottom, reclining as if she had never felt more comfortable in her life. My men filled the basin with scorching hot water, making a twisted solution of red and pink.

"I knelt by her side, fishing water from below to clean her body. It was there that she told me her name. Eoned, a merchant's daughter from the West. Her father had swindled money and goods from as many people as had made his acquaintance. His renown followed him though, and they were always pushing farther east to escape his pursuers. They had made it as far east as Merida when her father's deeds finally caught up with them. A failed sale of faulty armor to a member of the King's Guard. They gave him an option: face justice back west or hand over his daughter. From around her neck, she produced a golden locket. She allowed me to open it for her. On one side was a picture of her mother, clearly where she had received her beauty. On the other, cracked glass where her father once stood.

'He told me they were good men. Just men. He told me they would watch out for me. He told me he would return to retrieve me. And last, he told me to obey.' At this, she spat off the side of the tub. She turned and looked at the two undead soldiers by the door. 'Are these your slaves?'

'They are my thralls. They do as they are told. Others in my army are here for the opportunities that come with waging destruction upon those that would see them enslaved. They are free to go as they please.'

'And do they? Do they leave?'

'Never.'

"Eoned stood from the tub, the bloody water dripping onto the carpet, her red footprints tracking to the bed. She climbed onto the silken bed, inviting me with her eyes to join her. A shame spread across my body. 'That will not be necessary, Eoned.' She knelt at the end of the bed, a look of confusion on her face. 'It is not your body that I desire. It is your spirit.' I retrieved my cloak from the floor and covered her nakedness. 'This vengeance you seek, in exchange for your spirit. It is what I offer.'

"She climbed off the mattress and paced the room. After a few minutes, she rushed to my side. 'You would need an army the likes of which this world has ever known to right what has wronged me.' I could feel my jaw shift backward. I led her through the halls to the doors of the castle. She shielded her eyes from the sun as I pushed open the doors. The fields in front of us were strewn with the slaughter of battle. I left her to regain her sight, ambling down the stairs toward the fields. I raised my hands to the sky, bringing thousands of new soldiers to their feet as my horde howled into the morning sky. After every one of my victims had risen to my army, I turned to Eoned. She remained on the stairs, peering over my forces.

'Yes. I believe this will suffice.'"

Sir Lewis stirred in his seat, his chin resting on a balled fist. He squinted at the dead wizard.

"It would appear that you have something to say, knight," grumbled Drugghod. Sir Lewis scrambled to rebuke his powerful foe, mainly by waving his arms and shaking his head. "Out with it."

"Well, it is just that from what I have learned of you in a short time is that this army with which you control does not actually matter to you. In fact, you have described your motive for destruction as simply a part of your being. Yet, a young girl speaks to you of the atrocities inflicted upon her, and you bend to her bidding? And this deal you made, your army for her spirit. Are you saying you are capable of consuming souls?"

"Not that I am aware of." Drugghod's jaw clicked backward. His bony finger gently caressed the pointed crown in front of him. "During those fleeting minutes at Windsburgh, sitting on the throne and contemplating retirement, I felt a pang of human emotion missing from my life for decades. I cannot be certain, but I believe it was the pointed needle of fear."

"Fear? Of what?"

"I had forgotten why I had started my conquest, and it left me with the terrifying task of deciphering why exactly I was on this mortal coil."

Sir Lewis snapped his fingers. A skeleton shifted behind him. "I think I get it. You were going to be bored! And if anything, this Eoned would certainly bring some entertainment."

Drugghod scratched a line into his finger with the point of his crown. "Perhaps, Sir Lewis of the Hills. Perhaps. But I had little time to ponder my admittedly strange reaction to Eoned. We had work to do.

"You will have read of what comes next. With Eoned at my right hand and an army of the undead behind us, we launched an offensive on the western continent that will never be matched in history. We tracked through Eoned's history, moving from city to city, and removing from them all who stood in our way. In Merida, we found the Knight's Guard who had ripped her from her family. She again surprised me when she offered them mercy for information about her family. The knight's captain told us of a small island named Terratia just northwest of the capital city of Guardia. For his honesty, she allowed him to leave. As far as I know, it is the only mercy she has ever bestowed a man.

"The siege of Guardia would take months, if not years. I brought my army to its door and ordered my captains to begin the attack. The night of our arrival, Eoned asked me if she could go to Terratia alone. I told her that no member of my horde was beholden to me. All were free to leave at their will. But, good knight, the needle of fear came back to me then. And it was not something for which I was prepared. She cradled my face in her hands and wept for me. It would not have been possible for us to couple, but this was a moment of solidarity that I would not have traded for anything."

Drugghod folded his hands together, his head dipping low toward the table. Sir Lewis felt an odd urge to console the wizard. "I have read accounts of the siege of Guardia. It seemed to have been simply overwhelmed in a matter of days. Yet, you say it might have taken a year. How did you manage such a task?"

Drugghod leaned back in his chair. "It would have taken longer, yes. But your lot decided to stop being so damn noble and fight dirty.

"A scout from Guardia showed up at our camp waving a white flag. In his hand was a golden locket and a scroll from the king. 'Your head for the bitch,' it read.

"It turned out that the man Eoned spared went straight to the King of Guardia and told him where we were headed. Terratia is a small island, and there is only one port in and out. Eoned was a ferocious woman, but she could not overwhelm the garrison that was waiting for her. It was a mistake to leave her alone. It was my mistake. And it was mine to rectify in any way I could."

Sir Lewis held his hand to his lips. "I struggle to believe my ancestors would carry out such an act. I do not think you have lied to me about any details up to now, and I can think of no reason for you to. The kingdom of Guardia brought shame to our people. That is not our way."

"Looking back on it now, I don't blame them. They had to do something. We had sacked a dozen cities on our way to the capital, raising more undead along the way. They had to try something, and try they did." Drugghod slowly raised a finger to the knight, his jaw settling forward and his shoulders rising high to where his ears used to be. "But the mistake they made is trifling with entities about which they know nothing.

"That night, I went to the top of a hill overlooking the city and buried Eoned's locket deep in the earth. The next morning, those among my horde with blood in their veins escorted me to the city gates. I instructed them to accept Eoned and to take her to the hill. Eoned had become as much of a leader as I for them, and they told me of their desires to avenge this act. They had spoken in her tongue, even to me, by then. It was a nice thing to hear.

"The heavy city gates pulled open, archers knocking arrows on her walls. A dozen spearmen surrounded me; edges pointed toward me. The knight's guard from Merida was close behind. They had rewarded him for his information with golden armor and, I'm sure, a title of nobility.

'Drop your weapons, wizard.'

'I don't carry any, worm.'

"The spearmen stepped a foot closer. I made it easier for everyone involved. I rustled the clothes off my back and folded them neatly on the ground, resting my crown on top. Apparently satisfied I was unequipped, the knight's guard guided me into the city. The people of Guardia peered between fingers and fences as they took in my wicked nakedness. It thrilled me that I still had a few teeth remaining to flash in their direction. As we reached the city castle, the king had moved his throne to its steps. He held a long chain with Eoned shackled at the end, a collar around her neck. She was wearing purple around one eye.

'I didn't think you would come, Drugghod the Deviant. I suppose this lush is more important to you than I thought. Though from what I can see between your legs, I'm not sure what good she'd do you.' His court laughed at my expense. I tried to meet Eoned's eyes, but she avoided my gaze. 'Well, sorcerer? Nothing to say? No final tricks up your sleeve?'

'I haven't got any sleeves, you horse's ass. Now live up to your end of the bargain. I brought my head. You release Eoned.'

"Your king rolled his eyes, dissuaded by my disinterest in his wit. 'Fine. If you won't provide me with a bit of fun, I'll have to take it myself.' Your king tossed Eoned's chain to the King's Guard, who began leading her past me. She retched and clawed at him, but he beat her away with a pole. Still, her attention I could not find. 'Bring me the axe!' The court burst into cheers. I took to my knees and offered to the king my spine. Eoned kicked out at the guard and finally broke from his grasp. She ran and fell into my arms. The court awed and wailed at our misfortune.

"I told her something then that I had never uttered before and will never utter again. But that was for her ears and not yours, knight. They pulled her from me just as the king was raising his axe. My last sight was of Eoned biting the knight's guard between his legs. My head was cut off in complete joy."

Sir Lewis looked at the wizard in disbelief. "So, you died? But, you were already dead. How does that work?"

Drugghod leaned forward, his bony elbows on the table. "If you would recall from my story, your king called me Drugghod the Deviant. But, you know me as—"

"The Deceptor," Sir Lewis chimed in.

"Indeed. Now, I cannot be exactly certain as to the details of the following information as I was indisposed at the time. The king chopped my head off, and my undead horde fell to the ground at once. He held up his end of the bargain and escorted Eoned out of the city, which was probably in their best interest as she was attempting to murder all of them. Once she had reached the city gates, they released her to my captains. Seeing as the siege had been halted, they left the gates open, placing my head on a pike at the entrance instead. As ordered, my captains took Eoned to the hill over the city. I learned later that one of them told Eoned that I had buried something in the ground there. She dug through the earth until she found what I had left for her. It would not have taken long for her to notice that the locket would not close. Inside of the locket where her father used to sit, I had placed a red crystal. She would not have known what it was, but she would have known that it was important.

Since she is much smarter than anyone I have ever known, she ordered my captains to prepare to siege the city. Since she is much more commanding than anyone else, they did as they were told.

"That night, Eoned stood overlooking the city clutching the golden locket. She was singing a song that I had only heard her sing in her sleep. I know this because I tore myself from under the ground with which she stood.

'My liege. You kept us waiting,' she sang.

'Apologies, my queen. I got a bit lost along the way.'

"She turned to me with a crooked smile underneath a swollen face. 'Am I a queen now?'

'I suppose not quite. But, we can remedy that.'

"I raised my armies with only the sweet sounds of clicking bones and weapons being hoisted. We waltzed through the front gates undeterred. Indeed, knight, we took the city in only a few days. But, it was a bit more painful than you can imagine."

Sir Lewis leaned back in his chair, mouth agape. "The red crystal. In the locket. It keeps you tethered to this world. With or without your head."

"Yes, Sir Lewis of the Hills. When I became what I am today, I gave a part of myself to the crystal. As long as it remains intact, so do I. With a brief relapse, of course."

Sir Lewis pushed his chair back from the table, leaning forward until his elbows hit his knees. He studied the dead wizard as if some final secret awaited his arrival.

"If I asked you where the golden locket is, would you tell me?"

"I would."

Sir Lewis clenched his jaw until he nearly pinched a nerve. He jumped to his feet, leaning over the table toward Drugghod. "Where is the golden locket?"

Drugghod tapped the tip of his steel crown. "I do not know."

Sir Lewis nodded eight times before throwing his hands in the air and walking from the table. He stared at the throne looking for answers, fists clenched to his hips. His gaze fell first to the stone floor, then to his waist. A green ribbon hung from his belt, given to him by the magistrate's daughter before his quest began. He turned to the Drugghod, whose gaze was fixed on the ceiling.

"You gave it to her. You gave it to Eoned?" Drugghod's head tilted toward the knight. Sir Lewis barked out a single laugh and rejoined the table. "By the gods, you might be more human than you think."

Drugghod the Deceptor returned the man's laugh, though it was not clear to Sir Lewis whether it was genuine. "I did. And I have not seen it since. But our story together has yet to be completed. Perhaps in the void, we will find our answer.

"We had succeeded beyond any aspiration possible. The entire southern and western continent was under our control. We fortified the city and settled into a new role as lords of that land. Eoned commanded my troops with full impunity; we were equals in all elements of rule. Those cast out by your kind came offering their allegiance for our protection. There was the occasional skirmish or civil disagreement, but all was squashed by the might of our undead army.

"With all of our success came precisely what I had yearned so much for: contentment. But, that goal was always a singular one of my own; it was not shared by my queen. Eoned grew restless. So much blood was shed on our journey. It was hard for her to control what had burned inside of her for so long. But that is the thing about vengeance they do not tell you—it is ever so temporary.

"One day, a tribe of orcs came to our court. They had found a weakness in the human defenses to the north. They aimed to reclaim their land. I dismissed them, for taking more land from the north would only weaken our position in the rest of the continent. Eoned stepped forward from her throne. 'The dead army shall ride north in two days. It is time that we extend our hand.'

"Her legend was just as strong as mine. She was the human who ravaged her own people for slighting her. The orcs would follow her. Alas, I would not. She was angry at first; we had not had nary a disagreement in the many years we had known each other. Never before had she expressed anger toward me. There was nothing I could do to persuade her. There was nothing I could do to keep her with me. You are correct in saying that I am more human than I think. For whatever I felt that night was very human indeed.

"The next morning, she greeted me with a smile. She ordered two horses to be saddled and let the captains know we would return the next morning. As we exited the heavy gates of Guardia together, I knew it would be for the last time. She took me northwest to Terratia. I had sent a small garrison to control the ports, but to allow any residents to come and go as they please.

"Eoned knocked on the door of the hut. I stood by the horses; I knew what emotions my presence brought to people. Her mother opened the door. She held the same beauty as the drawing in the locket, and her eyes gleamed with a purity I had forgotten existed in this world. She shuddered when she saw me. For eyes of that purity are marked by the likes of me. I left her to her family and took the long ride to Guardia.

"When she arrived back the next morning, my armies and I stood inside the city gates, with the orcs among their rank. She dismounted and cautiously approached me. 'What is this, Drugghod?'

'Any member of this army is free to leave at any time. This has always been the rule. As you know, I cannot join you. I will not. But, I can send a few pieces of me with you.' The undead clicked their bones together. Eoned turned to witness her undead forces. I draped the golden locket around her neck. 'As long as you wear this locket, the largest strength the world has ever seen will march with you. But if they are to fall, to the ground they will stay.' I rested my hand on her shoulder. She gripped it and took a deep breath.

'And if I fall?'

'I will take a small group to Windsburgh. To the place where we first met. If the humans find me there, then I will know you have fallen. And if they strike me down, I will perish for good.'

"Eoned turned to me and tried to tear the locket from her neck. 'Please, Drugghod—'

'I will not live in a world without you in it. So go and take from it what you need.'"

Drugghod flicked at his crown. He slowly stood and walked back toward his throne. "In the years following, there was very little noise from around the southern continent. I took this as a good sign, but I detest hope and refuse to let it settle. One day, the sound of horses echoed around the castle. Later, the abominations below fell four human knights wearing the colors of the north. And so I knew my queen had fallen."

Sir Lewis cracked the knuckles on his right hand. "That isn't entirely certain, Drugghod." The dead wizard turned sharply toward the knight. The knight reattached his heavy gauntlets and tightened his boots. "Her armies did indeed fall. But, they did not find her. They had her cornered to the east at the base of the Burmasen Mountains. When they ran down the last of her army, she was nowhere to be found. They think she climbed the mountain to escape her fate, but no one could last long on those peaks."

As Sir Lewis bent to brush the skeletal debris from his boots, Drugghod rested a hand on his shoulder. The knight turned abruptly to find the dead wizard's face to be twisted into what could only be described as a smile. "I must thank you, Sir Lewis of the Hills. You have provided me with something I never thought possible." He lifted the heavy steel crown to his head with ease.

Sir Lewis instinctively rested a hand on his sword and backed toward the door. "And what would that be exactly?"

"A reason to exist." Drugghod followed the knight slowly toward the back of the hall, his long arms bent behind his back. "I told Eoned only once of my life before this one. Of my fall to the evil forces that bred inside of me. Of my trials on the Burmasen Mountains. Of how I became a *lich*."

Sir Lewis bolted for the door. Drugghod's arms raised to the ceiling. Four skeletons barred the exit, with thirty more behind him. Drugghod sauntered to his throne, resting his head on his fist.

"Drugghod, please! Allow me to climb the Burmasen Mountain and find the crystal! Allow me to end our misery!"

"Allow me to save you the time, human."

As the partygoers tore the knight apart, Drugghod returned to his favorite activity: waiting for Eoned's return.

About the Author

Roger Landes is a fantasy and science fiction writer from Chicago. He is best known as the co-creator of the serial comic book *The Last Herald* from Odyssey Comics. He currently resides in Minneapolis with his wife and two parakeets.

DANY
COMIC

JUST DESSERTS

BY CHARLOTTE H. LEE

Nellara burped and licked her lips. The goat meat had been tough, but the flavour divine. She rubbed her soft grey belly feathers, her lips curving into a satisfied smile. All too often, she'd scatter most of what she stole rather than eat it, letting the crows and gulls squabble over tainted food while she went hungry. Hades's directive for harpies to steal the food of evildoers before bringing them to face the Judges was sweet justice, but often the food was as repulsive to her as she was to her bounties. Perhaps an assignment with a good cook was a sign that she was moving up the pecking order.

From her perch atop a craggy promontory, Nellara could see the entire channel. Choppy, black water reflected towering charcoal clouds, making the day as dark as the hearts of those she hunted. Air, heavy with humidity, made the pirates' skin glisten as they dropped anchor and made ready to land on the sandy peninsula at the south end of the island. Murderous hands passed empty water casks over the gunwale to those waiting in dories below. One burly sailor missed a barrel, the crack and splintering carrying easily to her with no wind to drown the sound. He snarled answering curses when his mates protested the precious loss. Nellara leaned forward eagerly, her silvered wings rising for a down-sweep, watching to see how steeply the sailor would pay for his mistake.

The sailors turned their attention back to catching the falling barrels, their mutters lost in the distance. Nellara sighed and steeled herself to wait for the cover of night. Her luminous wings sagged back from where they'd been poised, disappointment making them heavier. She'd eaten and groomed her comely plumage clean of the merest trace of dust and grime. Now she would sleep. Later was soon enough to bear the disgust and fear with which the sailors would look upon her.

Nellara woke to shouts of laughter coming from the point. She opened her eyes to a night so dark that the bonfire on the distant beach shone like a beacon in the deepest torture pit of Tartarus. Sailors clustered about the fire, roasting whatever meats they'd caught. Mismatched songs rose to a cacophony that set her teeth on edge. She shook out her wings. Heavy droplets from the evening rain cascaded from her in a wide, arching spray. She sidled to the edge of the promontory, eyes scanning the starless sky. The storm had paused, but its torrent would begin again before long. Soon the bonfire would be out, giving her enough cover to take several in a single night. With luck, the cook was still aboard the ship. She hoped he'd be last. Stealing tasty food was preferable to mouldy or soured rations.

Nellara's patience was rewarded when one of the pirates wandered away from the fire, no doubt looking for a place to relieve himself. She tipped over the edge of the cliff. As silently as a shadow, she spread her wings, letting the smooth leading edges of her full wingspan cleave cleanly through the air until she was but a forearm's length above the waves. Careful to keep both arms tucked tight to her body, she skimmed the water, using the heat rising off the night ocean to keep her aloft. Eyes on the lone sailor, she swung wide around the point and swooped down the far side of the beach, unnoticed by those ringing the fire.

The lone pirate's unsteady steps across the damp sand were as loud as a trumpet. Nellara back-winged lightly to land, thick foot talons gouging grooves in the sand. She waited with a predator's patience for him to reach her in the dark. Thoughts of his bounty price made her lips stretch in an anticipatory smile.

"Oh. Miss, where did you come from?" The young pirate halted and peered about when he came upon her, as if he would be able to discover her vessel if he looked hard enough. "A lady as pretty as you shouldn't be out here all alone." He paused, scratching at dark curls behind his ear. "If you're hoping for rescue from that lot, you're better off shipwrecked here."

Pretty? Surprise froze Nellara's tongue. Never had she been described so. Hideous. Nightmarish hag. Harpy. This sailor must be drunker than she'd thought. An unbidden yearning rose up for a moment: that he could see her as pretty, a clearheaded observation rather than an inebriated wish.

"Are you cold?" He shrugged a threadbare coat off broad shoulders and staggered forward to swing it over hers. "Oh," he said when he caught sight of her wings. He gulped, letting the coat swing against his muscular legs. He stood there staring at her with eyes nearly as black as the night, taking in her full form. Nellara couldn't guess what her own face showed, but his was a curious mixture of hope, realization, disappointment and resignation.

"We haven't been losing men to the sea, have we?" he asked, his tone calm and a little sad. She shook her head.

"I thought harpies were supposed to be ugly. Old and ugly. You aren't. You're young. And beautiful." He stopped, closed his eyes, and gave his head the briefest of shakes. When he looked at her again, he produced a faint half-smile. "I've been long hoping for rescue, but I'd expected it would mean a return to my home rather than to Hades's gates."

"I'm sorry," she said, not knowing what else to say.

"No matter," he said. "Even the Asphodel Meadows would be an improvement over the last few months."

"I can take you last, if you'd prefer."

"No," he said, lifting his hand to wave off her offer. "I'd rather go now than have to spend another night with that loathsome crew."

Nellara nodded and held out her arms. He stepped into them, embracing her as she embraced him. He pressed his cheek to hers, and she could smell the sea in his hair. A weight settled on her heart. She crouched, felt him move with her, following her lead. With doubt beginning to stir in the pit of her belly, she sprang into the air, knowing she shouldn't be surprised that the weight on her heart hadn't impeded her launch.

Returning home with a prize was usually cause to celebrate. The bounty for a soul bound for Tartarus was a meal worth lingering over, each mouthful a glorious symphony of flavours exquisitely balanced and nuanced. A hedonistic orgy of scent, sensation and taste. A bounty meal, accompanied by the finest pressings of wines painstakingly paired to each succulent dish and the sweetest music available to all of creation, was what every harpy lived for. A meal prepared especially to the tastes of the bounty hunter, served on dishes crafted from silver, sent every harpy out to hunt evildoers.

Not once in her life had Nellara questioned the nobility of her role in justice for the wronged, nor had she ever felt guilt for collecting bounties.

Until now.

She and her charge stood in the line facing Minos upon his throne, waiting for her turn to speak. The familiar words of her usual litany for condemnation came easily to mind, while the words of supplication for reprieve were a jumbled mess in her head.

The pair in line before them moved past the Judges; a gaunt sister harpy dragging along a man weeping for mercy from those who gave none. Minos turned to Nellara, nodding in her direction. Impassive brown eyes peering out from behind his golden bull mask moved to the young man at her side. The words she sought would not come, and Minos returned his stony gaze to her. She remained speechless despite several preparatory breaths taken and released unused.

"So Nellara, your zeal seems in abeyance this day," he said, finally. "I must mark this moment. It is a first."

Nellara ducked her head, trying to hide the flush that crept up her cheeks. Despite her intention to remain still, her wings ruffled before she could pull them tight to her back.

"Lukos, step forward."

Shame battled with guilt in her breast. She hadn't even asked her captive his name. Lukos stepped up next to her. From the corner of her eye, she could see his fingertips straying in her direction, as if he were reaching out for solace. Or courage. Shame won the fight for her heart when the fingertips pulled away to form a fist at his side.

"Until your capture by Crathis and his crew, you lived the life of a decent man. Not a great man, but kind to those dependent on you and trustworthy to those who hired you. If you had continued to live that life, you would be judged fit for Asphodel Meadows."

Nellara glanced up, disbelief pulling her brows together. She looked at Lukos and stifled the urge to put her arm around him when she saw the colour drain from his face. She turned back to Minos, her rising protest checked when he began speaking again.

"You did not directly harm a single innocent life while you toiled in his galley, but you failed to stop him and his crew from harming countless souls. As the ship's cook, you could have easily sent all aboard to me for judgement at any time during the last five seasons. Instead, you chose to do nothing but what the murderers demanded of you. You performed your tasks to the best of your ability. While you did not do it out of support for their activities, you did do it to protect your own safety. You improved the lives of evildoers, saving yourself at the cost of hundreds of innocents. These are not the actions of a good man." Minos paused and glared Nellara back into silence when she drew breath to speak. "Judgement has been passed upon you. You are sentenced to Tartarus, where the punishment for your complicity will be visited upon you by Cronus for all eternity."

Minos tipped his sceptre forward, letting it fall upon Lukos's forehead. The young man cried out in pain and fell to his knees, his brow smoking from its new brand—a deer to represent cowardice in the face of danger. Tears of pain tracked down his cheeks and fell to the ground, darkening the stone.

"Please, Minos," Nellara said, her voice wavering, "must it be for all eternity? Would not a hundred or a thousand years be enough? He is still so young. He made a mistake."

"Do not question my judgement, harpy!" Minos ground his words out through clenched teeth, eyes blazing at her temerity. "I have spoken, and so it shall be." He banged his fist on the chair arm, the resulting boom echoing through the chamber and drawing the attention of his fellow Judges, Aeacus and Rhadamanthus, from their pronouncements. Mutters rustled through the cavern, bouncing off stone walls and bronze gates. Behind the Judges, Cerberus raised and cocked his three heads, all six canine ears pricking forward in curiosity.

Nellara swallowed, eyes wide with fear. Minos wasn't known for temperance or patience—it had been boiled out of him during his death. She gave a jerky nod and, gathering up Lukos with an arm about his waist, she led him beyond Minos's dais. The back of her neck prickled with the fear of reprisal until she was safely beyond reach.

"Thank you for trying, my lady. May I remember you in my dreams as Nellara?" The brand on Lukos's forehead had stopped smoking, though his eyes remained clouded with pain. The weight on her heart doubled at the thought that his pain was only just beginning.

"I wish I could do more for you, Lukos. I wish I had done something worthy of you remembering me at all." Nellara tried to smile, but her cheeks felt wooden.

"Ah, beautiful lady, you have done more for me by your protest than any has ever done for me before." He smiled at her weakly. With a sigh, he pulled away from her to stand on his own, then reached for her hand. "I will pray to Hades for another chance at life to repair my soul. Only he can override the dictate of a Judge. Now please, give me a smile that I can take with me. A gift that not even Cronus could take away."

Nellara gave him her best effort at a real smile, trying to hide her knowledge that Cronus could—and would—take away every happy memory Lukos had.

"Now, my dear, this simply will not do! Are you ill? Why do you not eat?"

Nellara looked up from the sofrito she'd been pushing around her plate with a hunk of soft, herbed bread. A pang of guilt sent a flush to her cheeks when she saw the genuine concern on Vaelete's plump face. Grease glistened around the matron's mouth, the lamb rib clutched in her hand momentarily forgotten because of Nellara's shocking lack of appetite.

"I don't understand something, Auntie," Nellara said.

Vaelete cocked her head, the grooves between her brows smoothing away as the concern faded to gentle kindness.

"What is it, child?"

"The last soul I brought back called me pretty. I truly believe he saw me that way. That's never happened before, and he obviously wasn't blind."

Vaelete nodded and sighed, lowering the lamb rib to her plate. She wet her napkin in the dipping bowl and gently wiped her face clean. Nellara waited patiently, recognizing the older harpy's fastidious grooming as a delay for thought.

"It was bound to happen to you eventually, though I had hoped you would be older and fatter before it did." Vaelete sighed again and shook her head sadly. "Sometimes good people get mixed up in bad business. They don't mean to, and they can't always escape quickly. If they escape soon enough, their soul takes no lasting harm. But if they don't, their soul darkens even if they don't intend to do wrong themselves. Dark souls see us as old and ugly because that's what they have become themselves. They can't see true beauty any longer."

"So, if a soul saw me as beautiful, it means that the soul wasn't yet lost?"

Vaelete fidgeted in her seat, wing feathers ruffling up and smoothing, fingers drumming on the table. She reached for her glass of wine, avoiding Nellara's eyes.

"It is up to the Furies to decide that, my dear. Only they can say whether the soul had the chance of escaping or if the darkening was inevitable. The Judges hear their words before passing sentence on any soul. Trust in them, my dear. They know."

Nellara nodded, outwardly accepting Vaelete's advice. She ate her meal, then, feigning enjoyment though it tasted of betrayal and injustice. The reward for Lukos's soul would not sit well in her belly, she feared.

None of the rest of the pirate ship's crew had seen Nellara as anything other than a monster. That should have made her reward meals worth any abuse. Instead, since Lukos's capture, each of her returns to the Underworld—with its accompanying discharge of a darkened soul—had been like adding a pinch too much salt to a honeyed sauce. Everything tasted off.

Nellara huddled in her nest. Even the sweet sound of her sisters' songs permeating the aviary wasn't enough to distract her from her growing misery. Preening over her smooth and silky grey feathers after a luxurious grooming no longer interested her. The last time she'd eaten anything delightful had been Lukos's goat meat. Goat meat. Chewy, stringy goat meat. But the taste had made even the endless chewing a pleasure. Where once she had revelled and gorged on food that made every unpleasantness worth suffering, now she chewed mechanically without satisfaction.

What she wouldn't give to have Lukos prepare her next meal.

Nellara stiffened, eyes wide and feathers ruffled large. Prickles rose on her arms, and a shiver ran down her back, spreading her tail feathers. What *would* she give to have him cook for her? She couldn't shake the heretical thought. What she would give to have him do more than cook sent a flush of burning heat to her neck and face. A desire for pleasures beyond the culinary became a titillating concept that made all future meals seem trivial and banal.

Squeezing her eyes closed, Nellara forced herself to think of the thousands of banquets she'd immersed herself in before she'd taken Lukos's soul. Surely one day, she would again appreciate the just rewards for her work? Unbidden, the thought that she *knew* she would appreciate Lukos's efforts wormed its way into her head. She gritted her teeth and tried to shoo it away. Beating the temptation to press her hands over her ears, she forced herself to relax and focus on anything other than food. Or Lukos. After several minutes a new possibility struck her, and she scrambled out of her nest.

Nellara spent the next several minutes combing through her bed, searching for elm leaves. If she could blame these thoughts on the false dreams they brought, she could easily go back to the life she'd known, content with her purpose and its attendant rewards. When she found herself beginning the search for the third time, she gave up. There were no elm leaves here. No sister had snuck any into her nest as a prank.

Was she crazy? If, on the wildest, slimmest hope, she could successfully retrieve Lukos from Tartarus, where would they go? Where could they hide from Hades and all his minions? Nellara snorted. She was a minion herself, she should know. This would take some thinking. Maybe, if she was lucky, just thinking it through would bring her appetite for the more usual bestial pleasures back.

"Well, you seem to have gotten over whatever has been bothering you of late," Xylinore whispered from the Judgement line next to Nellara's.

"Why do you say that?" Nellara asked, glancing about to see if anyone else had heard the older harpy's comment. If they had, they paid no mind.

"You aren't so hunched and long in the face. For the last few weeks, you've been looking like you have a permanent stomach ache."

Nellara shrugged and shifted the strap of her satchel. "My last assignment was a starving pirate ship. It bothers me when there isn't enough to eat. There wasn't even anything worth throwing to the crows!" She scoffed and wrinkled her nose. "Have you ever smelled a ship of starving men? It put me off food through the whole commission. Next time I'll make sure I take the cook last!"

Xylinore grinned at her and chuckled. "I remember those days. I'll gladly stick to greasy politicians and petty tyrants, I think. At least their food is always plentiful, and well worth stealing." Xylinore's line shuffled forward, and the harpy moved on with her charge, giving Nellara a bright smile in farewell.

As Nellara passed under the elm with her own prisoner, she whispered a command for him to break off a low-hanging branch. He gulped, glancing at the centaurs who roamed through the lines, bows clutched in hands strong enough to pull a man's head from his body. When she repeated the command with a reminder of their deal, he reached a shaky hand above his head and ripped a thin branch free.

"What are you doing?" Nellara raised her voice and her charge cowered, the branch held before him as a shield. The alerted centaur watching from three rows over lowered his bow and turned away when Nellara raised her wings and snatched the branch from the snivelling wretch. Flexing her wings to keep anyone from watching her hands, she stowed the elm branch into her satchel while she reached for the scruff of the sorry soul's neck.

"That won't help you," she said loudly, shaking him and then hauling him forward to catch up with the line that had shuffled ahead. "Cronus won't let you hide from his punishments with false dreams." Under her breath, Nellara said, "You have kept your part of the bargain. I will keep mine."

This time the proper verses for leniency should come easily. She'd practised it often enough over the last few months. Not that she thought for a moment Minos would pay them any more heed this time than any other. The murderer she escorted didn't know that, though.

Once Minos passed the expected sentence, with only a long blink to mark his impatience with her now-regular intonation for leniency, Nellara marched the sobbing excuse of a man to the sphinx-sized bronze gate beyond the Judge Line. After passing through the sky-scraping pillars that marked the entrance to Tartarus, they continued across a bleak, stony plain to the waiting Hecatonchire.

The hundred-handed giant towered over them, numerous shackles clasped in various fists—some human, most less so. She imagined those hands passing the elm leaves she'd hidden away in her satchel from hand to hand. Would the dozen or so from the branch be enough to let the Hecatonchire sleep in a paradise filled with the pleasures untold it yearned for, or would her bribe be refused as too little? All she could do now was pray that the bribe would be enough to convince the guardian to let her out of Tartarus with a sentenced soul in company.

Beside her, the captive whimpered, as condemned souls always did. Nellara's nose flared in disgust. Lukos hadn't whimpered. He'd met the monstrosity looming before them with his chin high, though she had seen the rapid beat of his pulse in his neck.

Grip-hands reached for the pathetic prisoner, engulfing him and smothering his screams. The gate guardian brought the murderer close to an eye-hand, studying the human's features, memorizing them. Smell-hands stroked him, committing yet another's soul aroma to its endless catalogue of evildoers. Lukos hadn't screamed. He hadn't struggled. He'd quietly accepted his consequences and suffered through the handling without complaint.

The Hecatonchire roared when the creature in its grasp bit a taste-hand's protruding tongue, drawing green blood that sizzled as it struck the earth. Nellara took advantage of the distraction and sidled out of its line of sight, taking to wing as the giant dropped a leg-hand's knee to the ground to wrestle the shackles onto the shrieking evildoer.

Four hard downstrokes, and then Nellara found an updraft, taking her high into the air above a barren, lonely landscape. She curved her back and yawed into a circle, eyes sweeping the horizon for any hint of which direction to go.

Far off to the north, a glint of light drew her eye. The River Cocytus wound its way through Tartarus, its icy waters expelling light and goodness before flowing down into the Phlegethon.

Clutching the satchel close to her chest, Nellara swallowed her fear and beat her wings northward. Below her, the rocky desert scrolled past, its rising heat aiding her flight as much as it baked her body. Taking care to avoid touching the elm's leaves, she reached into her satchel for her waterskin and scarf. With one eye on the growing glint and, careful not to spill the precious water, she wet the scarf then tied it around her mouth and nose.

On she flew, dampening the scarf every few minutes to stave off the worst ravages of the arid wind. A glint of white light in the distance grew into a band. It stretched across the horizon and reflected back a sun forever locked in zenith. Dampening the scarf did much to ease the parching of nose and throat tissues but did nothing to stop the desiccation of her skin. The fierce sun baked it, turning what was once smooth and supple into flaking patches marred by cracks and grooves.

From time to time, feathers from Nellara's chest, back, legs and wings came loose and swirled away in eddies of hot wind. If she didn't reach the river soon, she risked losing glittering secondary flight feathers in addition to the tertiary, contour and down feathers she'd already lost.

When, at last, she could make out the shore edge of the Cocytus, Nellara was tiring and contemplating the continuation of her journey on foot. She'd run out of water, and the cracks in her skin were weeping blood. The loss of secondary flight feathers made the beats of her wings weaker, so she had to work harder. Her back ached from the effort. Each stroke gave her less lift than the one before; already, she was barely more than a dozen forearms above the ground.

Nellara held the satchel to her almost-bare torso and let herself drop to the ground. Blood oozed down her arms and chest, soaked into the remaining down feathers and plastered them to her body in a lumpy, ugly red-black covering. If she'd had enough moisture left to her, she would have wept. All she could do was hope that her feathers would grow back one day.

The stones under Nellara's talons were sharp and hot against her feet. She trudged across the remaining distance to the river's edge, stumbling often as she kicked against rocks that leapt up to trip her. Fatigue dragged against every muscle, and only the smell of the water drew her forward. Rational thought was beyond her animal need for hydration, and she couldn't remember why she'd made the journey. The entire reason for her existence was to get to the river. There was nothing more.

Pain lanced up Nellara's leg and she stumbled, falling heavily into a patch of scorching sand. She cried out but didn't have the strength to rise again. Behind eyelids too heavy to open, the blazing sun burned scarlet.

"Nellara." A voice was calling her from far away. "Nellara, can you hear me?" The voice was deep. Male. A voice she'd been seeking. "Nellara, wake up." Why did she hurt so? Every inch of her body burned as if it had been seared then set to roast. The voice called her name again and she struggled to consciousness, aware now of the brightness of the light beyond her eyelids that had coloured her dreams such a frightening shade of red.

"Lukos?" Nellara tried to open her eyes, but they held fast. She reached a hand to rub them, but the voice's owner blocked her movement, urging her to stay still. A damp cloth, icy cold and wet against her hot skin, was pressed to her eyes. She stiffened at the intensity of the relief from both pain and light, gasping against the near-painful deliciousness of it.

Patterns dancing against Nellara's eyelids bemused her until another wet cloth was pressed against her lips. She opened her mouth, eager to draw in the moisture, willing it to ease the pain of the desiccated tissues in her mouth and throat.

"Lukos?" Nellara asked again when she had drawn out all the water she could from the cloth.

"Yes. Don't try to talk or open your eyes just yet. After I get you into the river, you can tell me how you've come to be here."

Another cloth against her mouth. She drew its water while Lukos replaced the one against her eyes, carefully wiping away grit and salt from her lashes.

Strong arms slid between her and the sand. Nellara cried out against the pain of it, then bit her lip in an attempt to stifle future cries as Lukos heaved to his feet. She couldn't stop the whimpers from sounding in her throat as he carried her the last steps to Cocytus's shore. Cool air wafting up from below her warned her an instant before the rushing surface of the water slapped her flayed skin. It was more than she could bear and she slipped away to unconsciousness again, where pain couldn't touch her.

A gentle stroke of a thumb against Nellara's cheek woke her, drawing her from sleep on a luxurious journey. The cool water was a gentle cushion under her and a soft blanket between her and the merciless sun. Lukos stood over her, blocking the sun from her face, his arms hooked around her underarms to hold her to him.

So many of her glorious feathers had been lost, leaving behind only scattered, blood-soaked down, making her loathe to open her eyes. She couldn't bear the sight of her nakedness. Would Lukos appreciate all that she had suffered to free him, or would he shrug it off as nothing compared to his? On and on, she argued with herself until the water's cool embrace chilled her to her core.

With her teeth chattering, Nellara finally opened her eyes to peer up at Lukos. His eyes were closed, fatigue etching deep grooves around his mouth. Chastened, she shifted her weight, struggling to bring her feet down. Lukos's eyes opened and the fatigue lines smoothed away as the shine of joy suffused his face. He lifted her, straining and grunting in his effort to stay upright against the force of the Cocytus's current. A single talon snagged against a large stone of the riverbed, and Nellara dug her grip down around a smooth rock, the weight of it enough to give her time to grasp another rock with her other foot.

Lukos's hands lingered on her elbows; fingers sun-warm against her chilled bare skin. Hope warred with concern on his face, his eyes pleading, though she was a little afraid to know what they pled for.

Unwilling still to see the devastation her journey had caused to her plumage but too cowed to meet Lukos's gaze, she glanced about.

The sun beat down on them, a fiery disk pummelling the endless expanse of burning sand and jagged rocks. The only break in the heat shimmering around them was the wide ribbon of Cocytus. Reason enough to stay where they were. How would they escape if she couldn't fly them out? There was no hope for flight as denuded as she was, and the desert too vast to cross on foot. The elm branch stashed in her satchel was useless if they couldn't get to the gate to use it.

"Why have you come, Nellara?" Lukos asked, his voice gentle but insistent.

"I came for you," she answered, barely above a whisper.

Lukos captured her hands and brought them to his lips. He pressed a kiss to her fingers, and she risked a glance at him. His bronzed face was wreathed in a smile so wide splits appeared in dry, cracked lips. Her knees nearly buckled in relief, only the knowledge that she could be swept away by the current keeping them stiff enough to hold her upright.

"Those words make my heart sing a song I'd never thought to hear again," Lukos said, his eyes full of emotion. "You honour me with your sacrifice." His voice broke with an unshed sob and he cleared his throat.

With tentative fingers, Nellara reached out to stroke his cheek. The sunbaked skin along his high cheekbone was rough under her touch, flakes loosening to drift away into the stagnant air. The deer brand marring the smooth plain of his forehead had healed into a raised, pulpy ridge. She touched it and shed a tear, knowing that it had been an unfair judgement. His bravery before the Hecantonchire had proven that to her beyond doubt.

"I don't know how yet, but I will take you to the Asphodel Meadows," she said. "Minos was wrong to send you into Cronus's clutches." Her brows came together in puzzlement. "Although, your punishment is not as great as I had feared it would be. You are alone here?"

Lukos nodded. "Yes. I have walked and walked, staying mostly in the shallows. Sometimes it felt as though I had not moved, for the scene never changes." He looked about, squinting against the sun. "It wasn't until I saw you that I was sure that my punishment wasn't to walk the bank of the Cocytus in an unending loop." He brought his gaze back to her. "Ever since I found you, I've been thinking of how I could get you home. This is not an existence you deserve to endure." He shook his head. "There must be a way for you to carry more water with you so you can return safely. Now that I know I have your forgiveness, I can earn my redemption with an open heart."

"But I came to get you out! I won't leave without you!"

Lukos squeezed his eyes shut, tears leaking from their corners. "You must! Return home. Pray for me." He kissed her fingers again. "I will not flee from my fate. I will not run away as a coward. I've spent enough of my life living that way. I will not do so any longer."

"I can't fly," Nellara whispered. "My flight feathers are gone, lost to this unyielding sun."

The confusion on Lukos's face made Nellara's breath catch in her throat. With dread a stone in her stomach, she looked down. Shock made her deaf to her own shout of surprise. Where before her contour feathers had flowed over her breasts, belly and legs in a soft, uniform grey, now they shone bright white with touches of gold and silver sparkling under the fierce sun. She craned her neck to catch sight of her wings, extending them to catch the full glory of the peacock blue leading edge feathers that graduated through jewelled purple and ended with a crimson trailing edge. She twisted her upper body to catch a glimpse of tail feathers that matched the glowing hues of her wings.

A chuckle from a short distance away startled them both. Nellara clutched at Lukos, still too disoriented to feel stable on her feet. Only moments before, they had been alone for as far as the eye could see. Now a man, seated on a gilded chair under a canopy watched them from the river bank. A lightly clad boy fanned him with an intricately woven and painted vane, its edging wrapped in shimmering silk. Judging by the golden circlet nestled over the man's elegantly coiffed, shoulder-length brown curls, there was only one possibility of who it could be.

"Hades," Nellara murmured.

"Yes, harpy," the Olympian said, his voice carrying easily over the rushing water. Genuine mirth lent his sharply angled face a warmth she would never have expected from the Lord of the Dead.

"It is rare," Hades went on while Nellara and Lukos continued to stare at him, both frozen—Nellara with guilt and Lukos with shock—"that my own creatures surprise me. Harpy loyalties tend to be restricted to their stomachs, so to watch this scenario play out has been more entertainment than I've had in countless years."

A thousand thoughts flickered through Nellara's mind, all of them too quick for her to catch and make sense of. She stood rooted to the ground, breath coming harshly. Hades studied them, sipping from a jewel-encrusted goblet, while they remained speechless. Lukos found his tongue first.

"My Lord," he said, pausing only to swallow hard, "you do us a great honour by revealing yourself to us." Lukos turned to face the god, his nervousness obvious by rapid blinking and a face drained of colour. He seemed to draw strength from his crushing grip on Nellara's hand and pushed his shoulders back, standing taller in the knee-deep water.

Hades waved a negligent hand, dismissing the nicety. He shifted his gaze to Nellara, cocking an eyebrow in a clear invitation to speak.

"My Lord, thank you for restoring me. I give the greatest thanks for your generosity in gifting me such magnificent plumage." Nellara bowed deeply from the waist, wings loosening from their tight folds on her back, and let her eyes drop from her Lord. She held the bow longer than courtesy required, both to show her genuine appreciation of her own new glory and to buy herself enough time to think now that her brain was functioning once more. When, at last, she straightened, Hades was watching her through narrowed golden eyes.

"You disagreed with Minos's judgement enough to risk eternal damnation for the rescue of another." Hades crooked a finger to beckon her to him. She tensed, shooting a glance at Lukos. Her lover—she could call him that now, the emotion she read in his eyes couldn't be mistaken for anything else—gave her an encouraging smile and let go of her hands. He sent her forward with a gentle push towards the shaded throne, then laced his fingers and held them loosely before him.

Nellara squared her shoulders, turned back to Hades, and nodded. "I did, My Lord," she said, stepping forward as she'd been bid. She stopped short of the hide that covered the ground around the throne, not sure if the invitation included sharing his shade. Her god's lip twitched at that. He beckoned her forward again, nodding to the servant boy. Nellara stepped into the delicious respite from the sun, mindful not to gouge the cool, soft hide beneath her feet. The boy presented her with a goblet. Bliss spread through her from core to fingertips at the sweet and smoky bouquet of her favourite wine.

"And will you accept whatever punishment I deem appropriate, or will you seek to subvert that, too?" Hades asked in a voice dangerously soft, his eyes as cold as the river behind her. Nellara swallowed hard with a mouth suddenly as dry as the desert surrounding them, the wine turned sour.

"Yes, My Lord. Your word is final in all things."

Hades raised his voice, his gaze keeping Nellara in place. "And you, Lukos, what would you do if Nellara were to be sentenced to the Mourning Fields for trying to circumvent your sentence? Would you try to break her out from an eternity of anguish for seeking an impossible love, or would you submit to the fair and just punishments you each have been given?"

Nellara's down ruffled contour feathers despite how hard she tried to appear calm. She debated which was the best answer and which answer she wanted Lukos to give. The silence stretched on, Hades displaying more patience than she had expected him to possess. She suspected there was a touch of dark humour at play behind his stony face, tumbled in with a fair dose of curiosity.

"My Lord," Lukos began at last, "I am grateful to you for restoring my beloved's health, and for granting me the boon of learning that she returns my love for her."

Nellara's heart squeezed tight in joyous pain. Her feathers smoothing at the confirmation she'd not needed, but yearned to hear anyway. "I feel that she would be best served if I honoured my sentence. I should continue my time in Tartarus until I am deemed worthy of redemption. Once I have earned it, I would gladly join her in the Mourning Fields or wherever else she may be sent. I will remain devoted to her no matter where my soul labours."

Hades flicked his gaze between them. "Such a romantic sentiment. It seems your love is not unrequited, Nellara." He paused, golden eyes boring into Nellara's as if he would read her thoughts as one would read an epic poem. She caught and held her breath when he began speaking again, this time a sardonic smile playing about his lips and a glint of humour appearing in his eyes. "It seems the Mourning Fields would not be an appropriate choice."

Nellara let her breath out in a relieved rush and held a long blink to gain some semblance of composure.

"What is also clear is that your time spent in lamentation has not been wasted," Hades said, shifting his gaze to Lukos. Hope flared on Lukos's face and in Nellara's heart. Hades rose to his feet, lifting his goblet in salute to each of them. "Lukos of Abydos, you have earned Redemption from Cocytus. Not only have you done it in a way that proves you have learned the dangers of succumbing to cowardice, but you've also learned the requirements of heroism."

Nellara gasped. Joy flooded through her so intensely that tears sprang to her eyes, blurring her vision into a meaningless blend of light and dark.

Hades's nod acknowledged her realization. "Yes, Nellara. I am also satisfied that you have learned to serve more than just your own selfish wants. Regardless of whether your love was returned, you would not have continued the duties of a harpy." He paused. "I shouldn't be surprised that the first of you creatures to learn to love more than her stomach chose a cook," he said, shrugging and shaking his head ruefully. "You may join this man in Elysium where together you may choose to remain or return to a terrestrial life in the form of your choice."

Nellara fell to her knees, stammering her thanks over clasped hands. At Hades's nod of acknowledgement, she shot to her feet and whirled to her lover. The radiant joy on his face sent her flying into Lukos's arms. She giggled when the sweet words he whispered into her hair were descriptions of the desserts he would create to show her just how much he loved her.

About the Author

Charlotte H. Lee's current home base is British Columbia's Lower Mainland, where she gleefully hides from Canadian winters. Her stories have appeared in Little Blue Marble, Metaphorosis, The Overcast, and others. You can find links to her published work atwww.charlottehlee. com.

DANY
COMICS

Death in the Highlands

by Melrose Dowdy

"Help me God, if you hear a pitiful beggar like me," Calum cried into the winds. His fists closed around a locket with a long chain. "Or anyone who hears me! I am a man at his end, a fool without hope." He opened the locket in his hands with care. Inside, an aged miniature painting of his wife, Cara, looked back at him with a stoic face. The real Cara possessed no such poise. Tuberculosis—the white plague—gripped her. She suffered the final throes of death that Calum refused to accept. No world worth living in could allow this. No life existed for him without her.

Calum stood beside his horse and leaned into it, a ragged cob horse whose breath came out in warm puffs. He felt each snowflake bite through the holes in his gloves. He looked down at Cara's face, so silent and serene in the locket, and remembered her choked cries for help.

Doctor Logan Saunders lived miles away. The weather and dark night would make the journey perilous. In the distance, the last glimmers of the sun bathed the horizon in sanguine light. The snow glowed pink and orange, and rare trees cast long, bony shadows across the landscape. Worse things lurked among the hills than the cold or dark.

"God, grant her the grace to make it to Christmas. Let me cook for her and spoil her one last time. Or if anyone else hears me tonight, hear my plea. Let her live. Let her live!"

A vicious laughter came across the hills. Calum turned his head in search of the culprit, but he saw no one. He understood every nook in this land where voices might hide.

He mounted his horse and used the reins to guide it beyond the stables. He took one final look at his home, a humble stone abode with a thatch roof. A single candle illuminated his bedroom, where his wife lay in wait for Death. No such rendezvous would happen tonight. Calum bolted his horse out of the yard and toward the village.

Calum rode through a barren landscape where nothing interrupted the blustery winds. In an age past, trees covered this landscape. Developments in the village required wood, and that meant the deforestation of the region. White specks of snow swirled and fell around him. Tall figures stood in the snow in the distance, a family, or a congregation of some kind. Calum didn't slow his pace for them. The snow passed through them as if they had no physical presence. The last traces of the sun's light glowed around their edges. They moved as if burdened by a grievous weight. Their faces hung long and low as if they melted with grief. Calum took a closer look and realized more of them emerged from the snow, glowing as if illuminated by candles in the evening dark.

"Then you've come for me," Calum called out. "You've found me at my most broken state and have come to take me away." He looked upon the Sluagh, the unforgiven dead who haunted the lands with restless fury. They looked at him with hunger and contempt. A woman emerged. The wind pulled at her hair slowly as if she lived in a slower stream of time.

"How could you abandon her?" her voice echoed. "You've left your wife to die alone. Her darkest moment, and she's suffering alone."

Calum reached into his belted tartan and gripped his pistol. The Sluagh had the sanctimonious presence of a holy mass, but they only ever had the worst intentions. "Amy Kinkaid," he said her name. "I remember you."

"And do you remember the way you abandoned the croft? The way you thought you were better than us and didn't fight the clearance with us?"

"There was no sense fighting the clearance. No man on earth had the power. British law destroys what other nations need armies to destroy."

"They brought the army, beat us, and torched our homes. Did you see the flames touch the sky?"

The skeletal remains of crofting homes stood among the Sluagh. Humble stacks of stones that once held thatched roofs dotted the landscape. Without their roofs, they looked barren and frigid, incapable of supporting life. Calum shook his head. This must have been a trick of the Sluagh. The crofting homes were miles and years away; he hadn't seen them since 1819. A tacksman paid renters to leave the land and replaced them with sheep. Calum relocated to the southwest border, to the outskirts of a humble highland village. The Sluagh couldn't fool him now, not while his heart still burned for Cara.

"I have a deep well of regret and shame, Amy. I'm a pitiful echo of my father killed at Culloden. It's been a century of despair. I had no idea the sun could set so many times without rising, but I won't have you rubbing it in. I won't be suckered by your Sluagh magic." Calum held his pistol at his side.

"I loved you once, and you abandoned me."

"You never said as much then. I have too much spirit for you to take me now. So long as Cara might live, I won't be moved by a single specter from Hell." Calum fired the pistol into the air, and the Sluagh howled. They shifted like seafoam on the tide. In the moment of their distraction, Calum charged his horse through them. They reached with bony fingers, but his horse moved too swiftly. The ghastly crofting houses dissipated in the snow.

In a few moments' time, he rode into the clearing near the village. He looked back and saw the Sluagh in the distance, a drifting mass of glowing shapes dotting the hills.

Regretful memories of his earliest years flooded his thoughts. The landowners in those days found it cheaper to replace tenants with sheep. Many good people left the country. Many were forced out. The land was once deforested, and now it stood unpopulated. His whole life had been a journey from the northwest corner of the highlands to any place where he could survive. Every move left behind ghosts and grew his guilt.

Snow and wind roared over Calum's ears without resistance from the landscape. He pushed his horse faster until it arrived at the doctor's home, a white-walled cottage with a vivid green door. Calum ached with pain in his joints as he stepped down from his horse. The bitter cold made it so much worse; he felt Death's breath on his neck. "Doctor Logan Saunders! Doctor Logan Saunders! Cara is dying! For God's sake, do something!" His breath came out thick and white on the cold air.

The thought of his wife's raspy, strained breathing pained him. He didn't possess the stillness of character to watch her die, but those scratchy breaths lingered in his thoughts. He couldn't escape them.

"Wake up!" Calum yelled. "Cara is dying!"

Illuminated by a single candle in his hand, the doctor's head emerged from the green door of the cottage. He scowled at Calum. "Be quiet now! Only ghosts and Sluagh are out at this hour. Are you off your head?"

Calum leaned into the doorway and grabbed the doctor by his shirt. "She's dying, doctor! My Cara won't make the night."

"Who has the nerve to dress like that in this age?" The doctor looked down at Calum's belted tartan.

"Few living, and many more dead." Calum pushed the doctor into his home for a respite out of the screaming winds. With dead silence in the home, the conversation carried a grave clarity.

"What is it you want me to do? I have been by your side for every step of her illness. I cannot do a thing for her; she is in the Lord's hands now."

"There must be something with all your learning that you can do. You've studied and practiced medicine for decades, too much to stand powerless when something so common comes for a man's wife."

"What's the problem here?" the doctor's wife asked as she arrived in the room. She wore only a nightgown and stared at Calum with shocked eyes.

In the distance, Calum heard the sound of children talking. He realized the depth of trouble he'd caused this family. He released the doctor from his grip.

He looked about the home of the doctor and saw blessings he didn't have. Art over the mantle. Fine china. Even the doctor and his wife seemed thicker, healthier. Doctor Saunders had wealth and the ability to navigate the nasty age he lived in. Calum did not.

Calum felt the ache in his ribs for deep nourishment. He remembered the way he ate when times were better. Calum felt a swell of disgust for the doctor, a man at once so privileged and yet powerless. The impulse to threaten the doctor with his pistol stirred in his thoughts, but the wife and children gave him pause. The awful reality occurred to him: the doctor had done everything he could, and tuberculosis had no cure.

"We're in the belly of the whale. She can't breathe. She dies as I watch her."

"In the morning, we can finalize everything; you have to be—"

"Finalize?"

"I can only offer a prayer for you now. There's nothing man or beast can do to cure the white plague."

Calum's breath burned his throat and nose, and he realized how loudly he'd yelled earlier, and how much the cold hurt him. "No." He shook his head. "No, I've prayed enough. If God sees this and does nothing—"

He stopped himself. Each breath pained him. "I am a Catholic man and will not blaspheme in your home."

"Can I offer you a drink for the road home?" the doctor offered.

"I've done enough of that too." Calum turned from the doctor and shut the door behind him. He stood in the swirling snow and listened to his horse catch its breath. The journey here had taxed the animal. He saw Calum and ducked his head down, as if to shrink himself away and not draw attention. Then he slipped further away, and Calum realized that something spooked him. He looked over his shoulder and saw the figure of a clan soldier in a belted tartan.

A distinct red tartan covered the man from knee to shoulder, and a blood-red hat topped his head. One hand rested on the basket hilt of his claymore, and the other held a studded targe. The studs of the shield glimmered in the moonlight. When he drew nearer, Calum realized that his face was grossly misshapen.

"Powrie, redcap. I know you."

"Do you now?" he asked.

"You're a MacDonald from Keppoch. Come to follow me all the way to the border to harass me about failure, have you?"

"I watched thousands of men move against the government that threatened to take away everything that I loved in 1746. I saw them losing and I died. You might understand. Now you are weak and losing too. Coward. You let the doctor speak weakness into your ear."

"I can't force him to cure tuberculosis with a pistol to his head. It's the eleventh hour, the bottom of the well."

"Despair makes a fine cover for guilt. It stuns you to inaction. There is your future. Will you watch the snow and do nothing?" The redcap pointed at the road in the distance, where a dark figure rode on horseback.

Calum squinted and looked in the direction of the dark rider. He wore a black cloak that fell over his shoulders and the sides of the horse. The figure seemed deformed with a hunchback, but Calum looked closer and recognized the shape of the rider's black wings. The rider balanced a long scythe over his lap. Most of his horse seemed white as snow, but a sour green tint shone in its fur where the moonlight struck it. This was Death on a pale horse, and he rode in the direction of Calum's home. Calum's heart sank as he saw the fate of his wife unfolding before him. Death rode with a slow, methodical stride, as though Cara's departure was no urgent matter.

"Would you have me shoot and stab Death itself?" Calum asked the redcap.

"Cara will die."

"You're trying to provoke me into a gruesome end because you love violence."

The redcap raised a finger to make a point, but he said nothing. A gnarly smile curled around his mouth. He stepped back into the snow and vanished.

Calum stared at Death again. The winds teased the edges of its black cloak and the feathers in its wings. Calum worried that he would defy God's will by intervening. The thought struck him as powerfully and quickly as a bolt of lightning. Could he be damned forever for fighting God's plan?

If Death reached Cara, no life remained for Calum, either. A squat home of gapped stones and whistling thatch waited for him, and without Cara, he could not withstand it. Their children vanished years ago for better lives in the lowlands, in England, and across the ocean. No life existed for Calum without Cara. He understood why the redcap smiled; Calum had no choice. He leaped onto his horse with renewed vigor and snapped the reins to burst the horse forward.

Death kept his slow pace, but Calum raced forward. The hooves of his horse pounded the snowy ground, and the horse panted loudly enough for his breath to echo in the hills. Death moved as though deaf and disinterested. The wretched details became clearer up close. Calum saw the dusty markings on his wings, the cryptic pattern on his cloak, and the bony fingers gripping his scythe. The sheer ugliness of the creature stunned Calum into inaction as they crossed paths. His horse charged past Death, and Calum took a good look into his empty eye sockets. Worms crawled over his bony skull.

Calum's horse galloped ahead and cut Death off on the road. He gripped his pistol, and after a moment of loading, he stopped his horse in the road. He summoned all of his courage to shout, "Stop there!"

Death made no change in his pace. His horse trotted slowly in the direction of Calum's home.

Calum lifted his pistol and took aim at the creature's very center. Anxiety hit him again. Did he fight an unholy battle against the natural order of things? He feared for his own eternal soul, but he couldn't stop. He loved Cara more than he feared God. Any cosmic plan that involved her death pitted him against the cosmos. He pulled the trigger. The gunshot cracked loudly in the darkness, and a plume of gunpowder rose from the pistol.

Death rode forward, unfazed. Even without eyes, it felt as though Death looked straight into Calum now.

Calum tucked his pistol away and unsheathed his dirk. He felt the familiar oak handle in his grip and the counterbalance of the foot-long blade extending forward. He commanded his horse into a charge and cried out. Did Death have a heart to stab or intestines to remove? If not, the dirk remained sturdy enough to crush a skull. Those were the irrational thoughts that raced through Calum's mind as Death expanded into something broader and crueler than a storm cloud.

Death's wings stretched out to their full reach, the size of several men placed end to end. His jaw opened and released a shrieking howl unlike anything Calum had ever heard. Death rose from his horse and reached for his scythe.

Calum lifted his feet up on the saddle of his horse, crouched like a tiger, took aim, and leaped. He struck out with his dirk, but the blade found nothing of substance to strike.

His body struck the snow with a hard slam, and he rolled down an embankment. He looked back to see his horse charging away. With the speed and grace of a well-practiced man, he reloaded his pistol and got up on one knee. His body hurt, but he didn't have time to check for broken bones. He had leaped from a charging horse and rolled with the grace of a mountain boulder.

Death paused in his path and rose above his horse to look down on Calum. His cloak swirled and flipped about in the winds with the temperamental snow that seemed to enter a strange vortex as if everything nearby yielded to his will. Death pointed at Calum with a bony finger and raised his scythe in the other hand.

Calum had wasted one bullet on Death, and his knife had found nothing material to stab. He pointed his pistol yet again and gripped his dirk in his other hand as if they meant something. The awful feeling of defeat returned to him. He recalled the vicious smile of the redcap and the futility the doctor tried to warn him about. Now he stared down Death in the middle of a highland winter night.

"You've come to take my Cara, have you?" Calum yelled at Death. "Well, I won't let you have her! Not so long as I live!"

Death hovered over his horse for a time before he drifted toward Calum and the earth as if allowing gravity a pinch of his authority. When his feet set down on the snow, he knelt down and allowed his cloak to envelope him. Scythe, wings, and cloak disappeared in a mass of black feathers that burst into the form of black birds scattering in the snow. Calum raised his hands to shield himself from them. In their midst, they left the form of a pale woman. She stared into Calum with frigid eyes. Something moved within her, but Calum could not know what.

"You don't have to fight me, Highlander," she said. "I will talk to you now."

"Are you Death still? The one who comes for my Cara?"

"I am."

"Then I must give you a fight, even if you are a lady now. I've seen what you are, and I can't forget it."

"And was it fruitful when you fought me first?"

"Aye. You were an ugly thing first, and now you're a lady."

Death laughed and said, "By my choice! I am not humbled, only charmed."

Calum heard her and thought of the way cats played with their meals. "I'm not a thing to fool around with."

"And I have never been one to fool around. You love her?"

"She is all I love. When I left the Northwest and came to the kelping world with nothing but my clothes, she welcomed me. She loved me when I was wretched and filthy with the smell of fish and burned kelp. I came to her after working the alkali out of the seaweed, and still, she loved and fed me without judgment. How can you let harm befall a woman whose well of love runs so deep? The kelp sold for nothing when the industry collapsed. We became destitute together and cling now to our crumbling home like barnacles on a beached whale. She loves me now, even as we share a paltry meal each day and the weight slips from our bones."

Humbled by his grief, Calum tucked his dirk and gun away. "All the waters of the ocean placed on a scale couldn't equal the gravity of loss I've felt. So many of those I love have returned to dust. And even if I could see them again, I would never want to see them as they've suffered here. I'm a man disjointed from his world. If you take Cara, the love that anchors me to this vale of tears will vanish. I'll be brittle kelp dashed on sea stones." Calum crawled to Death with his hands reaching. "Please allow me to die instead."

Death froze in place and said nothing for a time. She blinked her eyes slowly as if a pleasant aroma came to her nose. She must have relished something about his pain, but she answered, "No."

"Have you no idea what you're condemning me to? Everyone I know has left me except for her. You're robbing the Earth of the Sun. There's no cosmic order where that's acceptable."

"Death compels the most profound passions. All of creation took six days, but the end of days could last an aeon. Even the fall of Rome took centuries. I teach you love and tenacity. You stand at the collapse of an ancient order for these hills, at the end of a sacred union in your home, and soon you will pass too."

"Life has been a series of dreams in twilight. The horizon is an island of dreams on fire. The dirt at my feet is a hungry tomb. The air is a frost that kills the buds of any flowering thing. You must know the hour I will die."

"I've come for Cara MacDonell tonight. I'll come for you on December 13th of 1844."

"Eight years from now?"

"Aren't you happy with your time? I cannot give you more."

"You haven't understood. You're ancient enough to know the cosmic structure of life and death, but you don't know a thing about daily life. The carpenter builds the home, but the ant knows every knot and grain in the wood. Only a smart person could be as stupid as you. I will not live a day without her, but you've asked me for nearly a decade? She's been my sole purpose for breathing the acrid air of this dead world for decades. You say I'll live eight more years, but here you are, and here I am. Make a deal with this decrepit old man. Come for us both at the same time, and I will join you without a fuss in four years, not eight."

A smile formed at the corners of her mouth. Calum saw his persistence and passion warming something in her, and her resolve must have loosened.

"No," she said.

Calum recoiled. "I have no use for the years beyond Cara's death. I'm beyond dead, a soul in purgatory, the moment she's in the earth." Calum clasped his hands together, in his face a desperate man. "I've been thankful for every moment you've allowed me to have with her. Even the sourest argument we've shared has invigorated my purpose. Her acts of love are beyond my deserving. Please leave her be this night and come back for us both in two years. On that night, take every blade of grass in the field; any livestock I may own; the heather she loves so much; everything that crawls in the dirt; but take us together. Don't suffer me a day here without her."

Death stepped away from Calum to regain her composure.

"I will not punish you for the crime of loving a woman too much. Everything here moves with love and dies of love." Death returned to her horse and retrieved a flask from a satchel. She brought the flask to Calum and opened it, saying nothing. She took a sip for herself. She exhaled into the cold air, but her breath could not be seen. "We will share one drink from this flask, the three of us, and I will come for you both at the same time on December 13th of 1838."

"Two years from now," Calum realized out loud. Death granted him his desperate wish.

She handed him the flask, and he found its metal cold. The drink was a deep red, but it tasted nothing like wine as it splashed on his tongue. He'd experienced nothing like it in his life. It was bitter, but not offensive.

"Deliver the drink to her now. With it, we are bonded together in this pact. If she refuses the drink, or if I change my mind, then our deal is forfeit." Death leaned forward and pointed Calum to his horse.

"Change your mind?"

"I am moved by the sentiments that compel you, but I am still Death. Try to anticipate Death, and you try to chart the course of a snowflake to see where it will fall."

Calum didn't like the sound of uncertainty in her words. With the flask firmly in his grasp, he whistled for his horse. He walked briskly in the direction he last saw his horse running, and when it returned to him, he forgot his age and leaped up the side of the horse to mount it. Then began the desperate race home to return to his dying beloved.

His horse struggled for each breath in tandem with the rhythmic beat of his hooves on the snow. Falling snow stung Calum's face. He worried that Death might have changed her mind. He feared what may have happened to Cara when he couldn't stand to sit by her any longer. She couldn't have had long to live when he left.

He came upon the clearing where the dirt path led to his stony home. He saw the familiar window boxes with brown and barren stems and a dim candlelight in the bedroom window. The door to his home stood open, and he wondered if he'd left it that way in his panic. He looked down in the snow to see messy footprints followed by the imprint of a dress's hem. Cara had walked outside after he left.

Fear crept up in him. The dim glow of the Sluagh caught his attention. They emerged from the snow and peered at him with their long, grievous faces. Warm light outlined them as if from some other time and place. Calum knew they came for the weak. He steeled his heart and looked onward.

Cara lay in the snow on her stomach and ribs. She turned her neck with the last of her strength to point her nose and mouth into the air and breathe. She must have escaped the house for fresh air outside. The elements would kill her with enough time.

Calum leaped down from his horse with the flask in hand. He shook it to check that enough remained for her. The drink sloshed around inside the flask. He kneeled beside her and turned her over so she could drink. He placed his ear next to her mouth to make sure that she still breathed at all. A painful, scratchy breath entered and left her mouth.

"God, let me have your mercy now," Calum said as he opened the flask, though he knew God was not the one whose mercy he had bartered.

Cara reached up her arm and pushed the flask away.

Calum feared she might knock it into the snow and spill it out. He recalled Death's terms. Cara could not refuse the drink. "Listen to me, Cara! This will save your life!"

Cara shook her head. She refused a drink that looked like whisky. She had never been fond of it.

"Cara, it's not whisky. I've come back with medicine—from the doctor. It will keep you alive."

She calmed herself and listened to his advice. Calum took the back of her head in one hand and gently poured the drink into her mouth with the other. In moments, Cara coughed and cleared her throat. She hadn't possessed the strength to do that in some time. The breath left her nose and mouth in white puffs, and the suffering left her face. Calum recalled the way she looked years previous; her pain melted away in front of him.

Calum looked around at the Sluagh, whose bodies dissipated in the snow. They took their ethereal glow with them, leaving only darkness and swirling snowflakes behind. Calum saw their defeat; they couldn't claim him so long as his heart remained strong. So long as he could be with Cara. He placed his arms underneath his wife and lifted her up as if he were in his youth again. He pulled her body close and stood. She regained her warmth, and Calum felt as though he stood next to a fireplace.

"Who are they?" Cara whispered into his ear. She leaned into him and tightened her arms around his neck.

"No one and nothing, now. They cannot touch us."

He carried her inside as the last remaining Sluagh vanished. Calum kicked the door open with his foot and then kicked it closed behind them when they entered. He walked to the bed and placed her on it with care. Her head fell on her pillow, and she breathed with ease. He watched the rise and fall of her chest and saw that his deal with Death had been honored.

"You're breathing now," he said.

"Clearer than ever. The medicine is magic."

"It is."

A spell of silence passed between them when they shared a mutual affection. She might have had reason to be angry at him for leaving her, but he returned with a cure. With her pain gone, she rested at ease, and Calum marveled at the miracle of her. He took her hand in both of his and held it close to his face.

"Calum?" she asked with a hushed voice of concern. "Is everything going to be okay?"

He couldn't look into her eyes. He wanted to be certain of the answer, but he couldn't be. He knew the end of Death's bargain—that both of them would die in two years. That wasn't much time. Years slipped past him faster now than receding waves. He thought of the pain that she had just endured; she nearly died an agonizing death in front of him. It wouldn't do to let her suffer even an ounce of anxiety.

"Everything will be okay," he promised.

About the Author

Melrose Dowdy is an illustrator working primarily in digital media and an author of speculative fiction. After obtaining an education in fine art, Melrose began a cross-country journey in the USA seeking out the most inspirational art and stories to inspire greater creativity. Melrose stalks the Internet like a regular ghost and often shares art on Twitter and various Discord servers.

DORIAN

BY JOHNATHON HEART

I am in the parking lot preparing myself for the anxiety of entering my own apartment when something small and dark rushes in ahead of me. It slams the door behind it.

I freeze. My keys dangle from my fingers. I couldn't identify the running thing. It moved too fast. In the orange glow of the streetlamp, it didn't look human.

A second passes, then two. By the third, I wonder if it really happened. My muffled ringtone breaks the silence.

I reach into my disorganized purse, hoping it isn't him. I find the phone from its blue-white backlight and see the text before I even pull it out.

[Emery]
Need to take out trash when u get home plz. Thx.

He used to text in full words.

And he should know that I'm home by now. I got off work thirty minutes ago. I remember his schedule. I know he'll be at the office for another hour and a half. That he'll pick up dinner on the way back and pull in at around seven thirty, depending on traffic.

How does he forget so much easier?

My hand's on the doorknob now. Emery always leaves the damn door unlocked. I hassled him for it, back when we talked. It serves him right that there's a home invader.

If it exists. At this point, I'm pretty sure it doesn't. I saw it out of the corner of my eye, and it happened too fast to be real. A hallucination.

All that certainty lasts until I open the door and see how dark it is.

"Hello?" I say. Smart. He'll pop out from behind a corner, knife in hand and say: "Oh, sorry. Wrong house! My mistake!"

"Hey," I call again, just before entering and flipping the light switch. The kitchen/living room combo greets me. I grimace at every filthy surface. I always told him to clean his shit up, before. But now I can't say that. I have to be polite when we speak. Though we usually don't.

Good god, there's likely an intruder in my home, and I'm still obsessing over this breakup.

I ball my keys up in my fist. Just the way nice girls should in order to not get raped, and step over Emery's PS5/my Netflix box. I check under the kitchenette. Dirty dishes, but no intruder.

I search the bathroom. Pull aside the shower curtain and see my soaps removed (again) but no Hitchcockian shower-psycho. There's nothing in the bedroom closet we share, or under the bed I'll be sleeping in tonight while he takes his turn on the couch.

I open the door to his office, glance once, and don't turn on the light before closing the door.

I imagined it.

I pull out leftover chicken pesto from last night and microwave it. I turn on the PS5 and sign on as "CapnEmerz." I watch a dumb, endless sitcom as I eat.

He enters. He walks past me, blocking the screen for a half second, and opens the fridge to see that I've killed the chicken. He checks the trash and sees that I haven't taken it out. He puts a pot on the stove and starts boiling water. Probably pasta.

Another episode passes.

"I'm sorry," he says from the dinner table as the credits roll.

I stand up and walk to the bedroom.

Just until the end of the lease.

Warmth. The kind of warmth you get from being comfortably close to a fire. A smell like the lovechild of charcoal and rose with a pinch of vanilla.

A man in a red and black suit. His orange eyes sparkle. His black hair in a perfect coif. He has a short, neatly trimmed beard, and he's smiling. His face stays in view even as everything around him shifts. His hands are warm. His lips, too. When he removes his jacket, he reveals a slight but prominent six-pack dotted with dark body hair. His belt slides off next. His pants with it. His arms are warm, and so are his sides.

But when he enters me, he's cold.

I wake sweating and coming down from an orgasm.

My phone buzzes. After giving myself three deep, shuddering breaths, I check it.

[Emery]
Everything ok? U screamed.

I throw the phone across the room and allow myself a few more breaths. My clothes and the sheets are soaked through. Mostly sweat. Mostly.

The charcoal scent lingers.

Last night I saw Emery cooking and felt the urge to grab his ass. I haven't had sex in three months. I wish we'd done it one more time before the end instead of having a dead bedroom for the last few weeks. The one thing you're never ready for is losing access to sex. Maybe because it seems so shallow in comparison to all the heartbreak and depression and everything else you actually brace yourself for. The frustration sneaks up on you, then jumps and fucks you the way you suddenly wish a man would.

In a dumb, horny moment, I imagined hooking up with him. I reminded myself why that couldn't happen and it led to an equally dumb, sad moment in which I teared up again. I fast-walked to the bathroom before he could notice.

You get good at quiet crying.

The man in the suit comes back the very next night.

"I'm sorry if it was too intense last time," he says, in an almost-British accent. "Earth-shattering, and all that. I can be gentler if needed."

"This is weird. I don't have sequel dreams," I say.

We're in the waiting room I work in. All the chairs are empty. A steady stream of bubbles rises in the water cooler. The gaps between the bubbles are too rhythmic. You can practically time it.

The scent is back. I don't know where it's coming from.

"Sequel dreams?" the man asks. "Lucillia, this isn't a dream."

"My name's Lucy. That's my legal name. It's not short for anything," I say.

I look him over again. He's attractive, but he's got a small mole on his forehead. Is this really the best my brain can do?

"I see, then. Lucy." He looks around. "This is...?"

"My job. Are we going to fuck here?"

He glances back, and for a moment——I might have imagined this, but then again, I'm imagining all of this——he seems surprised. Then his confidence flashes back, and he smirks. "If you want to."

I think I do, but not enough to say so. This isn't one of my fantasies. Office sex is easier to fetishize when you actually have an office.

As if I asked for it aloud, we're now on a tropical beach. Sea air mixes with the rosy scent. There's a palm tree next to a folding chair and a beach towel. An umbrella shades them both. White sand leads to clear water that's ankle-deep a mile out. It all has a screensaver-esque quality.

"Is this preferable?" he says.

"But the intent here is sex," I say. "Like, that's what this is leading up to."

He raises a perfectly groomed eyebrow. "Is that a problem?"

"I guess not." There. It's out in the open. Maybe that was all I wanted. "But I haven't made up my mind yet."

In dreams, there's no pregnancy and no STDs. Sex is only ever mind-blowing. Why am I hesitant?

Because I'm so stuck in my own misery that I can't even let loose in what's obviously supposed to be a sex dream.

"You seemed to have few reservations last night," he says.

"That wasn't as lucid."

"Would you like less lucidity, Lady Lucy?"

"Oh, boo." I frown at him. His jacket's gone. His white dinner shirt is unbuttoned and blowing in the breeze. "You're terrible. I don't mean that in the roguish or charming way. You're just actually terrible."

He produces a pair of sunglasses from nowhere, unfolds them with a hard shake, then puts them on his face. Despite how they hide his exotic eyes, he pulls it off. "You didn't answer my question."

"No," I say. "Honestly, I'm down to just talk, for now. You seem at least interesting."

"Even though I'm terrible?"

"Abhorrent. What's your name?"

"Would you kill me if I told you I had many names?" He grins.

"God, yes, I would. And then myself for imagining you. Give me one."

"One name?" He looks up into the sky, which is suddenly a ceiling.

A mirrored ceiling. There are candles burning, and they're the only things that light the bedroom. The flickering glow shows silk sheets and plush cushions.

Biting his full lip, he says, "Dorian."

"At least it's not Damian. Or Darius."

"Yes, but only because I became tired of them both." He removes his sunglasses.

"This is the part where you tell me you're a vampire," I say.

"Too bad I'm not one." But when he grins, his teeth are fanged. "Unless you have that fetish."

"I'm not sixteen anymore. Put those away."

He closes his mouth. His lips puff out as he runs his tongue over his teeth. I imagine that tongue. Moving. When he is finished, he gives me an open-mouthed, perfectly white grin. The fangs are gone.

"Nice party trick," I say.

"I have others." He sits back on the mattress and pats the space next to him.

I sit in his lap instead.

He raises an eyebrow. "You surprise me."

"Too forward?" I say.

"I'm not complaining."

Maybe I *want* to feel like I'm sixteen right now. Hormonal and impulsive.

And with that thought, I'm instantly freed from whatever was holding me back. I kiss him. A real man might stop me, no matter how much he wanted me. My pacing is sudden and slutty, impatient and needy. But Dorian, overdeveloped as he is, is still my fantasy. His kisses are soft but intense, with slight tongue that teases and draws me in. He's on top now, and our clothes are gone. Orange eyes lock onto mine. He leans in as he enters me—still cold—and I feel his lips again.

The sex is a descent into incoherence, becoming the frantic fever dream I wanted. I'll remember the cold penis (which doesn't ruin it) and the rosy charcoal scent becoming heavier than it ever was. I press my face against his shoulder to confirm that it's coming from him.

Then I bite him. Hard.

I'm awake. I already know I came again.

Emery doesn't text me this time, thank god.

I sing in the shower. I dance while brushing my teeth. Even pouring cereal becomes a festive occasion. I know it's stupid. It'd be dumb enough to be in a good mood from sex, but *fictional dream sex* is a really pathetic comfort.

But I'm observing all that self-criticism from a removed place. I consider it the way you'd consider throwing away some nostalgic childhood piece of junk when you're downsizing. I toss it. It's gone.

So I'm happy from fake dream sex. So what?

When Emery comes out of the bedroom and pours coffee right next to me, my eyes don't turn to him. He can get coffee. It doesn't matter.

I feel his eyes on me as he sits at the table and drinks. I don't react. And I know he's going to take it as encouragement. He's been trying to talk to me for months. That possibility doesn't seem so terrifying now.

"I'm sorry if I ever make you uncomfortable. It's just hard," he breaks. "To adjust."

"Yeah," I say.

"I should never have said those things to you. I've been thinking about it. You do things in relationships that are just... ridiculously hurtful, right? Things you wouldn't do to someone you hated. But then you do them to someone you love. It's fucked."

"It is." I'm still looking away. "It wasn't just you. I'm sorry."

We've had this conversation. We said almost the exact same things.

Maybe he wants to have it again. If it didn't provide closure last time, maybe hammering the nail in harder will really cap things off. It ends the same way. Trailing off instead of concluding.

It almost brings me back down again. Almost.

"I have to go to work," I say.

He blinks. As if taken aback. "Okay, good luck."

I leave humming. In the door lite's half-reflection, I see him put his face in his hands. I swing the door open, and he's gone.

"So you make a habit of seducing people," I say to Dorian that night.

"Yes." He lounges on a plush, purple cushion on a raised bed surrounded by diaphanous curtains, all in a room that looks like something out of *Arabian Nights*. "Does it bother you?"

I'm sitting on the bed, wearing a skimpy belly dancer's costume. Is this really *my* fantasy? It seems very male-centric. "I admit, it makes me feel kind of replaceable."

"Would it help to know that you're the only woman I'm speaking to now?" he asks.

"Yes, but it doesn't resolve it," I say. "This only ends one way, doesn't it? You stop showing up in my dreams, and you move on to someone else's. Everything ends, like it always does, and I'm left with nothing again."

I'm not as upset as I probably should be. Maybe it's because, at the end of the day, he *is* just a dream... Why am I pretending that he'd live anywhere but inside *my* head?

"Again?" he asks. "You have nothing, now?"

"In the romantic sense, at least. I mean, I had Emery. And he was good, at first."

"Your ex-lover."

"Sure," I say, for as melodramatic as the word *lover* makes it sound. "But as time went on... it just... deteriorated. I can't put it any other way. Every disagreement turned into an argument. And then the arguments got toxic. I don't know where it started. He'd come home and play video games and refuse to talk to me. He'd make me do all the chores. I'd have to be responsible for both of us." This is the first time I'm saying it out loud. But there's no catharsis. Instead, it's like I'm trying to dig into a concrete mountain.

The truth is just that we were miserable once we moved in together. We weren't happy. That's all there is to it, that's all that I know, and I can't understand anything else about it.

He lies down from his half-sitting position and stares up at the ceiling.

"Have you ever been in love?" I ask him.

"I love you," he says. Not passionately. Just a statement of fact.

"You don't know me," I say.

"Love is never dependent on knowing someone," he says. "And I love every woman I've known. I am born to seduce them. And you'd be shocked to find how few women respond to anything less than genuine love."

"What are you, a male succubus?"

"An incubus," he corrects.

"Oh." It doesn't surprise me, all things considered. "So you've loved a lot of women."

"So many."

"And have you... been with any of them? Romantically. Not just sexually."

"No."

I'm not equipped to handle all the heartbreak in that *No*. It's more than mine. It's stronger and somehow fresher. But I'm still dealing with my own. Should we be trauma-bonding? Because that's not happening. Right now, I want to be further from him. Physically, emotionally, both.

Still I say, "You seem... sadder than last night, in general."

"I am," he says.

"Is it for the same reason? You're eventually going to leave?"

"Maybe. But didn't you say it always ends?"

"I did."

Really I said it not wanting to believe it, hoping that he'd argue with me. But he's not the person—demon—to do that, is he?

And with all the great timing I had last night, I climb on top of him, and we commence the delirious dream-fuck.

It goes on like that. And despite my miserable home life, for once I'm not miserable.

As time goes on, though, Dorian and I talk less. Whatever connection might have been there is fading as my desire for connection fades. I do my best not to think about his feelings as the dreams begin and immediately lead to sex. Some nights, the orgasm doesn't wake me. In the continuing dream, I'll see him sitting on the side of the bed, naked and looking at his hands. Or pacing across the scenery, his strangely cold penis jiggling with each step. He looks out windows, wiping his face with his wrist.

After two weeks of silence, I talk to him again.

"Dorian, are you okay?" I ask.

"I'm not sure," he murmurs, sitting naked in an armchair.

"What's going on?"

He shakes his head then glances out the window again. We're in an elaborate study, with oak flooring and a red Persian rug. A roaring fireplace and towering bookcases.

Before I can ask again, he speaks. "There are tragic things inside you."

"Inside *me*?"

He nods. "It hurts. When I take them."

I let that sit for a second. I mull it over. I think about what I've read and heard. What I've experienced. I don't speak aloud the question that comes to mind. I hold it back for minutes.

When I release it, it's on pure impulse. "Dorian. Are you taking my soul?"

"Pieces of it," he says.

"... That's... that's not good. That's really, *really* not good."

I stand up. I start pacing. I reconsider everything I've felt in the past few weeks. My changing mental state.

"It's not as bad as you think." His slumped eyes follow me.

"It's not as..." I stop and look at him. "Okay, let's define a soul. What is a soul?"

"Pretty much what you think it is. You. And yes, I'm consuming it. Partially."

"Okay." And now I'm angry, rage flooding in until I'm furious. "You just told me that you are *eating* me."

"*Part* of you."

"So if I chopped off your arm and ate it, your argument would be that it wasn't that bad because it was only *part* of you?"

"Perhaps if it was vestigial, or I didn't want it. Lucy, I've been taking your sadness."

I stop. I run my hands through my perfect dream hair. My mind allows it to be disheveled and ruined. Thank you, me. Whatever me there is that's left.

"Lucy, please. If you must call me a parasite, then I'm a benign one."

"No," I whisper. "You can't just... *eat* my emotions and assume I'm supposed to thank you. Tell me this is just a dream, and you aren't real."

And for the first time, that idea comforts me. That all this could be some illusion that could just fade away.

"I am real," he says. Then, without any real anger, "Lucy, please understand. This misery didn't start with your relationship or your job. It's been with you for your entire life. I've seen that. Just let me take it, please. We can bear it together."

Part of me whispers that he's right. It terrifies me. He's inside my head. And that's invasive and repulsive. But nothing that he's saying is wrong.

I've never been happy. Until now.

"You didn't even ask," I whisper. "I didn't consent to this at all."

"No, you didn't. Would you forgive me if I told you I was scared?"

"Scared that I'd say no? Yes. I understand that."

"You do?" His lips curve, readying a smile.

I hesitate. Is there any coming back from this, really?

No. Some instinct screams. *This needs to be the end.*

Then that's it. And I can't hold back. Not with something like this.

"I get it," I say. "But I don't forgive you."

His lips freeze, then droop. He blinks hard. When his eyes open, their orange color is brighter. Vicious. "Do you not even see what I've been sacrificing for you?"

"You didn't tell me."

"I told you now!"

"It's too late."

There's a pressurized sting behind my eyes. It's unfair. In a dream-world, I should be able to stop myself from crying.

"I'm not leaving. I love you. And I'm so tired of leaving every time I find a home. Please, Lucy. Just let me stay." His vicious eyes dull themselves into morose orange puddles. His fingers reach to me, opening wide, begging.

A home. At first, I'm unsure of why that unsettles me so much. And then I remember the thing that I saw running through my door weeks ago.

"You *invaded* my apartment?" I suck it all in. The tears and the misery and the brokenness. I stand straighter. "Dorian, nothing positive can start from that."

A link that I wasn't aware of withers. It's still there, but brittle, in the process of breaking.

"I love you," he repeats. "I'm staying. You should want me to. I make you happy."

It's childlike, and so is his face now. All his sophisticated language and demeanor has evaporated. He's a desperate, thirsty thing, far from human, that wants to consume me.

"I'm waking up," I say. "You can't keep me in a dream. I'll just wake up. And I am. I'm waking——"

I'm awake. The bed is covered in sweat. Different sweat, for a different reason. I look at the clock. Four a.m.

I tear the house apart looking for him. Fuck it if I wake Emery. Fuck it if his real demon form is dangerous. He needs to get out of my home.

How big is he? Does it matter? Does he obey the laws of physics, or could he be hiding in the pipes? I search the gross corner of the garage. The space underneath the toilet.

Until there's one place left.

Emery's office.

The door creaks as it opens. On the other side, I see them. All the photos.

It seems unfair, more than anything else. I deleted all that I could. But he allows his to just sit there. We talked about it, terribly and awkwardly, like all our conversations, and I learned that he has no regrets. It was a period of his life that he doesn't want to forget.

Fuck that philosophy, because now I have to look at it.

They're sitting on shelves and hanging on walls just the way they would be if we were some enthusiastic married couple with a family. Standing with him on the shore of Lake Tahoe. Sitting with him on the branch of a tree we'd climbed together. Kissing his cheek on a beach in the sunset. Some are aesthetically gorgeous. I promised I'd hang onto them for that reason alone. I promised a lot of things.

I look under the desk, in the drawers. When I open Emery's too-big closet, there's a shriek. The glint of an eye behind some boxes and low-hanging shirts. I push past them, and my hand grabs something soft.

I'm holding his throat. He tries to shriek again, but my grip tightens. I'm surprised at my own violence, but if I let go, he'll run. I fumble my hand along the wall and flip the light switch.

What I'm holding is not a handsome man, and never was.

It *is* humanoid. It has the wings, tail, and horns of a demon. Its ears are large and pointed. Its feet and hands are oversized and clawed. Its skin is grey. It's the size of a medium dog.

It has his orange eyes.

"... Dorian?"

I let go of its throat. My hands wrap around its torso. It grimaces. I expect a high or nasal voice to go along with that long, pointed nose.

But in a voice far deeper than its frame should warrant, it says, "Yes."

"You were this? The whole time, this was you?"

"I'm sorry." It frowns.

"You're leaving," I say. "Now."

It blinks and looks away. "But I love you."

Hearing it say that is one of the most painful things I've ever experienced.

"I just wanted to make you happy," it whispers.

I find my words again. "You'll make me happy by *leaving*."

"No. I won't."

Despite everything, that ridiculous voice inside me argues. It wants me to forget all of this. It wants life to be simple, just this once.

"I want to rewind time to when you thought I was beautiful," the imp says. "When I was a miracle coming to someone who desperately needed one. For once, for you, I wanted that to last forever."

The photos behind me are closing in. They're going to surround me with horrible whispers that used to be happy. Remind me of how destiny brought us together, how we were meant to be together, how we were meant to stay together, forever.

I close my eyes and force it out. "I'll make myself happy. Or I won't be happy at all. Now go."

My fingers open. He lands on his feet.

Dorian scans my face. I don't know what he's... it's looking for, but after a few seconds, its eyes waver and its face turns away. I've won.

The window opens. The demon spreads its wings, then flaps them. Its body lifts. Once it's above my head, it swoops out the window. Its stupid pointed tail is the last thing I see.

I'm alone in Emery's office.

I take each of the photos and drop them in the garbage bin outside. Then I take out the trash and put another bag on top to cover them. The trash truck should come before he notices.

I lie in my bed once I'm done. I call into work. It'll be fine. I've never used my PTO. I stare at the ceiling until I fall asleep.

Dorian is there. But I know this one is just a dream. Just me.

"I'm moving out, probably," I say. "Waiting for the lease to end isn't worth this."

Dream-Dorian says nothing.

"I'm still not sorry, you know. But I do feel sorry for you. Those things aren't mutually exclusive."

When I wake up, the sadness is back. Like someone was plugging it before, and the cork's been removed. In the living room, Emery makes breakfast, eats, then leaves for work. I tell myself I should go too. Then I remember that I already called in. I'll binge something on Netflix today, instead.

The scent of charcoal and rose with that vanilla accent is gone. I didn't know it was still there. After two weeks, it blended with the constant sensory static of living.

Now, I recognize it by its absence.

About the Author

Johnathon Heart is the pseudonym of a former editor-in-chief. They are featured in a variety of horror and fantasy anthologies such as Bleed Error, The Best of Bizarro, Soulmate Syndrome, Factor Four, and Depths of Love: Love Thy Enemy. They have pieces upcoming from Eerie River and AZK studios. They hope that you (yes, you) have discovered, or will discover, joy and love.

DANY COMICS

WHAT LIES UNDER THE CANDLELIGHT

BY MIA RAM

If you had lived in Glenridding as I once did, in the shadow of the mountains, you still would not have known of the palace.

Built of stone right atop a mountain, you would not have known what it was like to reach out a window and run your hand through a cloud, cool mist trailing your fingers. You wouldn't have known of its thousands of rooms or hanging gardens. You wouldn't have known of the crimson roses that grew in the floor cracks, the spires from which you could see the whole of Britain, or its magic lanterns that flickered to life with a single command. You wouldn't have known that any object not of the palace was forbidden from being carried into it.

You would not have known that the palace was ancient. It stood before the word of Christ was brought to Britain's shores and before Roman feet trod on our emerald hills. It stood when the Old Gods still reigned. When Cernunnos rode wild through the woodlands as the Lord of Beasts, when Eostre brought forth Spring with torrents of rain and savage wonders, when Belenus first commanded a dance above flames, and when Thunor wrought thunder with his hammer.

The palace bore witness to it all.

You would not have been able to see the winding path to the mountain in the clouds unless you were as exceptionally unlucky as my father. The palace had survived many centuries, hidden and remaining so by enchantment. But enchantments, tightly woven though they may be, eventually rip and tear as time takes its due. Tiny, yet just big enough for the occasional traveler to slip through.

If you had been as unlucky as my father, and if you had been caught trespassing by the Master of the palace, perhaps you would have struck the same bargain he did. Perhaps, in exchange for your own freedom, you too, would have traded the most precious thing you had.

I had been living in the palace five days shy of a year when I found the thing that would change it all.

Behind the palace was a small forest that I had taken to exploring during my morning walks. It was one of the many little rituals I'd been forced to acquire since my arrival. My husband was many things to me by then. He was master, prisoner, prince, and stranger all at once. Master, for the palace and all within answered to him. Prisoner, because he could not leave under the laws of the enchantment. Prince, for he told me that was what he once was, and that he ruled over a kingdom in the valley with an iron heart. And stranger, for he could never be found during the day.

With this, he was insistent. He told me that I wouldn't be able to love him if I saw him in the sunlight. Instead, he would visit me at night, in utter darkness.

So I hadn't the slightest idea what he looked like.

I did try to find him during the day for the first few weeks. He would lock himself away in hidden wings of the palace, and as I was merely his bride, the doors refused to open at my command. His always took priority.

I had to find other ways to ease my boredom. Fortunately for me, the palace held far more amusements than had ever existed within my father's little cottage in Glenridding. I entertained myself with the many magicked items throughout the rooms. I would watch invisible hands clean and cook, watch the pots and pans spontaneously filling with luxurious foods and spices from all corners of the world. There were harps and flutes that played themselves, filling the air with haunted melodies that I could tell were from a time before time. I could step before any mirror in the palace, shut my eyes as I imagined the loveliest gown I could, and when I opened my eyes, I would be wearing it. Even the tapestries were enchanted, with the woven figures playing out scenes like actors on a silken stage.

But the forest delighted me most of all. There always were new paths weaved between the trees for me to explore, and I could walk for hours before being led back home to the palace.

When I found it, I had already been wandering half the day. The sun was dappled on the path, and vines hung down from branches like curtains. I came across a stream and took off my slippers, dipping my feet in the cool waters. At first, I took no notice of the breeze, only concerning myself with the minnows darting around my toes in silvery flashes. Yet quickly, the breeze kicked up into a wind, furiously stirring the leaves as the water flowed more fiercely. I was caught in a miniature storm swirling all about me.

If this had happened on my first day, perhaps I would have been frightened. But once you've lived in an enchanted palace for nearly a year, bizarre occurrences tend to lose their bite. I tilted my head back with a shrug, letting the wind tear through my hair and enjoying the sudden gust. And then, just as I closed my eyes, it swept past my ear—

"Lady of the House..."

I opened my eyes immediately, looking for the source of the voice. It was not my husband's, for he would never venture out the palace walls, particularly not during the day. Nor could I pin it to any of the creatures of the wood. It was too light, a disembodied whisper.

"Lady of the House..."

"Who's there?" I stayed frozen with my feet in the stream. "Where are you?"

"Everywhere and all around. I flew the world's four corners and all the way 'round the moon to find you. Lady of the House, look down in the water..."

I glanced down. There was something at the bottom of the streambed, half-buried in the silt.

"My Lady, roll up your sleeves and pluck it from the stream."

"I take no commands from you, whatever you are," I replied. "And certainly not when you shroud yourself in secrecy. Come now, show yourself. You won't frighten me, if that's what troubles you. With all I've seen, there's little that can surprise me now."

"Oh, surprises remain, My Lady, surprises remain," said the voice. *"But my nature is no secret. I am the West Wind."*

"A talking wind?" I raised an eyebrow. "I suppose that is new. My husband has certainly never mentioned such a thing existing here."

"He would not have, My Lady. Your Prince of Beasts is a prince of secrets as well. He hides even his face."

"He has his reasons, I'm sure," I said, though I wasn't sure at all. "Who are you to question him, in any case?"

"A friend, My Lady. As a Wind, I desire freedom for all things. The birds of the wood told me of you. They told me the Prince keeps you like a dove in a cage, for his own selfish needs. That you have given your whole

life, while he will not so much as give you his true nature, seems very wrong to me.”

"I had little choice in the matter." I looked down again at the thing in the streambed. It glimmered in the light, golden in color.

"I, too, was once a prisoner here. When the world was wild, as it ought to be, and an enchantress bridled me into a jar. She used me to fly, to blow enemies away from the palace grounds, to carry messages across the land and sea. She would open the jar just a crack, and let just a sliver of me out. For a century, it was thus. It was not until Her hand slipped one day that I was fully free.”

"How horrifying! I can't imagine being trapped in a jar for a hundred years. I'm surprised you did not go mad."

"My Lady, I nearly did. But the enchantress carried me about with Her, and from the jar, I amused myself by observing and memorizing every inch of the palace and its grounds. And so, when I heard of your plight, I knew just the thing that could assist you. Down in the water, My Lady, down in the water.”

"But what is it?" I leaned down closer to look. I tentatively reached toward the water, dipping my hand in. I remembered one of the first rules my husband ever told me of the house. Nothing from outside the palace was to be brought in. Better not even to touch it. Yet I reached in. I wrapped my hand around it and pulled it out of the stream.

"A candle, My Lady.”

I rolled the candle in my palm, the wax smooth against my skin. A grin spread across my face. "You came all this way to tell me about a candle?"

"Yes, My Lady.”

"I'm sorry to disappoint you, but I've no need for candles. The palace is lit by glass lanterns in every hall and room."

"Indeed, My Lady? They must number many. Who lights these lanterns?”

"No one. They light or dim themselves by my husband's command."

"I see. How very efficient. Tell me, My Lady, what of your command? If your Prince commands darkness, and you command light, who do the lanterns obey?"

To this, I said nothing.

"As I thought. The lanterns may obey only the Prince, My Lady... but the candle will obey you."

I stared down at the wick of the candle, imagining fire. With a spark, a flame flickered to life.

I snuck the candle into the palace.

I told myself that the rule was petty, that I was only bringing the candle in for curiosity's sake. I didn't plan to *use* it. Only to keep something for myself. If only so that I would not dream of it waiting for me in the forest.

I kept it hidden beneath my mattress, and every night that the Prince came to visit, I had to hide my fear that he would somehow discover it, that he would sense its alien presence. But four nights passed, and he did not.

I tried to content myself. I tried to tell myself that it was enough to simply be able to trace the curve of his jaw or have his arms wrap around me, to feel him breathing beside me as he slept. I tried to treasure those scattered, precious moments with him before he disappeared once more, chased away by the twilight. After all, I could just imagine what he looked like, couldn't I? Couldn't imagination be enough?

All the while, I dreamed of the candle.

He was such a sound sleeper. Were I to light it, would he even notice?

On the night that marked my first year at the palace, I decided.

I waited until a few hours after midnight, when I was absolutely sure he was asleep. I didn't know what he would do if he were to find out I broke his cardinal rules, but I had no intention of finding out. I planned to light the candle for only a moment, just long enough to see him and remember his face, before blowing out the flame and casting the candle out a window.

As my Prince slept by my side, I pulled the candle out from under the mattress. Just as I had back in the forest, I stared down at the wick and imagined a flame. Within a moment, the candle was alight. With a trembling hand, I held the candle over the bed, and for the first time ever, I looked at my husband.

Oh.

He was beautiful.

He had golden locks of hair, a face so flawless you'd think him a sculpture come to life, and a gentle smile even in sleep. One hand rested on the pillow, with slender fingers befitting a musician. To think that such lips had met mine, that those hands had held me, and that I had never known!

I leaned in closer, in awe. His eyes were flitting beneath the lids. I knew he must have been dreaming then, and wondered what he dreamed. Already he lived in the realm of the fantastical, our own home a palace of dreams. Did he dream of what few things he didn't possess? Of the world beyond the mountain, of his kingdom in the valley, of me in the sunlight?

And what color were his eyes beneath those lids?

I continued to stare down, fancying that if I watched his sleeping face long enough, somehow I could know. So absorbed was I, that I didn't even notice when a drop of wax fell from the candle right on his bare chest.

His eyes flew open.

"W-what," he rasped, blue eyes staring up at me in shock. "You... what are you—"

"I'm sorry!" My voice and hand trembled as another drop of wax fell from the candle. Outside, a vicious wind began to batter the walls and window. "I just wanted to see you!"

"No, no!" He scrambled out of the bed toward the shadows. "You can't! Not for a year and a day!"

The wind outside grew harsher, rattling the window panes.

"A year and a day?" A third drop of wax dribbled down to my own hands, burning me.

"A year and a day..." His eyes fluttered, and he shivered as the wind finally blew the window open, tearing into the room. "I only needed one more day."

The flame blew out, and the candle fell from my hand as a storm ripped the wall away and tore through the room. Rain buffeted us, dark clouds choked the air as my Prince screamed and screamed, and just as I thought the wind was going to blow me away, a familiar voice whispered in my ear.

"Forgive me, My Lady. I never left the jar. I serve Her still."

With that, the wind knocked me from the room. I fell down to the balcony one floor below, my fall barely cushioned by the wind. I lay there limp and stared at the tiles on the floor. I don't know how long. My every muscle ached, and my head felt ready to burst. It wasn't until I realized that the sounds of the storm had quieted, along with my Prince's screams. Gritting my teeth, I rolled myself over onto my back and looked up at the floor above.

The wall was entirely gone, leaving the inside of the bedroom exposed like an open wound. The candle was lost. The rain and clouds were gone. The air was still. All I saw around me was infused with the silver glow of the moon. I kept watching, waiting, until finally, I saw a figure stumble out to the edge of the room.

The blue eyes were gone, the shape of his bared skull no longer human. Sickly white and smooth, his head resembled that of a stag's, only with cruel fangs dripping from his jaws. The sockets were empty and dark. Branch-like antlers sprouted from the sides and reached into the sky, towering above his head like a skeletal halo. From his back, a pair of dirty brown wings twitched. His hands had curved into blackened claws. His once-glowing skin was now grayed and dead, covered in patches of rotting scales and greasy fur. Everything of his body now reeked of death, every part of his body decaying or withered, a chimeric corpse.

His hands went to his throat, an agonized hiss escaping as he spoke to the air.

"Where are you? You and your fucking candle... *where are you?*"

I clasped my hands over my mouth. I didn't dare speak, didn't dare move or breathe. Above me, he tipped his head back, baring his fangs, and screamed into the night.

"I'll kill you! I swear to the gods, I—will—rip—you—apart!"

A thousand rooms meant a thousand places to hide.

A labyrinth allows one to disappear. I could slip from room to room, and hide within secret alcoves, underground passageways, and trick chambers. I crammed myself under beds and in wardrobes when I needed to steal a few precious moments of sleep. I learned how to crawl out the windows and climb my way down the palace walls to other levels. I discovered the dungeons and the old torture chambers, where ancient blood still stained the cobblestones and grinning skulls watched from the corners.

Walks in the woods became dangerous. It would be too easy to be caught in the open air, with nothing but the trees to shelter behind. The trees, the flowers, and the winding paths would not help me now. Nothing would when he was near. It was one of the ways I knew when to run. Doors would suddenly try to shut me in, the harps and flutes would sing their wailing songs to announce my presence, and the mirrors would crack when I passed them. Even the tapestries betrayed me. In place of their lighthearted plays, they now wove my likeness to show where in a room I was hiding or wove mocking versions of myself as a monstress, a dismembered corpse, a blood-drenched animal huddled in the forest.

The other way I knew when to run was to listen. He would often moan as he searched for me in the palace, the plod of his footsteps and drag of his wings accompanied by those low tones of pain. Once in a great while, he would scream out threats instead. They would echo through the halls and follow me as I ran.

"I'll rip you apart, like you're nothing... nothing but a ragdoll..."

I know you will, I'd think. *I know.*

"I'll cram that candle through your eye..."

If either of us could find it.

"I'll slit your throat, I'll carve out your insides, and I'll bash your head into the wall until..."

I know, my Prince. I know.

"I'll... I'll..." And slowly, his voice would give out.

Each and every threat played in my mind every waking moment, and I died a thousand promised deaths every day and every night. In my dreams, his hands were always around my neck. My eyes were always sunken beneath his thumbs. My heart was always bleeding between his teeth. It did not matter if we were on opposite ends of the palace. *He was with me.* His presence infused every pockmarked stone, every long and empty hall, every room and window. The palace was a vast, dying organism, and I was the parasite squirming within, regret close on my heels.

The hunt went on.

And on.

And on.

Days into weeks into months.

He was always just a little too near, and I was always just barely fast enough, just barely quiet enough, just barely clever enough.

But I couldn't be enough forever.

Kill him, be killed by him, or escape the palace. These were the only three endings.

To die by his hands, raked apart by claws or throat torn out by fangs, was a fear so great it outweighed the misery of life in the palace. I could not accept it.

I had already attempted to escape countless times, both in the golden days before I lit the candle and after. It was no use. The mountain itself kept me locked in, its jagged sides spiking up to block me from every route I tried. It could not be done.

That left only one choice. A terrifying choice, for he was a beast worse than what even my nightmares could conjure. But beasts can still be killed.

I wasn't stupid, at least not in this. Simply rushing him with a kitchen knife or attempting to bang him over the head with a brick would only end with his claws around my throat. No, I needed to learn of a weakness. I needed to know when he slept, where his pain was greatest, what he feared, and where he stumbled. I needed to study him.

It wasn't easy at first. I had to ignore the screaming instinct to run, the thing that had governed me and preserved my life. Seeking out a monster went against everything nature had molded me to be. But I did it.

He was below, drifting among one of the palace gardens, and I was above, sneaking in the shadows of the terraces. I had followed the sounds of his moaning, pulled through halls and halls. By the time I'd tracked him to the lower gardens, his wails had quieted to whimpers.

It was strange, watching instead of running. Here he did not lurch forward in bloodlust, fly with his ragged wings, or call to curse my name. He only sat among the roses.

He used to send me roses from the bushes, before the candle. Bright like rubies. They had withered to pale husks now. Everything in the garden had, all of it browned and twisted and brittle where once it had been a rainbow of flowers and endless green.

The Prince plucked two of the dead roses from the bush. He turned them over in his hand, feeling the petals between his fingers. Then, delicately, he placed one in each of his barren eye sockets.

I watched, transfixed, as he picked more and more roses. He pinned them on the tips of his antlers and wedged them between his feathers, piling on more and more. I inched closer to the terrace edge for a better look. Not watching where I was stepping, I tripped over an uneven cobblestone, a soft gasp escaping my lips as I staggered too far forward.

His head whipped up toward my direction and I froze. I was directly beneath the moonlight, directly in his line of sight.

For a moment, neither of us moved or spoke. Finally, he whispered three words.

"Are you here?"

I spun around and ran back the way I came, tearing down the halls. My heart was beating, fit to burst. A few beats of his wings and he could have had me, but that was fine. The risk was worth it, for I had confirmed a suspicion.

He was stone blind.

All I had to be was quiet, and I could watch him as much as I liked.

I preferred to watch from places high above and far below wherever he was. If he was perched on the spires, I stared up from the courtyard. If he was with the roses, I was at the peak of the tallest oak, nestled in the gnarled branches. The distance made things easier.

I can't imagine how I would have looked to him if he could have seen me. I had become the little monstress that the tapestries so loved to weave me as. The water in the baths and fountains no longer flowed clear, so all I had to bathe in and drink from was what few rancid pools remained. I was covered in grime from head to toe, my last dress so torn that I was half-naked, my hair a greasy mess of tangles that reached to the small of my back. I was pale now too. The sunlight was too bright, too harsh, and in any case, he never seemed to wander during the day. Old habits and all that. To accommodate, I, too, gave myself to the night. My vision sharpened in cold starlight. The secret chorus of the owls and the bats was my music. I could make myself small with the shadows, and I knew what it meant to live in the dark.

I could always see him, though.

Me, from the window of the tower, watching as the Prince returned from a forest path. I could see how those antlers weighed heavy on his head. I wondered, could I grab them from behind, use them to yank his head back and slit his throat? But perhaps they were weaker than they seemed. Perhaps they would snap right off if I pulled them. They were so stately, so entrancing with their sharp peaks. *So beautiful.* It would be a horrible shame to break the crown off his head.

The Prince, wandering the ballroom in silence as I watched from the room across the hall, staring through the open door. Those claws hung at his sides. Long and slender. I could imagine them clicking the keys of a piano, or plucking the string of a harp just gently enough not to snap it. He used them to navigate the whole of the palace. He dragged them along the walls, used them to investigate every object he came across, held them in the air to feel the winds of coming storms. His new way of seeing. I was sure I could bite the fingers right through if I had to, but I hoped I wouldn't have to. It would be a pity to mangle the well-tuned eyes at the ends of his arms.

The Prince, walking at the palace entrance where the grand staircase loomed, and me at the top of it. He was barefoot, dragging the tips of his toes over the tile designs, running his hands along the edges of the doors before throwing them open. Moonlight fell across the scales that crawled up the length of his chest, shoulders, and back. They shined, iridescent. I wondered if they were too hard for a knife to pierce. They covered his heart, just the place I would have wanted to strike. But what a tragedy it would be to fracture those lovely jewels upon his skin.

Always I followed, always I watched, even as the palace began to change around us. The halls gradually morphed into tunnels. The forest crept closer, and twisted trees sprouted in the middle of the bedrooms and ballrooms. Dark flowers grew on the ceiling, so hypnotic in their patterns that I could stare at them for hours. Strange fruit grew from the walls in white and blue and violet, tasting of ash and salt and blood. When I ate them, I had visions. Visions of corpses soaking the fields red, the air cloying with the scent of rotted flesh. Visions of a many-eyed, undulating monster burrowing into the heart of the earth, waiting. Visions of myself, ripping open throats with my own pair of fangs. Or of my own neck tipped back, my throat bared.

Animals invaded. Birds nested in every corner, rabbits and foxes made burrows beneath the floorboards, and serpents coiled around the ever-dimming lanterns. Even bats hung between the stalactites that began to drip from the ceilings.

Everything was warping and corroding. The mountain was taking the palace back in. But we had yet to finish the hunt.

The Prince, in the gardens, and I on the terrace once more. Standing in the midst of the ruins of our life, he stretched his wings. I wondered how high and far those wings could take him. I wondered how much he could carry when he flew. What if he didn't hate me? What if he could carry me and fly me home to the valley? What if we could both leave this place? But then again, there was no reason for him to leave now. There was nothing like him anywhere else in the world. He could never belong anywhere but here. And, perhaps, neither could I.

It was that night that I realized I could no longer remember his human face.

"Lady of the House... Lady of the House..."

I knew the voice as soon as I heard it.

"My Lady, please listen."

"Why should I?" I snapped. I was on one of the upper balconies, watching the darkling trees sway by the hand of the Wind. It was one of the few balconies left. Most of the rest were merely cliffs now.

"I can help you."

"Now there's a promise I've heard before," I said with a snort. I was surprised at how raspy and coarse my voice sounded. How long had it been since I had spoken aloud? I was surprised that I even remembered how to form the words.

"I can atone. My Lady, you are not the one this curse was meant to ensnare. You are only collateral. My Mistress has no quarrel with you. She has sent me to free you, for She is merciful."

"Forgive me if I doubt her 'mercy.' Particularly from the words of her captive. If she will not free you, why should she free me?" I asked. The West Wind swept softly against me.

"Who is to say She would not free me?"

"Have you asked her?"

"No."

I furrowed my brow. "Is it... is it that you *want* to remain in her jar?"

"No."

"Yet there you stay. Why?"

"I do not know, My Lady. I cannot leave."

I stood there for a moment in silence. I had learned too well that the West Wind knew how to wield honeyed words. The last time I had trusted it, it had kindled my destruction.

But the scales were too tough, the antlers too tall, the claws too slender. For all my watching, I had nothing.

"What have you come to offer me?" I asked the Wind.

"To offer? Nothing. But I have something to return."

A violent gust blew around me, whipping my hair so hard it lashed my face. Something familiar hit my hand. I rolled it in my palm, the wax smooth against my skin.

"If your Prince commands darkness, and you command light, what must you do?"

I knew I'd find him in the gardens again. Why hadn't I thought of it before? It would be so easy now, with the candle. I would sneak behind him, stepping soft like air, quiet like night. I would look at the wick and imagine fire and a flame would flicker to life, just as it did that night before, a year ago. I would hold the darkling flame to the feathers of his wings and set him alight.

And I would be free. It would all be over.

He was among the roses again but standing and haloed by the moon, all awash in icy, silver light. For the first time, I was not looking down from the terraces. I brought myself closer, closer, closer than I could have ever imagined. I gripped the candle so tight it was a miracle it didn't snap in half.

He didn't stir, didn't look backward. He had his head tipped back as though looking up at the sky.

Another step.

His feathers looked dry.

Another step.

It would be so easy.

Another step.

I was in the moonlight too now, inches away from his wings, away from *him*. So unfathomably close. I could see the slight rise and fall of his shoulders as he breathed.

I held the candle up, just a hair's breadth away from his feathers.

So easy, so easy. So close.

I stared at the wick of the candle.

So close.

I imagined fire.

I imagined fire.

I imagined fire.

And yet no flame appeared.

A soft gasp escaped me, a sound I would normally never have permitted, but I was insensible to everything in the world except for that candlewick. And, of course, my Prince heard me.

He turned in a flash, reaching out and snatching me by the wrist. I gasped again, the candle falling from my grip and rolling to his foot.

"You *are* here," he rasped, squeezing my wrist so hard I saw stars. I said nothing. I didn't want to give him the satisfaction of my voice, of hearing it tremble with fury or terror, whichever was stronger.

He held me there silently, waiting in vain for my answer. Then he paused. With one claw still gripping my wrist, he bent down and picked up the candle. I remembered then his old threats, his curses, all dripping with hatred not only for me but for that candle. I remembered what he had promised to do to me with it.

Yet I found I could not move, could not struggle against his grip or even blink. From so close, his antlers seemed even more refined, even sharper, a crown that could pierce a heart. The razor tips of his claws could cut my skin to ribbons in an instant, could impale my wrist if he curled them and squeezed. I lived all my thousand deaths again.

The Prince held the candle up in front of my face. At first, I thought he wanted me to do something with it, but he made no move to loosen his grip on me, and I had already failed to set it alight. Then I realized he was... staring at it. He had no eyes, no magic way to see, yet his empty sockets were aimed at the wick of the candle in dark focus. He stared, and stared, and stared.

With a spark, the flame flickered to life.

About the Author

Mia Ram is a fantasy and science fiction writer from Huntersville, North Carolina. Her work has been featured in multiple publications, including Metaphorosis Magazine and The NoSleep Podcast.

SHADES OF DORIAN

BY KEVIN FOLLIARD

An old soul, Gabriel preferred dim piano lounges to the ostentatious nightclubs that lined Chicago's Boystown neighborhood. He had been attending Columbia University on an art scholarship for a full semester, and it pained him to have made only superficial connections. He wasn't sure what he had expected exactly. To find some soulmate or best friend seemed far-fetched since both school and the scene were plagued with flighty boys and girls obsessed with their phones.

On Fridays, Gabriel skipped out on social invitations and instead frequented Chicago's Art Institute. There, he escaped into the moods, landscapes, and portraits of generations lost. Into even older souls who'd captured meaning in oil and canvas.

It was there, in Gallery 262, before Ivan Albright's iconic painting, that Gabriel, at last, made a meaningful connection. Albright's *Picture of Dorian Gray* had always struck him as the embodiment of decay and corruption with its blistering purples, browns, and grays. What about, "The painting possessed a festering that drew the eye——not life to it, but the reverse." Gabriel could not help but be seduced by his disgust for the figure, like an onlooker after a horrible car wreck. He dared not appreciate the ugliness.

The painting unnerved and thrilled him all at once, and he saw in it a mirror to his own detachment from his vapid peers, from his roots. Over the weeks, the painting had become a lens through which he viewed his life. His sense of self. It screamed something dark and unshakable. A shadow that stretched behind him no matter how far from the past he ventured.

This night, in the museum's waning hours, a man stood in stark contrast to Albright's portrait. A handsome college-aged student—no more than twenty—dressed in black slacks and a pressed gray button-down shirt. The gentleman's perfectly unkempt blond hair brushed the soft curvature of ivory cheeks. His metallic blue eyes targeted Gabriel. He gestured to the painting and said, in a voice warm as the autumn sun, "Do you find this compelling?"

Gabriel's heart quickened. "It's certainly striking."

"Mm." The gentleman eyed the painting and crossed the room. He rubbed his chin pensively, turned, and took in the piece from another angle. "I'm afraid I may come across as a snob, but it pales in comparison to the original."

Gabriel struggled to recall if there had been a famous painting of Oscar Wilde's character prior to Albright's piece, which had been featured in a Hollywood film in the 1940s. "I'm unfamiliar."

"With me?" The gentleman smiled. "I never introduced myself. How rude." He approached and extended his hand. "Dorian Gray."

Gabriel shook the young man's hand. "Dorian Gray" clasped with both hands. He had a strong grip and soft palms. They clutched hands a few precious extra moments. Gabriel flushed.

Was this an actor? A role-player, hired by the museum to explain the painting? "Well." Gabriel broke the handshake. "You certainly look the part." He sized him up. "I mean, this part, not..." He gestured to the painted Dorian, corrupted by sin. "Not that part."

"You don't believe me."

"From what I recall in high school English, Dorian Gray died when he stabbed the cursed portrait."

Dorian presented his Illinois driver's license, which *indeed* read "Dorian Gray," and included what Gabriel had to admit was the most captivating driver's license photo he had ever seen. Dorian snapped his wallet shut before Gabriel even thought to check the birthdate.

"Did you legally change your name to Dorian Gray? Or were your parents very... literary?"

"You think I'm strange. Quite frankly, I find the rest of the world mad in the worst possible way, minus perhaps my present company."

Gabriel smiled. "What makes you think that?"

"A compulsion. I saw your dark, discerning eyes from across the room. Your brow knit with analysis. Your delicate hands. I thought to myself, this man is observant. He might challenge me."

Gabriel opened his mouth but struggled for a response.

"Tell me your name."

"Gabriel."

"How angelic. Gabriel, this museum is closing," Dorian Gray said. "And I would like to buy you dinner. In fact, I insist upon it."

Dorian Gray neither ordered an Uber nor hailed a cab. He confidently led Gabriel down the front steps of the Art Institute, past towering stone lions, and opened the doors of a white limousine.

Gabriel attempted to conceal his astonishment. He ran his fingers across plush, velvety seats. As a poor kid from rural Arkansas, he had never set foot in a limo, not even for senior prom. "Where are we going?"

"Out to dinner." Dorian poured himself a glass of red wine from a minibar that lined the tinted windows. He offered a second glass. "Château Margaux?"

Gabriel shook his head. His heart pounded with a mix of fear and excitement. What had prompted him to follow this stranger? The limo? His pristine looks? His outrageous lie? Gabriel casually checked his phone. He should alert someone to where he was, but he wondered who would care. Certainly not his parents, who had all but disavowed him. He had no true friends among his classmates, only acquaintances.

"If you're sleuthing about me online, I'm afraid you'll be disappointed," Dorian said. "Social media is a poor man's vanity, Gabriel. Whyever should one sink to such depths?"

"I was only thinking of texting someone."

"To let them know you had climbed into a limo with who? A figment? A murderer? A madman?"

"Perhaps all of the above."

Dorian laughed. "I can only assure you that I am not imaginary."

Gabriel texted an email to himself. *At least if he thinks someone knows where I am,* he thought, *he won't try anything.*

The limo pulled into the alley behind a trendy sushi house in the West Loop. Dorian guided him through a back entrance to a small, private dining room. An attractive server in a gold and royal blue kimono presented a platter of sushi rolls and sashimi within moments of them sitting. Dorian graciously thanked her and asked that they not be disturbed. He then cast a devilish smile across the table. "I abhor waiting for things, don't you, Gabriel? Anticipation is the shackle of joy."

"What is joy without discipline?" Gabriel sampled a shrimp roll. It was exquisite.

"You intrigue me, Gabriel. What discipline has held you back in your young life? And once you achieve it, do you expect a return on the investment of pleasure? Or perhaps, will you find you've wasted years of precious youth?"

"You think I'm naive."

"Naivete is soil for the flowers of decadence, but no, I sense something far more intense behind those dark eyes, or I would never have chosen to dine with you."

"Quid pro quo then," Gabriel said. "Ask me anything and I'll answer, provided you're honest with me in return."

"I find that to be a terribly lopsided proposal, Gabriel, for you'll find little surprise in my own transparency. You seem to already know my story."

"I know the story of Dorian Gray, not of the man who sits across from me. And I confess, it's been a while since I read the book."

Dorian plucked a salmon roll with his chopsticks. "Books are beautifully tragic lies. I did so enjoy being deceived by them once."

"How old are you?" Gabriel asked.

"After a century and a half, one deliberately loses track. To avoid impropriety on my part, I've decided that you, Gabriel, are twenty-one, and I'll thank you not to correct that assumption. I've also made a handful of other observations, if you don't mind my sharing them."

"Please."

"You were not a deeply closeted child, raised in a rural setting, perhaps a farm. You've been granted thick skin from years of bullying. Your parents made little to no attempt to understand you, but you sought escape in creativity. You find now that you've transitioned to city life that you resent the shallow personalities of your urbane peers, and yet you have no love for your roots. You're lost in orbit, drifting from painting to painting in life's gallery, seeking one that calls to you."

Chills crept down Gabriel's spine. He felt the color drain from his face. The chopsticks trembled between his fingers, and he set them down.

"Observation becomes uncanny over the course of several lifetimes, Gabriel. I understand it's unnerving, but I assure you, I know little more about you. As I've only shared my observations, I still owe you a question. Was it my painting—*Albright's* painting of me, in fairness—that drew you in? And do you wonder now if you've somehow drawn me from it into your life?"

Gabriel took a deep, controlled breath. "I'm considering that now, yes. What are you then? Some kind of literary ghost? An elaborate hallucination?"

"I am Dorian Gray, a man of flesh and blood, love and loss, decadence and disappointment, independent of your fears and desires, Gabriel. You're most certainly an artist, and I suspect a painter."

Gabriel nodded.

Dorian beamed. "I knew from your stare and your fingers, your steely aloofness. You're like a beautiful walking scar. What I'm trying to determine is what horrid turn set you adrift in orbit. Oh, it was many things, certainly. The town, your parents, teachers, nasty children, but I sense a deeper, more succulent tragedy. A one-sided attraction, yes?"

Now Gabriel felt sick to his stomach. No longer could he believe this was an actor. He felt he was being peeled open. Dorian's dissection made his head spin. He reached for water.

"It's all right, Gabriel," Dorian whispered. "No one will bother us here. I own this restaurant. Your secrets are jewels I choose to admire in private."

"How much of the story is true?" Gabriel blurted out. "Oscar Wilde's novel, I mean."

Dorian sighed. His eyes drifted in bemusement. "Somewhere in the 90th percentile, I'd wager. It's been ages. Who should enjoy reading his own story but a complete narcissist? I do have a fondness for Wilde's rapacious wit, and an admiration for how he wrote himself out of the tale completely."

"You stabbed the painting," Gabriel said. "The painting from the story, and it aged you beyond death."

"I've stabbed many paintings in my more dramatic moments. There's truth in that scene. But you held my blood-warmed hand. You can see that I am alive."

"You haven't answered my question."

"You haven't answered mine." Dorian's cool demeanor broke into a sneer. "I will tell you—in fact, I will gladly show you—*all* of my secrets if you reveal yours." His cruel expression relaxed, and Dorian reached across the table. He slid his thumb across Gabriel's fingers. "This choice is yours, of course."

Gabriel let out a long, shaky breath. "There was a neighbor who I admired growing up. A much older man."

Dorian squeezed his hand. "Tell me about him."

"Mr. Murphy. He was a painter. He lived down the road, and he would set up a canvas to paint wildlife on warm days."

"A handsome man?"

Gabriel shook his head. "He was old. Fat. He had moles."

Dorian's eyebrows arched with disapproval, but still, he smiled. "To you, he was beautiful, because of what he could do."

Tears burned Gabriel's eyes. The image of Dorian's perfectly handsome face smeared and blurred, and Gabriel squeezed his eyes shut.

"You wished very much to be closer to him, and it frightened you."

Gabriel nodded.

"You don't have to go on if you don't wish to, Gabriel," Dorian said. "You can ask me something, if you'd like. Anything at all."

"No. It's okay. I... I want to tell you. I..."

"You have to unburden yourself. It will go no further than this room, I promise."

"Mr. Murphy was kind," Gabriel said. "He had no children. His wife passed away before I was born, and I think he was broken inside. But he always answered my questions about art. He taught me form, depth, light, composition."

"Your affection for Mr. Murphy deepened as you grew older," Dorian said.

Gabriel sniffled. Nodded. "It wasn't him that scared me so much as my compulsions."

"And what were you compelled to do?"

"I was fourteen. Growing bolder and more curious every day. I thought about Mr. Murphy at night. During school. He was haunting me."

"And you needed to banish the wicked thoughts," Dorian said. "You could only do that by confronting them."

"I decided... I would go over there on a warm summer morning when he'd be alone in his yard, always with a bottle of water by his art table. And... I drugged him." Tears spilled down Gabriel's cheek. He opened his eyes. Dorian rounded the table, knelt, and cradled Gabriel's hand. With the other hand, he dried his eyes with a silk napkin.

"It sounds like this was something you could not stop yourself from doing." Dorian caressed Gabriel's arm.

"I wanted to do so much more. I knew he had no interest in me, not in that way, and I felt it was the only way I could know... what it felt like. But when he passed out, before I could get to him... he fell. His head hit the corner of the patio wall. A pool of blood spread underneath him."

"Did you call for help?"

"I left him there." Gabriel sobbed.

Suddenly, Dorian's arms enveloped him. His hands slid along his back.

"It was an accident. I just thought he would fall asleep and..."

Dorian shushed him. "We'll never speak of it again unless you so desire."

Gabriel held Dorian tighter. He smelled of flowery cologne, roses and lilac.

"Thank you for this, Gabriel." Dorian inhaled deeply and then softly kissed him. Gabriel kissed back. Dorian's lips tasted like sweet wine. His hair feathered against Gabriel's cheek.

Dorian broke the embrace and gently pushed Gabriel back into his chair. "We should leave." Dorian stood and straightened his shirt. "I owe you a secret. A painting. And I desperately want to know what you think of it. But before we return to my estate, I would like to get to know you even better."

It was much later by the time the limo pulled up to Dorian's estate, far north of the city. Dorian had taken them to a private wing of the botanical gardens after hours. There, Gabriel had surrendered himself to Dorian's touch. Pleasure lingered in Gabriel's mind and body, and it was only as they pulled through iron gates that he started to wonder exactly where they were. When the limo door opened, he heard the crashing waves of Lake Michigan somewhere nearby. He guessed they were on some secluded property in an affluent north suburb. The house was an enormous colonial, set behind a twelve-foot brick perimeter. The limo dutifully turned and left them. The gates clanged shut.

Before Dorian opened the door, he eyed Gabriel with concern and squeezed his hand. "Brace yourself." Dorian led him into the foyer, past an elegant staircase, and into a parlor with an ornate gold fireplace, Persian rug, and elegant Victorian furniture. A polished grand piano gleamed in the moonlight. His host switched on the lights. "There it is."

A scalloped gallery frame hung on one wall. Within it, a hideous creature sat upright. Its skin bubbled and flaked like lava. A garden of horrors surrounded the figure. Slithering insects and spiders hid amid thorny vines and smiling, carnivorous plants. The being's claws dug at what appeared to be the eyes of bloody victims. It soon became apparent that the being sat on a throne of distorted human prey. Broken souls bent backward with shattered spines and protruding bones. Blood trickled from their pierced eye sockets down to hungry, monstrous flowers. The figure's smile sliced ear-to-ear across the boiled skin of his cruel face. Beady, devilish eyes glowed bright as magma. In the center of the painting, Gabriel noticed stabbing marks and slashes.

For a moment, Gabriel stood in shock. Then fell to his knees. His stomach turned. Dorian was already beside him with a gilded waste basket. Gabriel retched and vomited.

"Easy," Dorian said. "Not on the rug. There you go. That's a common reaction, Gabriel. It's all right. *That* is the original, and I confess, I grow increasingly proud of it over time. I've come to truly love it. It's horrid. It's exquisite. It's the epitome of honesty. To think that I once hid it in an attic seems the peak of absurdity now. But I have so few guests. Only those who I think might appreciate its power."

Gabriel dry heaved.

Dorian rubbed his back. "It's all right. It's only a painting. I'm right here. I'm the same man who kissed you and held you. Was I not correct, though? Albright's painting leaves something to be desired."

Gabriel nodded and wiped his mouth on his sleeve. He averted his eyes from the painting. Not because he was unable to look, but because he feared a second glance would suck him in. Would kill him.

"I promised you my secrets, and my secrets you shall have," Dorian whispered. "Follow me." Dorian crossed the room to the painting. At first, Gabriel recoiled. He had the sudden urge to flee. But Dorian pushed on the wall. There was the sound of stone and wood grinding, and the entire section of the wall—painting and all—turned inward.

Gabriel's stomach relaxed as the painting tilted out of view, revealing a dimly lit stone chamber. Dorian turned, grinned, and beckoned him. "You will love this. I promise you."

Gabriel's heart slammed his ribs. He yearned to follow Dorian, to learn absolutely everything about this man, to be held by him more. But he *knew* he should leave.

"Please, Gabriel." Dorian's eyes sagged with disappointment. Golden hair swept the curvature of his handsome face. "For that curious little boy so enthralled by Mr. Murphy's paintings. You owe this to yourself. There are pleasures beyond what I've shown you tonight. *Far* beyond."

Gabriel's feet moved independently of his conscious mind. Soon he was entering the cold cavern. He shuddered as he passed the painting. He felt its insidious eyes searing his flesh, but once Dorian rotated the wall fully back in place, an enormous weight lifted.

Gabriel wondered how any normal human being could bear the presence of that painting for long. "What greater secret can you possibly have than that?" he asked his host.

Dorian scoffed. "Please. There's nothing secret about that painting. Not anymore." He led Gabriel through the dark and down a flight of cellar stairs. They entered a room lit with oil lamps. Gabriel made out the dark, looming rectangles of canvases. Dorian hit a switch, and overhead lamps blazed to life, revealing a dank chamber with concrete and brick facades.

Scores of paintings surrounded them, all portraits of Dorian Gray in various stages of decay. None so hideous and far gone as the one Dorian proudly displayed in his parlor, but all of them snide, sneering, blistering. Several were aged and haggard, but human-looking. One painting seemed to be growing odd protrusions, devilish antlers which stabbed from the figure's forehead. The devious face had clearly once been Dorian's, but now...

Gabriel's breath fled. Did he want this for himself? To be young, beautiful forever? But only superficially? Was this all Dorian desired? An already corrupted companion with whom he could share his eternal youth? He reached out to touch the horns, to see if they were real, and in that moment, a metal collar clamped around his neck. Gabriel twisted in surprise. Slack chains clanked along the cold concrete floor.

Dorian backed away; hands held high. "It's all right, Gabriel. You're going to be all right."

Gabriel sunk his fingers into the metal collar and uselessly pried. He yanked at the chain, which wrapped and wound a stone pillar. Padlocks held the chains in place. Beside the pillar was a chair, an easel with a blank canvas, a palette, and a cup full of brushes. Jars of paint lined a small wooden shelf. "What are you doing?"

"Giving you closure," Dorian said. "Giving you penance. As I've done for so many." His host gestured to an alcove on the far side of the chamber, packed with yellowing bones. "Lifetimes of decadence surely cannot be contained in a single portrait, Gabriel. I require new talent. New blood."

Gabriel shook his head. He searched Dorian's steel blue eyes.

"You will remain here and you will paint me. You'll learn to love this room."

Gabriel shouted and yanked at the chain.

"Yell all you want. It only makes you more beautiful."

Gabriel choked and sobbed, stretching the chain in his attempt to break free.

"I love that you're afraid. I love that you're in despair. But there is purification in punishment, Gabriel. I brought you here because I can tell it's where you wish to be. You will know pleasure as much as pain in my care. You'll learn that the two can become almost indistinguishable. You will expand my gallery and enrich my life."

"Why?" Gabriel sobbed.

"Because. Art is born of shame and trauma. Because you yearn to be held captive by a powerful older man. And because... I am beautiful, and must be painted."

About the Author

Kevin M. Folliard is a Chicagoland writer whose fiction has been collected by The Horror Tree, The Dread Machine, Demain Publishing, Dark Owl Publishing, and more. His recent publications include his horror anthology *The Misery King's Closet*, his YA fantasy adventure novel *Grayson North: Frost-Keeper of the Windy City*, and his 2022 dinosaur adventure novel *Carnivore Keepers*. Kevin currently resides in the western suburbs of Chicago, IL, where he enjoys his day job in academia and membership in the La Grange Writers Group. You can learn more about his writing at www.KevinFolliard.com.

FIRST I WAS AFRAID, I WAS PETRIFIED

BY Rajiv Moté

Lie still, hero. The thornbush broke your fall. Don't try to open your eyes. I'll bandage them. You'll survive—I was blind once too. No, hero, the winged horse is gone. He soared toward Olympus after throwing you. He was never yours to keep. By what right do I say so? I knew his mother. Well enough to weep when that other "hero" returned with her head in a sack. You didn't know Pegasus was born of the gorgon? That beauty could come from horror? Your ideas of monsters and heroes come from poets spinning boasts into tales. Boasts of men who won't face the truth of what they do in the name of Olympus. But I knew the gorgon, and I loved her. She faced her fate with more courage than any so-called hero. I was a soldier, not a poet. But lie still while I bind your wounds and tell you a tale the poets will never sing.

I was on my knees, emptying myself of the sea on an unknown shore. My eyes stung from salt, and the sun was blinding, even with my eyes closed. I whispered gratitude to Poseidon, but it only brought another fit of coughing. I remembered the gale, our capsizing ship, and a light like a star beneath the waves, though that memory slipped away like a dream when I tried to fix on it.

"Here is another," said a girl's voice. "Could this be the one? Is it my time?" Her voice was sweet, but sad. It held a touch of fear.

"No, little sister," came another voice. Older, more sour. "That one will come from the sky. This one crawled from the sea, like the others."

So I was not the only survivor.

"Look at me," the first voice said, suddenly imperious and hard. Not a girl, then. A maiden, perhaps.

No matter which way I turned my head, the white light consumed everything. I climbed to my knees. "Where are you?"

"He remains flesh," said the maid, with a touch of wonder.

"Look, sister," came a third voice. Another woman, older than the maid, younger than the sour one I already thought of as the crone. "His eyes are white as spray." Compassion touched this one's voice. The mother then, to complete the trinity.

"He's blind," said the crone.

So I was. Eyes open or shut, even behind my hands, it was like staring into the noonday sun. I fought down panic with a soldier's discipline. "Please," I said. "My crewmen. You spoke of others." I struggled to climb to my feet, but my limbs wouldn't obey. A restless ocean wind filled my ears with whispering. It pebbled my wet skin.

The crone chuckled, a cruel sound. "Reach with your left hand."

My hand fumbled out, searching, until it felt oddly textured stone. I groped around it trying to understand what I was touching. Two bent stone pillars. Or a statue. The shape of a man.

"Be grateful your blindness protects you, soldier," said the mother.

I pulled myself to my feet, leaning on the statue, uncomprehending. My gooseflesh had nothing to do with the wind. There was danger here. My weapons were at the bottom of the sea.

"Protects him?" said the crone. "Hardly." Something massive dragged across the sand. A burly arm encircled my neck from behind. Not an arm—sinuous but boneless, and thick as a man's leg. It began to squeeze and lifted me off my feet by the throat. I clung to it to keep from strangling. "We'll have meat tonight," she said, her voice close to my ear. The wind hissed like a nest of vipers.

"Must we kill him?" said the maiden. "He's helpless as..." Her voice trailed into silence. Something wordless passed among the sisters.

"Hold, Stheno," said the mother. "I see an opportunity." Again, something dragged across the sand toward me. The hissing grew louder, as if I was surrounded by serpents. I felt a prick through my corselet at the base of my throat, sharp as the tip of a dagger. It dragged down, parting the tattered layers of linen until my ruined garment hung open.

I kicked and pulled against the thing around my neck, but it constricted until I surrendered, hanging limp and naked in its grasp. "What say you, little sister?" asked the mother. "Not so terrifying now?" I could feel a gaze sliding over my body like the crackle in the air before lightning strikes.

"He's pretty enough," said the crone's voice behind me, "sun-dark and lean like Apollo, if not so handsome."

"What would you have me do, sisters?" The maiden sounded on the verge of tears.

"On Ithaca, men present themselves for a woman's consideration," said the mother. "Touch him. See what a frail thing a man is."

"Do not move," whispered the crone into my ear. Her voice was echoed by the hissing that was certainly not wind. "Or I'll butcher you yet." The bond that held me rippled like muscles under soft leather. My hands still gripped it, holding me up, but I willed every other part of my body to relax. The tips of my toes dangled in the sand.

A hand, soft as a girl's, pressed against my chest, just below the coil suspending me. Slowly it moved down, shyly steering around a nipple, pausing to explore the rise of each muscle it found. Tracing each scar.

"He's hairy as a beast," whispered the maiden.

Her hand continued its roam, down over my navel, and then stopped, rising and falling on my quickened breaths.

"Confront your fear, sister," said the mother.

In spite of the crone's command, in spite of my terror, in spite of the coils ready to cut off my breath or snap my neck, I felt myself... stir.

The maiden withdrew her hand and gasped. Her sisters laughed, a harsh and terrifying sound.

"Look at it loll to the side, trying to raise its head," the crone cackled. "A blind, fat worm, playing at being a serpent." The hissing seemed to laugh along with her.

"You see? This is nothing to fear. Give it a squeeze."

I spasmed at her touch, and stiffened completely. I may have moaned.

"See how it strains toward your hand? He is unable to master it. It masters him, to its needs. Yet it is only a small bit of vulnerable flesh. This is true of all men, mortal or god."

"It is... it is ridiculous," the maiden said. "A serpent ought to laugh—not fear a worm."

At this, anger spiked through my terror, and though I could say nothing for lack of breath, and I dared not struggle, I willed myself down in defiance of their mockery.

"Oh," the maiden said. "He wilted."

"We've hurt his pride," the crone said. "Men wilt to our laughter. That is why they revel in our fear."

There was silence at that. I could not guess what passed among the sisters as I hung there, blind and fighting for air.

"I will make you a gift, little sister," the mother finally said. "The usurper of our father's throne and his pitiless niece used fear to corrupt and pervert your power. They turned it lethal to men, because they are what you fear. You misunderstand it. I would have you unlearn this damage. I would have you change the color of the black horse in your dreams."

Fingers of a different sort—cold and leathery—closed on my shaft, and it stiffened again with dismaying obedience. And then it stiffened further. It became harder and heavier than ever before, and neither fear, nor anger, nor mounting alarm stopped it. Her hand left me, and my upthrust manhood weighed like a stone.

"Release him, Stheno."

The coils around my neck loosened, and I dropped to my knees in the sand. I hurried to my feet, muscles working at last, and my hand moved to understand what had been done to me. There was a sound like a whip, and a coil jerked my hand away. A cold and leathery fist seized my other wrist and wrenched it behind my back.

"No," the mother said. "It is no longer yours to touch. It, and you, belong to your new mistress now. You will be fed. Washed. Given a fire at night. But you will not flee. And you will obey her in all things. Do you understand?"

"Please," I croaked.

"Do you understand?" hissed the crone, Stheno, behind me.

I nodded.

"What are you called, and from where do you hail?" demanded the mother.

"I am Eustathios," I said, trying to reclaim my pride. "A free citizen of Athens."

"*Her* city," Stheno hissed.

"Then, Eustathios," the mother continued, "captive of the Isle of Sarpedon. Kneel before our sister, your mistress, Medusa."

The sisters were true to their word. They fed me shellfish, olives, nuts, and fruits. Neither bird nor animal lived on the island for meat. The "mother," whose name was Euryale, stripped me of the remains of my clothing, prodded me into a stream, and insisted that Medusa wash me with her own hands. Though it was still heavy and hard as stone, my penis felt the sensation. Overcoming her shyness before my blind eyes, Medusa became amused at how it jerked to her slightest touch. She made a game of commanding me to stillness and coaxing movement despite my effort. As they marched me from beach, to stream, to a lonely bed of sand near a crackling fire, I was always aware of it hanging between my legs, weighty and unchanging as a marble carving, a sculptor's phallus in truth.

I lay awake for a long time, the white light still shining behind my eyelids, only the chill air informing me of night. Other than my tending and Medusa's games, I was mostly ignored. The sisters talked among themselves. I wasn't sure I was even watched. Even if I could navigate the steep, rocky terrain without sight, the ocean roared in every direction, and I had nowhere to go. I curled around the fire, warming myself as best I could.

I should have felt angry. Or humiliated. Or afraid. But the innocent delight Medusa took in my body, like a girl playing with a strange new toy, affected me. I would flee, if I found a way. I would murder the monster Stheno if given a chance. But as captivities went... I arrested the thought. A soldier did not submit so readily, even for goddesses, which the sisters surely were. But what choice did I have? I was blind. I had been a long time at sea.

Somewhere nearby, I heard Medusa whimper and groan in her sleep until I slipped into uneasy dreams of my own.

In the morning I was still blind, though I saw patches less bright than others. Hissing came from above me, close. Slowly, I climbed to my feet. The hissing receded. "Are you a goddess?" I asked.

"I am mortal," Medusa said. "My sisters are goddesses. We are daughters of Phorcys, who ruled the seas before the Olympian usurper."

I drew myself to my full height. I was blind and naked but still a soldier, and Medusa admitted she was no goddess. The hissing became angry. "Are there serpents near?"

"Yes," she said, but did not explain.

"What would you have of me, Medusa?"

Again I felt the crackle of her gaze, and I wondered what I would see if I could meet it. "Citizen of Athens. Servant of Athena." Her footsteps made no sound, but her voice slowly circled. "Stheno advises me to cut your manhood from you, and make you wear it on a thong around your neck." I turned my head to follow her voice. "Euryale wants me to make use of her gift. To learn to take my pleasure in my remaining time."

"Euryale is wise."

"I'm inclined to listen to Stheno," Medusa snapped. "Better that than to commit the same crime as my father's usurper."

"Do you mean Athena?" From the feel of her gaze, I could tell she had stopped. "I heard you cry her name at night," I said.

"I do not mean Athena," she whispered. "There is nothing I could do to match her cruelty." There was such bitterness in her voice, such pain.

"Medusa, I am a citizen of Athens, not a slave. I will die before being made one. But I swear on my honor, I will not harm you."

Medusa laughed scornfully. "Warrior, if your eyes worked, you would not bluster so." She resumed her circling. "You would not have survived our first meeting. And if you have any brains at all, you will kneel and be still. Now." The imperious voice was back.

There was something here, some leverage. I only needed to puzzle her out. I sank to one knee, again reminded of the weight between my legs as it brushed against my thigh. Then I settled to both knees, waiting. She came behind me and ran her fingers down my spine, circling each vertebra with a fingertip. I heard her kneel behind me.

"Such pride, even in submission. What would shame you, Athenian? What would terrify you? What would make you weep from pleasure?" Her hands parted my buttocks. I tensed. She reached around, pinched my nipple, and gave it a violent twist. The heavy head of my penis bobbed in response. "Oh. It misses me." Her hand closed around the shaft for a moment, but quickly withdrew. It spasmed helplessly. "I will not do this," she whispered into my ear. "Right is *not* about being more powerful." The nearby serpents added their whispers.

My body was trembling. My breath, rapid. I could have turned and seized her. Even blind, I could have torn off her clothing and plunged my stone phallus into her. And died for the crime, the same that some god had apparently visited on her. The same crime she resolved not to visit on me. For all her menace, she was young and inexperienced, angry and fumbling, but all the same, so righteous. So curious. It aroused in me a tenderness that, to this day, I cannot explain. Perhaps her sister was right. The stone between my legs mastered me.

"If that is your will," I said. "Is it?" I sought leverage, yes. But perhaps desire called desire.

There was silence as her gaze crackled on the back of my neck. Without a word, she stood and walked away. Uncertain of the invisible geography around me, I simply continued to kneel.

Euryale visited. I puzzled out the sound. Medusa's immortal sisters slithered like enormous serpents over the ground. "I bring food, Eustathios." She sounded happy. "You will need your strength." Something clattered in front of me, and I reached down to feel a woven rope basket. Inside were wet, rough stones. Shells. Oysters. I pried them open with my fingers and sucked down the flesh, uncooked. I was famished.

"Do you know the tale of Orestes and your city's protector?"

I shook my head and continued to eat.

"Orestes murdered his mother. Punishment for spilling kins' blood is meted out by my cousins, the Erinyes. But Orestes called on Athena to hear the accusation. You may know that Athena had no mother, having sprung from the head of Zeus. Therefore, in her judgment, woman is but the field in which man sows his seed. There is no more kinship than that. So Orestes was spared punishment, and my cousins returned to the depths of Erebus."

"We must abide by the rulings of the gods," I said carefully.

"So we must," Euryale said. "You are a soldier, not a farmer, so perhaps you have never plowed a field. Not in the actual sense."

Again I shook my head.

"A farmer who sows his seeds with care, who nurtures and waters the soil—who truly loves the land—may bring forth strong, healthy crops. But for one who sows carelessly, with violence and disregard, the land will only bear noxious weeds. Athena was wrong. Poisoned fields yield poisoned fruit. I want you to think on that."

I could only nod.

"Also consider that misused earth can be redeemed. If one takes care in the tilling."

"What are you telling me, Euryale?"

"I'm telling you to be kind to my sister. You may yet survive this."

"Kneel, Athenian," Medusa commanded. I obeyed. It was night, the air crisp, and the fire beside me warm. Her hands were on my shoulders, then my arms, caressing the muscles with a touch so light, I shivered. "Are you truly mine?" The fear and desire were plain in her voice.

"I am yours, Medusa." Her arms circled my chest, and I could feel her breasts press against my back, tiny nipples poking from under a thin garment. Her serpents hissed in my ears. They sounded… content.

"I will tell you a tale," she said. These sisters were fond of tales. "A young girl, beautiful, raised by the sea. Loving the sea as she would a father. Each day she sat beside it and stared at the waves. She dove, swam, and sported in it. And always, the waves held her up, and brought her gently back to shore no matter how far she swam." Her fingers ran through the hair on my chest, and she idly stroked a nipple.

"Years went by. The girl reached womanhood, and her body changed. So did the sea. It was not the sea she knew. It grew rougher. The waves tossed her, sometimes held her from shore until she panicked. Begged. When she watched the waves, she could feel them watching her back." Medusa's fingers pinched, and I gasped. She moved in front of me. Her foot nudged apart my knees, and the weight of my petrified phallus pulled it down to stand at an angle. I felt her legs straddle my thighs.

"One day, as she sat on a rock, dangling her toes in the water, something cold and wet wrapped around her ankles." I felt the gossamer garment slip down her legs and puddle about my thighs. She bent over me. Agitated hissing filled my ears. "Seaweed, mottled and foul, tried to pull her into the water. She broke the strands, cut them against the rock, and scrambled away."

Something encircled my wrists, pulled them up and together. Cool, scaled, and muscular. It continued to coil and lift, stretching my torso up and up with inescapable strength. In my blind eyes, a shadow resolved against the white light before me, like a flower with enormous, waving petals.

"Something rose from the water behind her. Like a great horse, but blue as the ocean, with seaweed for a mane and tail. The maiden fled, but it followed. She ran to the temple of Athena and threw herself at the feet of the statue, crying to the goddess to save her. But the horse entered the temple, its wet tendrils trailing behind it." Medusa crouched. I could feel the heat of her body near my face. "Are you mine?"

"I am yours," I repeated.

"Are you willing?"

"YES!"

I moaned. Loudly. Wet heat engulfed my phallus. It slid up and down, forcefully, and fingernails like claws dug into my stretched back. Medusa rode me furiously, and it was only when she released me, dismounted, and left me lying in the sand, unsatisfied, that I realized the hot splatters on my face had been her tears.

"Did the goddess ever answer her?" I asked. It was some time after midday, by the feel of the sun on my face. Shadows moved before my eyes. Sometimes I could guess their shape. I lay on my back in the sand, and Medusa sat beside me, playing her fingers through the hair above the phallus that lay like a stone between my legs, a thing apart, hers as much as mine.

She grasped a handful of hair and gave a sharp tug. An admonishment. "Oh, the goddess answered... after Poseidon had done as he wished and returned to the sea. Athena was furious that her temple had been defiled. But goddesses are like gods, and all others mighty; they excuse the strong and blame the weak. And Athena was cruel." Medusa's hand left my body, and her voice darkened. "Athena cursed the young woman, whose only crime was her beauty, transforming her into a monster so hideous, so loathsome, that any man who beheld her turned to stone."

I lay silent. The breeze blew cool over my body. Other than that, I heard only Medusa's breathing. "I'm sorry," I said.

"Cross your wrists above your head," she said, her voice stone. "Be silent." She straddled my hips. Two serpents crept up my chest and around each arm.

"Wait," I said. I heard an angry hiss. "I want to touch you."

"No."

"I do not agree to this unless I can touch you."

She didn't speak. She barely moved. But the serpents withdrew. I raised my hands to her hips. Soft. I followed the curve of her waist and cupped her breasts, feeling their warmth and weight in my hands. Her neck, long and elegant. A shudder went through her body. My fingers caressed her cheeks. They were smooth and wet. I traced the oval of her face until I felt the serpents I'd expected. I'd puzzled out that much. First, they fled my touch. But when I did not recoil, they gently tangled among my fingers, tickling my hands with their flicking tongues. My hands ran down, over her shoulders, and encountered soft feathers at her shoulder blades. "You have wings," I marveled.

I returned my hands to her hips. "Slowly now," I said. I moved her nether lips over the phallus, our phallus, slicking it with her nectar. Then I gradually lowered her onto it, holding her hips firmly so she could feel herself being filled. "Now rock, gently."

She moved as I guided her, languorously, until her breath caught, and she began rocking with more urgency. "Slowly," I said. "Don't chase it. Let it happen."

She did try. But soon she cried out, again and again, the sweetest song ever heard on this birdless island, until she collapsed on my chest, the phallus still inside her. I felt her heart beating against my skin. I could not share her climax. Whatever had been done to me allowed me to feel, but not release. I pulled her against me, stroking her back with its great, feathery wings.

I remembered something, but waited until our heartbeats slowed. "Medusa," I said. "When you found me on the beach, you asked if it was your time. Later, you mentioned the time remaining. What did you mean?"

She sighed. Without lifting her head from my chest, she said, "Cursed girls are all given foresight." I waited for her to explain. She did not.

"Now, Eustathios. Again. Faster this time."

My vision was slowly returning. I could make out shapes, though the white light made it hard for me to tell day from night except by the warmth of the air. The sisters included me in their conversations, sometimes asking my opinions like an old family servant. Most of it was incomprehensible, gossip about beings older than the gods of Olympus. But they were curious about Athens and what life was like there. I got the impression they had not seen a city for many mortal lifetimes. They wanted to know everything, from politics, to fashion, to art, to food.

Medusa and I coupled frequently. She allowed me in her bed, and would reach for me many times a night. She tried what positions occurred to her, had me pleasure her with my mouth, and switched her love-play between gentle and ferocious. I taught her what I knew, and found her an eager pupil. Her serpents became fond of me as well, coiling gently around me and tickling with their tongues. It was sweet agony. I could not spill seed through the phallus. But she was happy, and that made her sisters happy, even grim Stheno, though she sometimes jested about craving fresh meat.

Finally, when I began to see colors in addition to shapes, I told Medusa about my sight. She was silent for a long time. Then finally she said, "You must leave here."

"I could bandage my eyes," I said before I realized what she meant. She released me. I was free. And yet, not.

She took my face in her hands and kissed my mouth, a kiss as full of tenderness as desire. "No, Eustathios. The next part of my story has nothing to do with you."

Euryale slithered up from behind her. I recognized the way she moved, a sort of side-to-side swishing. "Yes, he must leave," she said. "But not for his sight. The time draws near, Medusa." Euryale sounded sad, as sad as I'd ever heard. "The one from the sky comes."

"Who is this?" I said. "What is to happen?" They ignored me.

"You have two days left together. Maybe three," Euryale said.

"But he must leave now," said Medusa. "If he sees me..."

"I've told you, you misapprehend your power. Neither what Poseidon nor what Athena did made you loathsome. They only made you afraid. Ashamed. I think you're beyond that now." Euryale paused. "Do you still dream of the horse?"

"Still black as smoke," Medusa said. "With wings of fire. He craves birth. I don't know how long I can hold him back."

"Let us see what our soldier can do about that."

The next morning, my sight returned. The white light, slowly dimming, extinguished overnight. I sat up, seeing the place for the first time. It was a bare-walled cave, lit only by the sunlight outside. The only furnishing was the bed, a heap of feathers, leaves, and moss. The sight broke my heart.

I felt Medusa lying next to me.

A sudden terror gripped me, but I steadied myself. Whatever I would see, I *knew* her. Nothing about her could horrify me. She was my own, my Medusa. I made myself look.

The serpents that were her hair began to rouse when I touched her smooth, pale cheek. I knew those cheeks, those lips, that proud chin, by touch. I recognized the sight of them. Her eyes opened, and she looked at me. The crackle in the air from her gaze pebbled my skin.

"You're beautiful," I told her. And she was. Her eyes were dark and serious for so young a face. Her body... I already knew and loved her every line and curve. The wings that had tickled my back were golden feathered, and the serpents she had instead of hair knew me with an intimacy only she herself shared.

Medusa gasped, her mouth hanging open. And then she screamed. For a moment, I thought she was the one who regained her sight and found me hideous. But no, it was a scream of delight, and she covered my face and neck and chest with kisses, the kind with teeth.

Euryale and Stheno eclipsed the light in the cave opening, and after bickering for precedence, slithered in on enormous serpentine bodies. I had imagined their appearance for so long, the sight did not surprise me. And I had lived naked and without privacy for weeks, so their presence did not bother me in the least.

"Well!" Stheno said. "At last, she understands."

"And none too soon," Euryale said seriously. "There remains one last thing." She slithered to the bed and pulled the covering down where my phallus had tented it. Before I could stop her, if I would even have dared, she ran her cool, scaly fingers from root to tip. It was like ice melting. It drooped, and I became fully flesh again.

"I dislike it this way," Medusa said. And she held my face between her hands and gazed into my eyes. Immediately I rose and hardened. I looked down. I was still flesh, stiffened only with desire.

"Tomorrow, we will have a boat for you," Stheno said. "But today, you still belong to her." There were no threats today. She was as happy as Euryale.

"But I can stay now... I can help."

"No," Medusa said. "Tomorrow, I will not permit you to touch me. But today…" Her serpents wriggled and her smile bared teeth.

"Take care in the tilling," Euryale told me as the sisters took their leave. Her voice was grave.

All day she drained me. She waited in cross frustration for my seed to rebuild, and then took it again. And again. I drank water by the bucket. She stuffed oysters down my throat as I pleasured her with my fingers. And at times, we just lay in the sun, one leg swung over the other's, watching clouds drift in the vibrant blue sky.

"The old sea, Phorcys, will protect you on your journey home," Medusa said. She rose on one elbow and laid her hand on my chest, above my heart. "Just as he protected you when you arrived. When he gifted you to me."

Abruptly a memory locked into place. I remembered the star under the waves that had blinded me, saving my life. In its midst, there was a shape that seemed sometimes a crab, sometimes a fish, and sometimes a man. I turned to look at her, and she met my smile. But her dark eyes were sad. I might have stayed had I understood. Tried to save her from the doom the cruel Olympians decreed. I kissed her and felt the crackle in the air between our bodies, a quickening of love for my own divine monster.

The next sunrise came too soon.

About the Author

Rajiv Moté is a writer and software professional living in Chicago with his wife, daughter, and a tiny dog. He is a member of SFWA and the Codex Writers, a columnist and podcaster for Dragonmount.com, and can still be found on Twitter at @RajivMote.

DANY
COMIC

LONG BLACK VEIL

BY JANUARY BAIN

Stormy waves whipped by the screeching North wind crashed into the shoreline far below the stone parapet. So loud and threatening to man or beast that even the birds of flight that gave her manor home its name had taken to their nest today, battened down by the weather. The rough surface of the widow's walk scraped Roslyn's palms. Her nerveless fingers clutched at the sharp edges. *It would be so easy*, she thought, staring at the void below. Nature's fierceness lashed the jagged subterranean rocks awaiting both the unwary and the weary. The salt air clung to her clammy skin, dampening her unadorned dress and soaking her long black veil. With an audible sigh, she shifted her gaze, staring now at the invisible grey point where the sky met the sea.

When she squinted, she fancied a long boat with high masts appearing like a ghost ship forever riding the tides, only to have the wishful mirage vanish again as it always did. That ship would never come home. Its crew was long buried beneath the weight of dark water, and creatures had long ago picked their bones clean in their unmarked grave.

The story told by Seamus last night around the Samhain's fire came back to her as she shivered, her throat tightening with longing. A story of three swans and a young boy. He'd followed them out to sea on a floating bit of driftwood until he was too far away from land to get back. When the three swans turned into beautiful women, he'd lived amongst them for five years, in the most wonderous of places, before becoming homesick. When he rejected the old crone promising vast riches and proved his loyalty, they relented and brought him back to the shore. But soon, he missed the beautiful white swans and stood sentinel, waiting day and night for their return, until one day, he was found dead on that very shore. Would it not have been better for him to have stayed there with them? Undergone the transformation and left this world forever?

An eerie church bell began to peel sharp and hurtful in the distance, its discordant notes spelling trouble, for it was only pressed into service when help was needed to aid those in danger. A boat and its crew had most likely floundered. Torn, she hesitated. The call of the water, the call of the swans infusing her with thoughts of immediate relief from constant pain. The melancholia deadened her limbs, and made each breath and movement as difficult as walking through the muddy, sucking bog of a swamp. What use could she be?

But the old way still stirred her blood—the need to help those in trouble—and she moved away from the threshold, leaving the doorway open behind her.

The wind whipped her long black veil about her pale face, obscuring her vision. It thrust its cold fingers into her long hair and pulled strands loose from the tight braid as she strode across the misty ground, her feet invisible below its thick greyness. The gusting breeze pushed her thick skirt against her limbs, forcing her to stop now and then to tug herself free of its binding.

Out of breath but forcing herself to go on, she reached the edge of the cliff that descended to the shoreline, careful to keep her feet from slipping out from under her on the slippery, moss-covered path as she made her way downward. The driftwood-strewn beach was awash with clansmen dressed in kilts and thick wool jackets and clanswomen dressed in long heavy dresses, all lining up with ropes tied as anchors. All in aid of hauling survivors or goods away from certain disaster. The ship in question lay listing on its side, nearly belly up, a gaping hole apparent. But what struck her at the moment was the name painted on the ship: *Swann*.

"Roslyn, good of you to join us, lass," Seamus said, his weathered skin creasing into a smile. A fisherman like most of the rest of the men and women assembled, he had been of some help to her during these long months that had turned into years of waiting for any word from the missing ship. He'd lost his wife six months back, dead in childbirth, and she knew he would not wait much longer for a new woman to warm his bed and care for his large brood. *Work is the answer for melancholy.* The words of her Gran messed with her mind.

But what if there's no energy left to start again?

There was no answer with her beloved Gran long gone and buried along with everyone she shared ancestry with. She took hold of the end of the thick rough rope and tied it about her thin waist, noting how shrunken she'd become these past months. Maybe she'd just vanish altogether and avoid any decision? She planted her feet, feeling the futility of the action. If the water wanted a person, it took them, no questions asked, no forgiveness possible.

She held to the land, helped by the weight of others, and felt the heartbeat of Mother Earth through the thin leather of her boots as she clung to the rope. The icy wind whipped her cheeks raw, yanked the veil from her head, and allowed it to skitter across the ground toward the water, where it sank beneath the waves. Was it a sign?

Endless hours passed, and the cold seeped further into her blood and bones, leaving her numb until dawn finally approached and the winds began to calm. They'd pulled many men and bodies from the greedy grasp of the sea, her and the neighbours, bearing down to find the strength that one never knew they had until it was tested.

But when the sun broke above the water, coming back to save them once again with its promised warmth, it highlighted the tired faces of the men and women surrounding her, turning their wan skin golden, and near took her breath away in the beauty it bestowed. It was a daily miracle, the arrival of the sun, that so often went unspoken. At that moment, she felt a part of creation, no less and no more than any other creature living under its sway.

"We saved a lot of them," Seamus said, standing by her side as they watched the waves for any final stragglers. "You did well, lass. You stood your ground. Saved a few swans." He made mention of the boat's name, making a small joke. Seamus was a good man though some spoke of his impatience and love of drink. A man of many stories and, most likely, many secrets. Like all men.

She nodded, too cold and too tired to speak. Maybe a bit muddled by the moment. A memory of another day anointed her eyelids. When her man had turned from striking the anvil with his giant hammer, sparks flying, and the iron glowing red hot. The moment he'd spotted her as she walked into the barn, locking his blue, blue glance with hers, and admired his chestnut hair shimmering in the glow from the furnace. The image died along with her flagging energy.

"There's another one. Looks dead to me," a villager shouted, pointing at the rocks near the shore. "He's caught up on that piece of driftwood."

A few of the men waded out to their hips and worked to free the body, shouting commands at each other as they bore the man to shore. A large man, raven-haired and long of limb. But what riveted her was the piece of veil he clutched in his hands. She leaned down to check if it was hers, noting her initials sewn into the fabric when his eyes opened, and they stared at one another for a brief, endless moment. Those blue eyes.

I know you.

"Where's this one going? The extra beds in town are about filled up with the sick and injured," one man asked, his voice weary and hoarse from exhaustion.

"Take him up to the manor. I'll nurse him," she said.

Seamus looked from the man to her, his expression still and closed. "No, you can't ask that of these men. You live up there," he used the tilt of his head to point out the obvious as if it were more a hindrance than a boon. Yes, she'd had the blessing of being born with an inheritance that kept the wolf from the door, but it didn't stop any tragedy from happening or make her loss any easier to bear. "Too difficult a journey for tired men. I'll take him in. Emily can care for him."

"Emily's twelve and too young to carry the full burden, Seamus. I'll stay today and for the night shifts until the man is better," she said.

He didn't quarrel with her decision, perhaps noting the firmness in her tone.

Roslyn followed the small, silent group to the Barnes residence, a middling cottage on the edge of Wickers Bog. She averted her eyes as they passed that haunted section of land that had claimed many a life, some accidental, some deliberate. When the men set him down on a cot in the back storage area, she waited for them to leave before requesting that Seamus bring hot water and rags to clean the man's wounds.

"Do you have any salve, Emily?" she asked the eldest daughter, who stared at her with huge doe eyes, wringing her small reddened hands.

The girl who'd carried the burden of her many siblings despite being small for her age, nodded and hurried away. Too much had been asked of her, far too young. But there was nothing else for it. Should she be giving up her life to make another's easier? She pushed the uncomfortable thought away and turned to the man who lay unconscious on the thin mattress, noting the pallor of his fine skin. He had the look of an aristocrat about him, of Lairds who bore up arms in defense of their ancestorial homes. An ugly purpling bruise marred the side of his forehead, the probable cause of his unconsciousness.

She reached for the strip of black veiling, but his fingers held firm, and she gave it up to work on removing his outer jacket and shirt to check for other wounds.

Emily crept back into the room, carrying a basin of steaming water and a few strips of sackcloth. They tended the man together, then when they'd done all they could, they covered him with a warm blanket.

"Who do you suppose he is?" Emily asked. "He has the fine clothes of a gentleman."

"Most likely the captain or owner of the vessel."

"Do you think he'll live?"

Roslyn's heart squeezed. "Maybe, lass, I don't know for certain. It's in God's hands now." She turned from staring at the man she felt she knew. "You go about your duties. I'll see to the man and take on the night times so that you can get your rest. You are already overburdened, Emily."

"No need, Roslyn. We can manage," Seamus insisted from the doorway, as if wanting to hurry her away. He looked at the man lying on the cot with a scowl, squinting his eyes.

"Soon as he's capable, I want him brought up to Cygnus Manor, Seamus," she said, surprising herself with her determination. A sudden urge to bear him away right this minute grew in her, gave her cause to worry and fret. Why this odd sense of danger, of dark things waiting in the wings?

"It wouldn't be right to have a strange man living in an unchaperoned house," he warned.

"You let me worry about that. Besides, there's cook and the housemaids to end that gossip."

Seamus pinched his mouth closed, his grey-colored eyes flashing a second of dark anger before he covered it up by excusing himself.

"Da says you're going to be our new mother and that we are all going to live in the fine manor and have new clothes to wear," Emily said when they were alone again.

The words surprised her, followed by the heat of anger. Seamus had no right to promise that. She'd only let him ask the question out of respect. She saw that now. There could be no future for them. She did not want to warm the man's bed. To make it right, she'd see the children cared for until they reached adulthood and send a generous sum to ease her rejection of their father.

She picked up a fresh piece of linen and wet it in the basin of water, wringing it out and then replacing the cloth on the sick man's forehead. When he opened his eyes again to stare into hers, she felt that same energizing jolt of electricity race through her.

The clamor of others rising and milling about in the main room reminded her of the houseful of children that needed tending.

"Go and prepare breakfast, Emily. I'll see to him."

"Da said you should not be left alone with him." The girl appeared too young and trusting to understand the urges of men. Or women.

"You can leave the door ajar. I'll be fine. The man's too spent to be any trouble."

She sat by his side listening to the roughness of someone splitting wood and other sounds of domestic activity. She kept watch, only eating a small amount of the food that Emily brought her at mealtimes. From time to time, she nodded off, exhaustion claiming her. She dreamed of swans and pure white feathers strewn on the water. When she finally had no choice but to relieve herself, she stood up and stretched to uncramp her limbs. Pins and needles prickled her flesh, the blood flow restricted by her long watch over her patient. No sound emitted from the room next door, and she wondered where the children had gone. The dim light coming through the small window of the shed suggested evening shadows had arrived.

"Don't leave me," a voice croaked. She startled, moving closer to the man and bending down beside the cot. His eyes were closed, his face flushed. Did he have a fever? She laid the back of her hand on his forehead to check when Seamus entered the room. She didn't hear him, so intent was she on observing her patient.

"You're going to be okay. What's your name?" she asked in her most soothing, gentlest voice.

"I dreamed of you," he said, opening his eyes and peering right into the depths of her soul. Mesmerized, she could not look away. "An angel come... to rescue me from the deep. Jamie Ross, at your service, captain... of the *Swann*."

"Jamie, I'm Roslyn, Lady of Cygnus Manor."

"I'll see to him. You need a break now, missus, to see to your own," Seamus interrupted like she had a brood of her own to tend.

Why had he done that? Suggested she was a married woman instead of a widow alone? Seamus only ever called her by her first name since he had been making a case for himself. Unease skittered across her flesh. She had to get Jamie away from this place, away from the dangers of Wickers Bog. The mosquito, plague-infested swamp had claimed too many lives.

If only she had turned Seamus down the first time he'd asked instead of letting things take root. She'd been too self-absorbed, too clouded by encroaching darkness to see what was right in front of her. Since they'd pulled Jamie out of the water, it was like the blinders had come off, revealing what life could yet still be.

"It's good you're feeling better, Jamie. A few days rest, and you'll be right as rain," she said to make her point.

"You should not promise a man health when God may still choose differently," Seamus chastised her, like he held sway over her.

"God has taken enough from me." She let the statement hang, uncaring for a moment of how another might take her words.

The overriding urge to bear Jamie up to Cygnus Manor fired her thoughts. "I will pay you to find the men to help me get the captain up to the manor," she said, avoiding Seamus's brooding glance. When had the man taken on such an aura? How had she'd been so blind these past months?

"That cannot be. No one's available. He stays put." When she glanced at Seamus, unable to stop herself, the depths of the longing she'd created became clear. The man wanted more, so much more than she could ever give him.

"Time for you to go home," Seamus insisted. "You need to rest."

"Before I do, I want him blessed by Father Hanigan, in case he takes a turn for the worst in my absence." She crossed her arms over her chest, her eyes pointing out the crucifix over the doorway. A desperate chess move he could not ignore.

"The good father has his hands full today, burying the dead. He wouldn't thank you kindly for adding another obligation to his plate. And there's no one about to take word to him anyway. The children are at the church, praying with the other good people for the poor drowned souls." He dismissed her words so easily that she was hard-pressed not to pick up the black veil and strangle the stubborn fool. The image was so unlike herself, she startled at the revelation.

"Then tell him I will bless the offering basket with a handsome tithing come this Sunday if he'll find the time this day."

"Give me the coin, and I'll see the deed done," he grunted

She quickly pulled a small bag of silver and gold from her inner waistcoat, handing it over. "There is more where that came from if this man is kept safe and sound."

"*That* is in God's hands," he said with keen piousness that grated her last nerve. "Now, I insist you must rest. I'll send word if there's any change."

No point in riling him further.

"I'll be back soon," she said, vacating the cottage.

"Wait until morning," he advised.

He watched her go. She had to force herself to keep placing one foot in front of the other, her body leaden and uncooperative, as she followed the narrow, well-beaten path around Wickers Bog. When she changed a glance back, he stood in the doorway, a sentinel of doom.

She increased her step, an image of doom rising in her mind as she circled the swamp, the drone of insects and chorus of frogs singing their invites to challengers accompanied her. The stench of bog gas, sharp and arid, grew stronger, assailing her senses. The bog held too many dark secrets. Too many bodies of those unwanted or deemed in the way. She would take the children on, she promised herself. Give them a better life. She raced around behind the cottage, her feet pounding and flattening the long grass. Her braid flapped against her back, spurring her on like a whip against an animal's hide. There was no time to run for help. She was on her own now, and with everything to lose, she was free to act.

Peering in the small, dusty window of the storeroom, she observed Jamie, his hands still clutching her precious veil. A dark shadow loomed over him. She watched, as the minutes dragged by, wondering if she was being foolish, mistaken in her thoughts. Exhaustion must be playing havoc with her mind, causing flights of fantasy or mistrust at will. Seamus was a good man, had been kind to her, incapable of harming another for gain. But even as she thought that, wished it were true for certain, doubts remained. In the dark of night when the self is revealed, she would have traded another's life for her own beloved's return.

Then Seamus began moving about the cramped space. He yanked her long black veil out of Jamie's hands and placed it over his face, pressing the damp cloth tightly to his nose and mouth. Jamie struggled against the lack of breath in his airway, his limbs flailing. She moved as fast as a swan could rise from the water, dashing around the front of the cabin and grabbing a sturdy length of fresh-cut firewood. Raising the heavy wood over her head, she tore into the storeroom and struck blindly at the man attempting to murder her last hope for happiness.

Catching Seamus by surprise, she gave him a fierce blow to the back of his skull, knocking him sideways into the wall and away from Jamie. He slumped against the floor, unmoving. Her heart sank when no sounds came from Jamie though his face was no longer covered by the death cowl.

Was she too late? Had the die been cast in stone? She crouched down beside Jamie and kissed his cold mouth, trying to bring the breath of life back. When he stirred long, terror-filled moments later, his air mingling with hers, her heart rejoiced.

Later, she sat and watched the body vanish under the hungry mud of Wickers Bog, sucked down into the deep by treachery and betrayal. When she rose on stronger legs and firmer resolve, she tucked the black veiling into her bodice. Then turned her face to the glory of the setting sun, where flames of red and gold anointed the western ridge and the swan tower of Cygnus Manor. Yes, they would leave this place, her, Jamie, and the children. Sail across the vast ocean to the New World and never come back.

Like the boy should have done in his story so long, long ago.

About the Author

January Bain has been fascinated with words since childhood when her mother took the time to read a chapter a night to her children from wonderful adventure books. She writes poetry, songs, and novels in a number of genres, has won an award for her mystery/thriller work, been blessed by her novels having been translated into other languages, with some in the process of being made into games. She first and foremost considers herself a storyteller, obsessed with understanding the motivations of her characters to bring her stories and poems to life. She hopes to inspire and touch hearts.

CHANGING OF THE GUARD

by Liam Hogan

I lie motionless in my coffin as my lover weighs his options. The quick strike of a stake through the heart? The prolonged agony of scorching sunlight? Or the brutal finality of decapitation, my head and body burnt in separate pyres?

The methods may vary, but the conclusion is the same. Because when you're immortal, there is no happy ending. No story ever truly ends. Not unless you fake it.

And the story has to be tied up, not for my sake, but for his. For my very mortal, very ephemeral lover, Andy Francis McPherson. So that he can go on with the rest of his all too short life… and so I don't have to watch as he gets old, his beauty fading with every sunset.

Over the centuries, I have died many times. And I have loved *so* very many times. Male and female, Black and White, and all shades between. Names shift with the fashions of the times; Jonathans become Jon, Elizabeths become Betty, Ellie, or Liz, and back again. My own name changes almost as often, though usually lagging somewhat behind. Currently, it is a rather staid *Cornelius* and in dire need of a refresh.

Faced with a flip-book of my lovers, some might judge me indiscriminate, but that would be unfair. I have a certain *type*. In addition to youth and vigour (each bringing their own short-lived semblance of immortality), coupled with the sort of pleasing looks that improve with every encounter, they are, above all, *good*. Not the false piety of priests, sanctimony donned with their Sunday vestments. Oh, I have seen what *they* get up to when they think there's no audience. None, except for a God I'm not sure even they believe in. To be a priest is to be an actor, too close to the rude mechanicals not to see the ugly scaffolding, the inelegant props. They know all too well how flimsy the set they dress is. Though I can't condone their behaviour, I understand it, because I, too, am an actor, though I would hope a more *honest* one.

I almost jerk in surprise when I feel Andy's tender lips press softly against my cold forehead. But I am an expert at playing dead, even as my body tries to stir into life, as I yearn to respond. It is a moment heavy with potential and existential threat; for my lover, rather than for me.

So when I feel the point of the stake trembling above my unbeating heart, I am *glad*. The danger has passed, and it will all be over soon; once he summons his nerve. Despite it all, despite everything I have done, there is no malice in his actions, only regret.

Because, like those who have come before him, Andy is good but not saintly. Good, but not so good he does not struggle with the temptations that I offer. They all know who and *what* I am, and that makes their struggles even more poignant. How they choose to end it, to end me, says more, I think, about how I've handled our relationship than about them, than about the purity or otherwise of their mortal souls.

The stake is by far the cleanest option.

Worst are those who employ others. The final scene acted out by strangers, ones with no compulsion about cleanliness or about avoiding my suffering. So-called vampire hunters; most often mere mercenaries in these enlightened times. I sometimes wonder how exactly I must have wronged my lover to be treated so, even as I mark the hired men for future, *discrete* retribution. I am prepared and willing to die for love and hold no grudge, but only if they do the deed themselves.

A fat tear drops onto my silk shirt, a shirt that is about to be ruined. I realise and acknowledge that thinking about such trivialities is my way of distracting from what comes next.

Some of it is smoke and mirrors. My little death—as fake as anything ever is. Why should one as powerful as I, as long-lived and legendarily hard to kill, dissolve to ash under even the brightest sunlight? The rays burn, true enough—dramatically so—but it would still take a long, long time for them to do any *permanent* damage. People see what they want to see, see what they expect. And the stories told about me, myths forged and renewed with each enactment, with each garbled telling, with each inevitable closing chapter, they strengthen that, even as they ought to leave people wondering how it is I get to meet my end anew.

Some of it, a sizeable, cathartic portion, is real. Real pain, real hurt. My shrieks are not entirely pretend. Sunlight is like acid on my skin, and my nerves are quite as sensitive as any mortal man's. There's a very good reason I avoid matinee performances. A stake is blunt, and the force required more than you might imagine, the shuddering jolt as it both crushes and pierces my chest—I would defy anyone not to writhe in brief torment. As for cutting off my head, that does not stop me from fearing and feeling the flames as they lick at *both* parts of me.

For the rest, I need behind-the-scenes help. My quartet of backstage familiars to put me back together. They are usually sullen about the whole business, especially those who have been with me for a while, feeling that I have not shown them the same regard as my lovers.

It is a fair complaint, but what can I say to it? A sycophant deserves exactly the amount of respect I show them. It is, in any case, the last service they will ever do for me; I need their blood, their life force to heal, to fully recover, as much as I need their silence to forge myself a new identity, a new beginning. A new name.

And if I am more savage with them than perhaps I need to be, if I grip them fiercely, feeling their bones splinter, if I feed more lustily than usual, surely that is to be expected? My lover has just left me, having dealt what (to them, at least) was thought to be a killing blow.

Breakups are hard. Especially on my familiars.

A shock, I am sure, when they were expecting a more generous reward, expecting to finally share in my immortality. One probably shouldn't play with one's food. A weakness of mine, I'm afraid. Not the worst. The truth is, what they want, I cannot give. The myth of transmissibility born of my many faked "regenerations" down the centuries. Even if I could, and if I did, I doubt they would thank me for it. Not in the long run. And the long run is what they're foolishly after. Perhaps, in the end—always in the end—it is a small mercy when I take away their unattainable desires before their cravings hollow them out, leaving only a bitter husk.

So I justify my actions to no one, not even to me.

There's a sharp intake of breath, and I steel myself for the fatal blow. Instead, the air escapes in a broken shudder. This is taking *forever*. Night is surely on its way, the clock is ticking, and I can not be expected to lie as still as this once the sun has set! I quell the urge to reach out, to console, to encourage. Or maybe to drag him into the coffin for one last, desperately needy fuck. Limbs constrained in a space designed for one, clothes tangling before being ripped free, the tight confines forcing even me, who has experienced everything there is to experience, to be inventive, to give more of myself than I am used to giving, no distance between us...

And then to lie, still blissfully entwined, still closer than I have been to anyone for a long, long time, and to murmur that *everything will be all right*.

But it is mere fantasy, and though I itch to fulfil it, I must stick to the role I have carved for myself. I must play my part until the curtain comes down. It is my own fault. I have been with Andy longer than most, longer than I should. Seven years. A blink in my extended lifetime, but a significant chunk of his. Seven years full of passion, of adventure, of extremes, fuller than most lives. My relationships average, I would guess, around three years. It is easy to become bored when you have seen and experienced it all. Some are as short as three months, some too repulsed at what I do to survive, or too repulsed at their own small part in my continued existence.

Some—and each one lingers in my memory like a foul smell—I am repulsed by. Those I have misjudged. Those whose goodness was nothing but an act (oh, the irony!) and who revel in the permission and privilege my reputation and wealth grant them. In their wake, I cry off both love and humanity. In their wake, as it was with Andy, I am always at my most vulnerable.

It isn't easy, finding the right supporting actor. Especially as they never quite know how much is real, how much is fantasy, and how much an erotic mirage that we both willingly buy into. Because that is what love is, what lovers *do*. In those uncertain borders, that is where I, and my story, come alive.

Seven years that could easily have become eight, nine, ten. And what then? That they age, and I do not, is the wedge that will always drive us apart. A wedge I insert, gently enough. Just the tip, long before the blunt end looms into view. After the seduction is complete, I always bite my lovers. It is the only way to convince them of what I truly am. But I only take a little of what they have to offer, however much they beg me to take more. A nip, really. A mere moment of intoxication, as my lover quivers beneath my touch, as I refuse to give in to my thirst. One must never lose control.

In truth, I do not need to feed all that often. Not as long as I look after myself, not as long as I avoid injury. Such as a stake through the heart... Blood is the glue that sticks me back together, however ruined this body, these slender, smooth limbs might be. Blood is the ultimate intimacy, the one and only thing capable of making my heart beat. Everything else is lesser, pale and wan, even if everything else is all that my lover and I can share; what fills the time, idle entertainments for body and mind. Sex is grand, but...

Despite this, and even in the honeymoon period of a new love, I hardly ever feed to excess. To that heady point where I can feel life flickering away even as the victim's heart gamely tries to push the vital fluid to my lips, the pulse that is echoed as though in empathy by my long-calcified heart. With such abstinence, my lovers have been known to believe that I am reformed; *saved* even. Love truly is blind.

And when I do thirst for blood, I am never bloodthirsty. I am not wasteful. (Except when it is *necessary*... as it will be shortly. Again, I am busy deluding myself as I stand back and critique my performance and the delivery of my lines.) Only those who live for a short time can afford the luxury of excess.

"I'm sorry..." comes the halting voice above me, and I am almost overwhelmed with fury, convinced that at the very last moment, Andy has lost his nerve. That he has found himself unable and un-willing to deliver the final lines. But it is not *betrayal* he is apologising for.

The first blow is far from timid. I convulse with exquisite, astonishing agony as finally, the stake is hammered in. My heart, under the pressure of the blunt wooden point, gives a solitary, stuttering beat, such that for an alarming moment, I might believe myself mortal again. Then the second blow, even fiercer, felt in every screaming cell of my body, puts an end to such an unlikely illusion, and I hear the crunch as the bloodied stake splinters the underside of the coffin. I would thank him, my Andy, my sweet lover, for being so bold, even as stars blaze supernovas behind my eyes and my thoughts—

—I'm back, a familiar's blood in my mouth and in the gaping void of my crushed chest. Every nerve is aflame in indignant protest as my heart spasms under the remembered assault, tearing itself apart even as it tries to reform. Above, as my eyes grapple for focus, dangles a scrawny wrist. A head bowed, eyes averted, a messy nest of lank, grey hair. The blood tastes of ashes, of incipient insanity, of a thousand picked scabs. *Bad blood.* Even so, my trembling, swollen tongue laps at it, probing the air as a rivulet splashes and drips from the clenched fist, across my face, onto my lips, into my mouth. Until finally I have the strength to crane my neck, until I can wrap my teeth around the proffered limb and properly *suck.* Feeling the warm liquid fill the aching hole in my chest, I *suck*, and *suck*; until there is nothing left to give.

When I come to once more, a passage of time that feels like millennia but can't be more than a dozen minutes, the familiar—his name, I think, was *Jasper*—is slumped against the side of the coffin. Sitting slowly, painfully, I press trembling fingers against his neck, seeking what I possess not, and nor, now, does he.

I spit, expelling a fat iron gobbet onto the crypt's cold stone floor. Jasper has been drinking the stale blood of others since I last supped on him, a forgotten number of moons ago. Insanity mixed with addiction and hopelessness, mixed with an echo, a stutter, of something far more ancient. The stake that was driven through my heart lies by his body, licked dry.

A doubly deluded fool then; believing that he was well on his way to becoming what I am. Believing the stagnant, black ichor that spilled from my wound would complete the transformation. Neither strategy has done him, or the blood his veins carry, any good. I need, I *hanker*, for less corrupt, livelier fare.

I don't have to look very far. Jasper must have drawn the short—or perhaps the long—straw. Two familiars wait, heads bowed and fingers fidgeting. Docile twin sisters of the night, ready to offer themselves up to me to complete my restoration. Which means there's one familiar missing: *Pietro*, the youngest and most tempting of the four. Annoying.

Such desertion is not uncommon. Though none of them know in advance that this is their final role in my long-running play, without even a curtain call to look forward to, my all-too-apparent demise is still reason enough to flee; to run, to hide.

No matter. I will hunt him down. I know his scent. I have tasted him, and he will be all too easy to track.

I drain these two more loyal acolytes, murmuring promises to keep them enthralled and passive even as one expires in front of the other (even after they've seen what became of Jasper). By the time their dowdy bodies slump to keep Jasper company, I am sated. The flesh over my heart is tender and raw but unpierced. The crushed bones have knitted themselves together, the organ itself as pristine (and as useless) as the day it halted.

Emerging into the rain-slicked courtyard, I suck down the heady cocktail of cemetery scents like a newborn. I'm actually disappointed to find the missing familiar hasn't gone far at all, and my hunt is over before it has even had a chance to begin.

But the scent is not that of a familiar. *Not* Pietro. It is—

"Cornelius."

"Andy...?"

He's *waiting* for me, half hidden in a ruined arch that overlooks the entrance to the crypt. Still wearing the fine silk scarf I gave him seven years ago to cover the twin marks at his throat. At the time, his only blemishes. Looking surprisingly calm for one who has just violently plunged a wooden stake into the heart of their undead lover and then watched them emerge from the shadows.

"How did you...?" I begin to say, lost for words for the first time in perhaps centuries. I am not prepared for an unexpected encore.

He shrugs. He might be calm, but he also looks tired, haggard. A forewarning of what the future holds for him and a reminder of what the cruel hand of time will etch permanent soon enough. "I *know* you, Cornelius. It's what I thought you might do."

I nod, an unaccustomed lump in my throat. "Forgive me?" I whisper.

He smiles and his years drift away, even as I notice the tinge of sorrow. This is not the easy smile that once attracted me to him, or the joyous laugh heard across a crowded room that lit up that night and many more that followed.

"I *understand*," he says. "If you wanted to end our relationship, you could have done so in a heartbeat, simply by ending my mortal life, as you have many others. But you didn't. Instead, you went to painful, almost theatrical lengths to protect my feelings."

I'm glad what little light there is washes the colour from the scene. Glad, too, that I do not, in any case, blush. "I didn't want to hurt you."

"I know. But you did, anyway. I am not you, Cornelius, untouched by the years. I age, I wither. And I have had to watch, these past six months, as you tried, and failed, to ignore each subtle sign, each small change, as you set about sabotaging everything we had. I have had to listen as you professed weariness at your eternal existence and dropped such heavy hints about how I might end it." He regards his fingers, the dark crescent moons of my blood dried beneath his nails, and looks away briefly.

"I think that, if you were capable of imparting that remarkable gift of yours, of preserving me as I was, or even now as I am, you would have offered it."

I shudder. He can not possibly know of what he speaks. "Would you have accepted such a gift?"

His eyes are back on mine and he offers the same tired smile. "I cannot say. Sometimes I think yes, of course. Who wouldn't?" There is a pause in which civilizations might crumble. "And then, sometimes I worry that however much two people love one another, it is not love if it is *forced* to last forever."

He *does* know. Oh, rare humanity! If I could shed a tear, I would. Seven years is suddenly all too short a span, and I wonder if I have acted in unseemly haste.

"Why did you...?" I gesture to the arch he stands within, his waiting, watching place.

Andy shakes his head briskly. "I wasn't going to. I played my part—the script you wrote for me—reluctantly, even to the bitter finale. But then I realised, as I prepared to scale the cemetery wall, to exit stage right, that I wanted, needed, the ending to be on *my* terms. Not yours."

He looks up into the night sky. The clouds that earlier shed their tears are parting. There is a glimmer of moonlight, a quarter crescent, a silver scythe, before it again buries its face in my shame. A sigh plumes in the suddenly chill air. "I thrilled at our time together, Cornelius. I would not trade it for the world. And yet, the very first time I set eyes upon you—do you remember?"

"Of course. New Year's Eve." I do not tell him that I saw him two months earlier than that. Halloween; the night I first heard him laugh. That I watched and waited and laid my careful plans, letting fate take the credit. That our first encounter was as scripted as our last was meant to be.

I half suspect he knows.

"Somehow, I was aware even then that it could not last. That there was a part of you that remained aloof, watching, perhaps even laughing." If he's waiting for me to protest, to deny it... then he would have had to wait far longer.

"And what now?" he asks into the silence. "Do you find another younger lover?"

I scowl. But that, too, is an act. How can I be offended when he speaks the truth?

"Not for a while. Not, probably, for a number of years." Not until I recruit a new set of familiars, reinvent myself to fit the times. Oddly necessary, especially when the rate of change is so very swift, technology that shines its light into every dark nook and cranny, that threatens to banish the night and those who make it their home.

He frowns. "Do not prolong the wait for my benefit—"

"It is not." I am inspired towards a confidence, one that will help me rescue my composure, restore my control. "I revel in the time I have between lovers as much as the time with them. And, in truth, I cannot predict when cupid will strike again. Though even when cupid *does* strike, I am not forced to act upon his capricious whims. I can afford to be choosy, to take my time."

He nods, slow and thoughtful. "I see. You do not like to be alone. So you surround yourself with others, eager to be admired, to be desired. And yet, company is bitter-sweet. No one experiences things the way *you* do. None suffer as you do."

He places his hand over my heart, the tingle of the new flesh, the quiver of the old. "I'm sorry."

I wave it away, this repeat of the words he muttered over my coffin, annoyed by his lack of originality, by the vain attempt at empathy. "Don't be. As you can see, I am—"

The warm hand lifts, the absence as sudden as a slap. "I'm sorry that you're not brave enough, Cornelius. You never were. To give yourself to me. To truly *share*. To be with me, whatever happens, whatever comes."

I frown, chastened, shocked, angered. "I have lived—"

"*No*, Cornelius. Or should I perhaps call you by one of your many other names? I'm not sure you *have* ever lived, any more than you have loved. I'm not sure you let yourself. Perhaps you don't even know how to shed the many masks that you always wear. But it doesn't, shouldn't, matter. Lovers know that one of them must pass first. It terrifies them, but it doesn't ever stop them from loving, nor does it make such cruel deceit as yours necessary."

He sucks in a deep breath and lets it out in a low whistle. "I have envied you. Envied and feared. But I also pity you. Even though I knew it was uneven, that I was the more loving one, I thought I would *always* love you, but now...?"

A shake of his head. A final look that tells me I will never see him smile ever again. "Now I'm not so sure. Goodbye, Cornelius."

He turns his back on me, a shocking, insulting dismissal. And then he is gone, the scarf tumbling into a puddle as the rain starts anew. All the things I should have said to him, all the things I should have done...

It is too late. They will haunt me for a very long time indeed.

About the Author

Liam Hogan is an award-winning short story writer, with stories in *Best of British Science Fiction* and in *Best of British Fantasy* (NewCon Press). He's been published by *Analog*, *Daily Science Fiction*, and *Flame Tree Press*. He helps host the live literary event Liars' League, volunteers at the creative writing charity Ministry of Stories and lives and avoids work in London. More details at http://happyendingnotguaranteed.blogspot. co.uk

DANY
COMIC

THE PROMISE

BY E.J DAWSON

Great-Aunt May's house sat on a hill of abandoned lots, derelict stores, and the detritus of a bygone era. The real estate value on old houses with a view should've punched through any preconceptions of a dead zone. Except that's exactly what it was; nobody who could have afforded it wanted a house in Merryweather Hills. Too far from the city, the local country stores were ravaged by nearby suburban supermalls. Too old, too expensive, too out of date.

A small village stuck between large towns. Stuck in time.

At a local traffic light were a bar, a post office, a Quickie-Mart, and a church. The mart looked like it'd stolen an antique building, an old hag of a thing attempting at youth with glittering neon lights.

I stopped there for cigarettes and whiskey but grabbed some chocolate too. I wouldn't need anything else.

Aunt May got her groceries delivered; Mother saw to that. A gardener and maintenance, all taken care of and paid for by the trust. But Great-Aunt May was getting too old to be left alone, according to my mother.

"You won't have to lift a finger."

"If you've taken care of everything, why am I going there?"

"The doctor says she needs someone to watch her, she's not a risk to anyone but herself, but if she falls, she'll need someone."

"You just want a free nurse. My doctorate does not make me a caregiver."

"I don't trust you to take care of yourself, much less an old lady, but you can call an ambulance."

Remembering the bitter words she'd said, I pressed my thumb against the thin band of gold on my fourth finger. A broken promise. Not mine, though. I was the foolishly faithful one.

I pressed the gas pedal on the car that was my one gain in the divorce from Darren and coaxed the little vehicle up the hill to Aunt May's old house.

For all the weather-beaten, brick-rotting, paint-faded, decaying carcasses of houses, Aunt May's stood pristine. The soft white of the walls remained worn but pretty. A slate roof in cobalt blue held all its tiles. Ivy climbed the gray stone fireplace up one side of the house. It wrapped around the first and second-story wrought iron balconies and lent the house a charming air. Not like the overgrown monstrosities to each side, their yards full of weeds and windows broken, sinking into the earth one day at a time. Probably vacant.

I parked in the drive, ensuring the hand brake engaged the steep hill, before getting out of the car. Lace covered the windows, but I needn't have worried about my arrival. Aunt May sat on a rocking chair on the porch.

"Great-Aunt May!" A slight reminiscent swell thudded in my heart. Aunt May smelled of lavender, always recommended second desserts, and never told a secret.

But the sparkly gaze of vague mischief and mysteries weathered under the burden of age. Her eyes were unfocused even as they gazed at me while I trotted up the stairs. Had her hair always been so white? I held out my hand to hers, ignoring her puzzled smile and wrapping her limp grip in my own. The lavender scent wafted over me, but beneath it came the edge of decay.

I smiled past it. "It's so nice to see you again."

"Sorry, m'dear, I know your face, but you aren't Beatrice." Her voice, croaky and trembling, set my own heart aflutter at her weakened state. Mom came around every two weeks but wouldn't while I was here. Avoided it like the plague, and only the trust fund kept her visiting.

"It's Lizzie—Elizabeth, Beatrice's daughter. Mom called to let you know I'd be staying here for a couple of months to keep you out of trouble." I cringed at the dumb joke as soon as I'd said it but smiled when she chuckled. She grasped a strand of my waist-length hair tumbling over my shoulder.

"Oh, you lovely young thing, you." She tugged the wreaths of my curling strawberry blonde hair. "You get this from your father. Your mother was darker, like I was before time took a turn on me."

Her hand ghosted over her own attempt at a French roll, hair so old it bore a brittle look, stuck to the skull beneath. Her age a sudden burden in the afternoon sunlight, I swallowed my pity to focus on the evening.

"Mom had some groceries delivered. I know you like to cook, but what if I gave it a turn for the evening, and you can tell me how you've been fairing?"

"Oh, that sounds lovely dear. I won't eat much, though. I don't feel up to food much these days. I don't... feel much at all." Her gaze darted over my shoulder, and her lips thinned, but when I turned to the far end of the porch, there was only the view and the wind.

We ate a dinner of reheated roast from Aunt May's latest delivery, over-salted to hide the blandness. Fatigue gnawed at my senses, but not as much as Aunt May, who poked her food, nibbling here and there.

A subtle kind of resentment not made of each other but circumstance hovered like the shadows over the dark kitchen. Thick, cloying as the scent of cooling meat.

"It's all right that I stay, isn't it?" I asked, wondering if she was aware I was there or if I was a nuisance to her quiet life. Mom never said what a state she was in the last few years.

Awareness rushed to her face, and she patted my hand. "Of course, dear, we just weren't expecting guests."

I frowned. "We?"

She waved her hand dismissively. "Oh, I mean, the people who organize everything for me, you know. We might need to get more groceries."

I smiled at her. "Don't worry about it. Mom's taken care of everything."

Including things to search the house for. The little list burned a hole in me the longer I stared at this frail, old, abandoned woman. Shoulders hunched, the tall, old kitchen gloomy around her, she was so very alone, and the starkness struck me until a shape emerged from the shadows.

Someone was behind her. I squinted into the dark, the one kitchen light bulb flickering. Panic thudded through me until I caught a trick of the light beside the big, old iron stove, long left to cool now that Aunt May had a microwave. Too tired. I shoved my knuckles into my sockets to shove aside the grit of sleep. After a late night crying and a full day of driving, I needed a drink and to study.

"I think I ought to go to bed." Aunt May rose, leaving behind most of her plate.

The announcement derailed my thoughts of the whiskey in my suitcase. "Do you need any help?"

"No dear, I hope you sleep well."

I cleaned away the dishes, glancing once more at the ominous shadow in the corner. I took a glass from the cabinet, chipped ice from the freezer, and checked the doors were locked.

I didn't want a trick of light to become a man. Out here, who would hear anything, and help wouldn't reach either of us in time. In the glass window, it was only my own gaze that failed to pierce the dark, yet I couldn't help my hands fisting, a shiver trickling over my skin as though someone, somewhere, stared back.

At eight thirty on the edge of campus, I would have already decided to stay in and study or go out. Here… all I had was a town of six streetlights, a strong glow on the horizon of the nearby Lakesmouth, and beckoning promises of fun on the horizon. Maybe I could go out and have random affairs too. It was a melancholy and stupid thought. Casual sex wasn't me.

In the bedroom Aunt May told me to take, I stood in an old dressing gown of hers, having taken the hottest shower I could convince the antiquated boiler in the basement to make. I drank whiskey, smoked, and wished for things to be other than they were.

I stared at the dull screen of my phone, with a signal, not that it did me any good.

One message from my best friend Belinda wishing me a good vacation. None from Darren.

Sipping whiskey left me drunk, lonely, and a little bit horny.

Was it stress? My period? Or just these empty houses, their ghosts, and that I was terrified of becoming one of them. Mom talked about how dark, depressing, and lonely the house was. That we'd offload it as soon as possible. Was I there to wait for Aunt May to die? Or was Mom trying to show me what happened to women who weren't married to men like Darren?

My throat tightened, and the lights on the horizon blurred. My hand fisted on my glass like I could strangle it. Strangle him. Or her. Let him feel the rage. But he wasn't here, and my tears were nothing to my mother. I leaned on the railing, cigarette between my fingertips, and blew smoke at the dark houses beside us.

Some town.

I tapped my ring against the railing. In hate, in a call for attention, or as a reminder I wasn't alone, and yet the red stamp on the papers in my laptop bag confirmed I was divorced. Unlovable.

The metal band of false commitment was warm on my finger, so familiar, pressing on me, constraining me, as echoes of the judge's verdict pounded my ears.

The metal was easy to tug off, and it was as satisfying as pulling at the scab of a wound. A fresh wash of blood rushed through me, like the emotion I might have once felt for him. I spun the ring between my forefinger and thumb, inhaled from the cylinder between my fingers, and blew the wafting gray smoke through the loop.

Dead. Empty. Hollow.

The words rang like Sunday bells of conscience. They sang into the farthest, darkest reaches of what I couldn't change about myself. He was gone, and the ring was nothing more than a promise we'd made, that he no longer kept. I tossed the ring into the overgrown grass of the neighboring yard, wrapping my gown against the cold, and retreated inside.

A bar heater warmed the room, and I dragged it close as I slipped into bed. The thick, flannel sheets on my face were quick to envelop me, snuggle me in, scents of lavender and mothballs. Heat built from my torso, down my limbs, to my feet wrapped in thick cotton socks, to my hands pressed beneath the pillow.

On the edge of sleep, whiskey, and regret shuffling me to the void, a heavy pulse touched my core.

A subtle throb, a hint at desire, a possibility of euphoria.

I dragged a hand down to my shirt and slid it between my thighs, the faint thought of sex a teasing edge. But fatigue from the drive overrode the hunger, and I pressed my thighs together, willing the sensation away.

Too warm, too safe, too much missing Darren's press against my back, his fingers tangling in my hair, as though he were here now...

Breakfast started with coffee, and thanks to Mom, I could chug percolated bliss. Dreams made of phantom figures left me craving warmth. Wanting arms around me. I'd woken more than once sure Darren had changed his mind, and was standing there, only to find myself alone. That morning I'd started at sounds, checked rooms that were empty, and took second glances down corridors as though someone stared at me. But every time I looked, no one was there.

Aunt May sat with her tea, staring down the hallway and nodding to herself. Mom mentioned she was always batty, but in her final years, she'd talk to someone who wasn't there if she thought she was alone. It's what pushed the doctor's verdict that gave Mom control of the trust.

I sat straighter in my chair, a reminder text from Mom pushing her agenda. "I am going to do a look around the house, go over a list Mom sent of repairs needed to see how bad they are, and then I have some work to do on my dissertation. Is that okay with you, Aunt May?"

Her head jerked as though I'd interrupted her. "Oh. What, dear? Yes, mmm, that's fine."

"Do you want to sit on the porch again?" I wanted to get her settled, and the idea of exploring the old house was tempting. The off-white walls and dark wooden cabinets and cupboards. The aging library and sullen basement. A much more appealing trove to delve into than the depressing notes from my lecturer to improve my thesis. My doctorate could wait. It was the last pass with final suggestions, and he'd given me an extension for mental health.

Aunt May rose shakily to her feet, tea in hand, slopping over the table. "I'll sit in the sun."

I helped Aunt May to the porch, put a blanket over her knees, and took out my phone to check the list Mom sent. The replacement of a rusting drainpipe. The broken floorboards about the balconies. A fitting in Aunt May's bathroom. That slow boiler.

And a list of antiques to start ticking off like she was preparing for an auction. It sickened me to do it, but she'd promised to let me keep studying. Staring at the darkened halls of the entrance, I stroked the face of the grandfather clock in the corridor. The last time I'd walked through there, I couldn't reach its face. Mom took me away and never brought me back, not after my grandmother died. A woman who'd never looked at me twice and hated her sister.

Aunt May was nothing more than a financial asset that'd pay for itself once she passed on. Staring at the frail old woman, it wouldn't be long.

A cruel thought. I didn't lie to myself about Mom's interest or my own. But I could love this house. Show it and Aunt May that I cared. I'd renovated the wreck Darren promised was a palace that he couldn't afford. Lovingly brought the old girl back into respectability with sweat, blood, and tears Darren insisted were overdramatic. He'd paid for it. I couldn't fight that. Aunt May's house came as an opportunity to use my hard-learned skills and brighten the old girl up a bit. I swanned from room to room, painting soft colors on stark white walls in my mind, reimagining this place as though I'd call it my own and Mom wouldn't sell it.

Out the window, Aunt May muttered to herself, but if I drew close, she grew silent. She'd never leave. Not until she died. Far as I remember, she'd never left.

Student debt begged me to wish her dead, but I didn't. Stealing the forgotten fortune of an insane old lady didn't look good on anyone, least of all my mother.

I'd do what I could for Aunt May, as long as the scandal of my divorce burned crimson on my mother's cheeks. Twenty-six and a divorcée.

What I'd give to be left alone like Aunt May.

A long tour of the house's semi-functioning state proved it was in far better repair than Aunt May could have maintained. The boiler was made in the late 1800s and still worked. The rot of the floorboards was only outside where frost and wet weather were bad. The rusted drainpipe had been sanded and repainted. The bathroom's fixtures were just old, and that was all. Cold water stroked my palm as I stared around the semi-perfect tiles. Hardly a crack.

A chill swept over my skin, and I turned, wondering if Aunt May was in the hall, but it was just a draft from the open window. I shut it, noting the hinges were silent as I slipped the lock shut. Everything about the old house was perfectly maintained. The genteel age. The cleanliness went beyond the once-weekly visit of a maid. Nothing was distinctly wrong, yet I couldn't shake an uncanny curiosity at the house.

Outside, across the fence, the rotting weatherboard creaked and groaned for the kind of love this house held. This wasn't some hired fixer from Lakesmouth. It was dedicated work. The odd prickle drew me out onto the porch where Aunt May dozed. I touched her shoulder until her eyelids fluttered, and she gazed up at me with a smile.

She held out her hand. "Is it lunchtime, dear?"

"Soon. Mom wants to do some fixing to make the house more comfortable." An easy white lie. "Who is the repairman? I want him to take a look at that boiler and see what we can do to replace it."

Her hand dropped to her lap. "Oh... just the people the local help send. I don't request anyone; Beatrice takes care of it all."

Her gaze focused on the horizon, and though I kept asking for names, she didn't have any.

"Hi, I'm calling for May Hough on 18 Fallowdown Crescent in Merryweather Hills, she has a handyman that comes to do repairs, and I just wanted to talk to him." It was my fourth call to local elderly services trying to track down who helped with the house.

"What's the reference number?"

"I... don't have it. I'm her great-niece, and I'm just trying to get an estimate on what it would take to replace the boiler."

"I can't see a name on file, dear, but I'm a temp. You've been relayed to the county office. I'll have to check with your local. What's your number so I can arrange a callback?"

I gave her the details and hung up.

"Lizzie, dear, there's some red wine in the cellar. You should get us a glass. I could use a drop."

I turned from the gourmet lasagna in the antiquated oven I'd got going and grinned at Aunt May. "If you like, any bottle in particular?"

"Any dear, let fate guide your choice."

With ambiguous directions, I turned from the kitchen to the cellar door and skipped down the stairs. In the cellar, I hunted for the wine rack and found dusty bottles on an ornate shelf. I touched the top, leaning down to study them in the low light. A bottle slid partway out. My weight must have moved the delicate frame, but fingerprints marred the dust on the bottle. I plucked it out, staring at the marks, wondering if Aunt May had wanted this one recently but put it back. It looked fancy, but I knew nothing about wines and headed upstairs, hoping she'd approve of my choice.

In the kitchen, I plucked open the drawers for a corkscrew and opened the bottle with a pop. I poured us each a glass, and with classic lasagna adding to its flavor, we toasted to nothing.

Aunt May placed her glass on the table. "Your mother sent you here because of a man."

I took a deep drink, and then another, not ready to talk about it. Aunt May had married once, but I'd never met him. I'd long suspected from Mom's odd behavior around Aunt May in my teens, there was more to it. I pushed the last piece of lasagna around my plate, deciding whether to answer.

Aunt May chuckled. "She isn't here to judge you, and I certainly won't."

Aunt May and her secrets. I'd foolishly forgotten. I laughed and ducked my head. "Yes. I'm divorced now, and Mom wanted me out of the country club circle this winter."

She rapped her knuckles on the table between us, and my head jerked up to look at her. When she gazed at me, right into me, the first time she'd looked fully at me, her blue eyes washed of color, almost gray, still pricked inside me. Sought out secrets too. "What happened?"

I dropped my gaze and twisted the stem of my glass. "He had an affair."

"No, he didn't."

My gaze shot to hers, and she imparted a knowing grimace.

"He had *many* affairs."

A crack in my facade opened. I blinked away the well that blurred my vision. "That's true. Not that it mattered to my mother." I finished my glass, and Aunt May nudged the bottle until I refilled and took another sip.

"He was a bastard," I confessed, nursing the second glass. "I was there for him, and he didn't care, or stop, and still tried to blame me for his... appetites."

"What about yours?"

The question stole my breath. Searched for hidden desires. Sunk down into me until I couldn't answer. It was as though she had a script to the inside of my head where questions I couldn't ask myself shouted into the numbness I'd use to muffle my unhappiness.

Aunt May wouldn't be dissuaded by my silence. "You aren't the first woman who found their husband... lacking."

A sharp bolt of awareness struck me. Her derisive tone, the twist to her lips. The grave of my great-uncle some twenty years ago. The visit two years prior to a bitter old man and his estranged wife.

"I suppose," I stuttered. "Maybe we were ill-suited."

"Maybe he didn't see you for who you truly are."

She stared at me, and sipped her wine, even as my mouth grew dry at her frankness, at my short, loveless marriage that left me wanton, hungry, and angry.

I turned away to clear away the dishes, and she didn't ask me again. I didn't ask what she meant.

The chill bit me as I walked out onto the balcony, and a chair I hadn't noticed before pulled me to the corner. I sat, drank my whiskey, and smoked. It wasn't a good idea after the wine, but I found I didn't care. I couldn't rub my ring and hate it like usual. Instead, I tried to imagine who I could be with rather than Darren. I wasn't like Aunt May, tied to some man until I was too old to leave.

What kind of a man would I want?

Someone who cared about me over his own desires.

An image built in my mind: dark hair, strong brow, intense eyes, lean physique. I painted him, as though he stood at the far end of the balcony, dressed in a loose suit, hands in his pockets, gaze fixed on me. I licked my lips, let my imagination build him, lust after him, and wished he was real.

He walked toward me.

My breath caught in my chest, a hard constriction, fingertips lax as I became transfixed by his gaze. Dark, hypnotic, mesmerizing. Hands loose by his side, he stood over me, towering, and stretched one hand to my face. I didn't know what he wanted or how he moved, but it didn't change that he was there. His fingertips pressed against my skin, and it was real. Too real.

The whiskey glass tumbled from my numb fingers to the porch before rolling over the edge and smashing onto the stones below. I flinched, blinked once, and the figure was gone. Drunk and exhausted, I went to bed, but he haunted my dreams.

"What are you doing, dear?"

I wobbled on the shaky stepladder, glancing over my shoulder at Aunt May as the morning sun streamed in, much to my annoyance. The pounding behind my eyes wasn't aided by the twinge of guilt at my search getting caught plundering the library bookshelves. "Mom sent an email; she wanted a specific picture of her mother."

It was the worst thing about her little list. It wasn't just antiques. There were personal items, as though Aunt May were somehow guilty of stealing something from Mom.

"Well, let's have a look then, shall we?" Aunt May hobbled to a chair at the round desk by the shelves, and I brought the albums down. She tugged them open, but rather than the newer albums, her hands strayed to the ones of her own youth. To when she was a girl. Reliving the past.

Belinda warned me to expect it from the elderly, and hearing about her growing up would be interesting. I let her scan the pages, Aunt May pointing at a few old photographs, stating names I didn't know, but I stopped her hand on one.

"Who is that?" My voice didn't tremble, but a spider of dread skittered up my spine. It was the man from the balcony, who'd walked through my dreams with a taunting smile, whispering a message I couldn't remember when I woke.

Her fingers ghosted over the picture, a young woman with a man behind her. "Not a relation."

I studied the picture, the woman. "That's you."

She sighed. "Once, when I was very young. Right after my aunt died."

"What was his name?"

She moved my hand aside and turned the page. "I don't remember."

After an exhausting day, too many bad emails with a reminder on the due date of my thesis, news on the financial settlement from my lawyer, and the council unable to find out who was fixing up the house, I sat out the back, glass in hand, chasing away yesterday's ghost with more whiskey. It was easier out here, down in the garden Aunt May couldn't reach, too far away for her to hear me crying.

I considered texting Darren in loneliness, asking why, before putting my phone aside. I needed something else. I willed the strange visitor from the previous evening to return, but my thoughts couldn't paint him again. In frustration I drank, sullen and uncared for. It drove me to one too many thoughts, blurry and lonely shadows that haunted me. I crawled into bed for the warmth and wept at my solitude.

A hand stroked my hair, patted my back, and drew the covers in close. Kissed my ear and whispered as my mind fell into oblivion.

"Soon you'll never be alone."

A rotting hangover and a chiding email from my professor left me pounding the keyboard to finish the last of my dissertation. All it needed after the last few days of solace and sobriety was a finishing touch. I drove to a nearby city, gathered fresh ingredients, and came home to Aunt May.

Aunt May stood by the kitchen door. "What's this?"

"Lobster, smoked salmon, caviar, white truffle tagliolini, and champagne." I dumped my hoard on the table and laid out the celebratory meal.

Aunt May laughed with giddy delight. "This is a feast for twelve!"

I grinned back. "We'll just have to do the best we can."

She took two glasses with the slow movements of the old, until I grabbed them and sat her at the kitchen table. "You just enjoy it."

She laughed. "What's the cause of such merriment?"

I popped the champagne. "Provided I pass, I've just earned my doctorate."

We beamed at one another as I poured. She held out her trembling glass to mine. "I always knew you were gifted."

I tapped my glass against hers, glad to share the celebration with someone. "Thank you."

"No degree will ever tell you that, but you have... more to you than your mother."

"Oh?" I paused at setting out the food.

"Oh yes... it takes quite the determination to accept one's true calling." She brushed her hand over her skirt. "Sometimes it takes everything."

Too much good food and champagne left me awake as Aunt May went to bed. I trawled through the library, finding the stack of albums, and turned the pages of my family history. The people of the past gazed back with monochromatic stares, until I got to the picture of the mysterious man.

"Who are you?" I brushed my fingertips over the page. An answering touch ghosted over my spine. I turned around, and no one was there.

Yet within me, an urge blossomed, and taking the half-empty champagne bottle, I climbed the stairs to my room. Slipping between the covers, I gazed out the window at a starry sky.

I laid in bed, unable to sleep, an edge of wakefulness churning my thoughts. That face, that man, the stranger who was nothing, trailed my thoughts all day. Caught between asleep and wakefulness, I gave into the longing to be touched.

Envisaged him once more, standing on the far side of the room, watching me.

He said nothing. No words were needed. He knew what I wanted.

I stripped off my clothes, safe from autumn's bite beneath the covers, but it reached me still, goose bumping my skin, an elicit prickling rocking over me as I shuddered. At the gesture, he stepped closer, hands above the covers, heat emanating until I lay in luxurious softness.

His voice commanded, and I obeyed, eyes drifting shut, lost in phantom touches, coming quietly undone from someone who wasn't even there.

"He's yours now."

I jerked my head from a pleasantly sleepy fugue as I entered the kitchen the next morning. Aunt May already sat there, a cup of tea before her.

Her gaze scanned me, barefoot to dressing-gown-clad shoulders to my mussed hair and satiated eyes.

I blinked away the lethargy of pleasure, still lost in the ghost of my dreams. "I'm sorry?"

She smiled. "It doesn't matter. I'm glad you slept well. He'll see to that."

"What are you talking about?"

"Nothing." She rose. "I think I'll sit outside a while... enjoy the sun."

"A storm is coming."

I stared at the black horizon, rubbing my arms against the chill. "We should go inside."

"No. I want to stay out here."

Aunt May was adamant. Even as the wind grew, raindrops fell, and lightning crackled over the sky.

"Please come inside," I begged.

"You don't know what it'll be like tonight."

I barely caught her words over the breeze. "What do you mean?"

"He's going to be so angry," she cried, voice breaking. "There's nothing I can do to stop it."

I came to stand before her, watching the tears track down her face. "Who do you mean?"

She kept crying. "It's too late now."

Unnerved by her tears, I lifted her bodily from the chair and took her inside to sit before the fire in the living room. I made tea as her tears quietened, and any offers of dinner were passed by.

"Since you like whiskey, there is some in the library."

I took a step back. I hadn't told her. Kept the bottle in my room and out of sight. It didn't matter.

"As you like."

I served us two glasses, and she drank half of hers, coughing a little.

"Easy now," I chided.

"Pour another."

Skeptical, I did as she asked, and I sat and waited as she stared at the flames until her breath quietened.

"Why are you so upset?"

Her gaze shifted to me. "You should go to bed. Lock your door. Don't open it."

Apprehension spiked within me. "I'm not going to do that."

She sighed. "Then help me to bed."

We climbed the stairs, her weight heavy on my arm, steps slow, but we got there, and I helped her change into a nightgown and get into bed. She sunk down into the mattress, skin almost translucent, the evening aging her by years.

I wanted to switch off the bedroom light, but the picture by her bed caught my attention.

A photograph of Aunt May, standing in the doorway to this house, but behind her was a figure. The same man from before. And in the picture, he scowled at the camera.

The lightning crashed, and the storm battered the house. I glanced up at a figure across the bed, the same man from my dreams, staring down at Aunt May. The lightning faded, and he was gone.

Breath whistling between my lips, I touched Aunt May's shoulder, still gazing at where he'd stood. "Aunt May?"

She didn't stir. She was gone.

"Dreadfully sorry, miss," the policeman said. "Had a few emergencies this evening."

I clutched my cardigan about my shoulders, the stretcher with Aunt May's body passing by. "No one's fault, officer."

"We'll send around a unit in the morning to get the rest of the details. If they don't come by, then you needn't worry."

I nodded, taking his card, retreating back into the house to lock the door now that the officials were gone.

The grandfather clock chimed the midnight hour. Hours since her passing.

The storm rolled overhead, not done despite Aunt May's death.

I tried calling Mom for the third time, and got voicemail. I'd already texted Belinda, who hadn't responded. In desperation for another human touch, I texted Darren.

[Lizzie]
I know we aren't talking, but I could use a human voice right now.

I let it go a few minutes, watched the read acknowledgment, and nothing else.

[Lizzie]
My great-aunt just died right in front of me.

My phone rang, Darren's number coming up. "Hello?"

"Oh, sweetheart, I'm so sorry."

An ache lanced through me at the sound of his voice, static making it almost unrecognizable in the storm. "It's okay." My voice broke. I dragged a hand over my face, even if he couldn't see me.

"Do you need me to come to you?"

"No, I'm okay. I just need to talk to someone."

"Why don't you talk to the man already there?"

I paused, dropping my hand from my face. "What?"

"Aunt May didn't leave you alone, and now she's gone, it's your turn." The voice twisted, and became something, *someone* else. Someone familiar, who'd coaxed me into illicit pleasure in my dreams. But it couldn't be...

"Darren?"

"Did you think she was alone?" It became a deeper baritone, an edge of hate in the voice, a furious nature I hadn't encountered. "Do you think... you are?"

I dropped the phone, leapt to my feet, and stared around the darkened library lit with a single lamp and the flashes of the storm. The policeman, he was right outside. It'd been minutes. He wouldn't be far. I snatched the card from the pocket of my cardigan and the phone from the floor.

A text message from Darren lit the screen.

[Darren]
Call whoever you like. Only I will answer.

I gazed about the room, backed into a corner, afraid of every shadow. But I had to know.

[Lizzie]
Who are you?

Lightning crackled, struck nearby, and the house shook down to its foundation. I screamed. The lights cut out, and all that was left was the dull glow of the screen.

[Darren]
I'm yours. And you're mine.

The ghost of the house came out of the shadows, and I blacked out.

Rain pattered on the windows. It tapped on my eardrums, tempting and sweet, but fear jerked me awake. Fear of a shadow that couldn't be real, a man who was in photographs but wasn't here. How Aunt May swore he'd be angry. How he'd come out of the dark for me.

Lightning flickered over the darkened room; antique furniture made ghastly. I lifted my head from a dusty pillow, a lingering scent of lavender clenching my heart. Aunt May. Who never told my mother about stolen sweets, second desserts, or that I liked a boy at school. Aunt May, who'd known about my loveless marriage even though she'd never met Darren. Aunt May, who kept a ghost in her house.

At that, I shot upright, staring around, seeking out the shadows. "Where are you?"

"Here."

He sat in a wingback chair, wreathed in shadow. Not handsome, but infinitely seductive. The angles of his face, a sharp nose, thin lips. Expressive. In the way his hands lay over the arms of the chair, his legs crossed. The way, after a while, I realized he didn't breathe.

"Who are you?"

He blinked, gaze falling to the floor before returning to my face. "I'm a promise."

"To who?"

"The women of your family who believe they are alone, unloved, and long for more."

My heart twisted so tightly I had to swallow against the constriction in my throat. "What do you mean?"

"I fell in love with one of your ancestors... and I was not human." He gripped the arms of the chair. "Your ancestor was defiled by men from an invading army, leaving her broken. I was on the losing side of deities in that war, but she found me, saved me, and gave me hope when I had nothing, abandoned by my gods. I gave what I thought was love to her in the form of a promise."

I couldn't look away, couldn't ignore the pain in his eyes. "What was the promise?"

He met my eyes, in the dark, in the quiet, and saw the thoughts only Aunt May uncovered. That I now knew deep inside he'd found and told Aunt May. "I would become her heart when no one else understood her, and I would follow the women of her womb to the end of time, for I served no god anymore. Only the whims of this kind woman. Do you understand me, Elizabeth?"

Aunt May was gone, and his promise remained. "Do... what do you mean when you say serve?"

He laced his fingers together, gaze penetrating every half-held desire in my head, rifling through them like a deck of cards. Yet no one person is such a simple concept, and like a reader first finds a library, he devoured the full spectrum of my mind until all I held was fear of what he knew. And longing.

My heart raced, and my skin was clammy. I didn't know if it was fear that prickled my skin, which dusted beads of sweat on my brow, but another part, deep, dark, and falling apart at his touch, longed to unfurl, to become some other woman I didn't know existed within me. I was a possibility. He was a promise.

"I will always pull you," he whispered, lips tight over the jaw I wanted to trace. "You will find it hard to stray from me. That is my part of the bond. But in return, I give you a place with no secrets, nothing held back, and no other desire than to do as you wish."

"Is this what you did to Aunt May?" The question burst out of me, carving an ache in my chest, wishing I wasn't about to be used again. But I couldn't take it back, had to ask for more. "Did you devour her desire like you just did to me? Do you think by knowing what I want you can control me?"

He laughed then. Full throated and sending my heart racing. And this time, it wasn't with fear, but a kind of exhilaration, like standing on the edge of a cliff, even as his eyes glowed, and I didn't know if he was a forgotten god or a damned demon.

"Who do you think fixed the house that Aunt May loved so very much?" He grinned as though he were a cat that had all the cream. "What little pleasure your aunt wanted from this world was to be left alone. And I granted it."

He rose from his couch, and I clutched the blanket over my shoulders, the blanket he must have placed there, as he crossed to stand before me as my mouth grew dry with lust, fear, and loneliness.

He brushed my hair from my face, and his touch made me shiver. "What do you think I would give for you?"

I didn't know, didn't have an answer, and he didn't need one. He knelt before me, peeled away my clothing like the layers of my soul. Uncovered me with every gasp, every cry, every tear that he licked away with a wicked tongue, and I wanted him that way. Wanted and was afraid of this immortal unraveling me one thread at a time, with a promise.

"According to Aunt May, Elizabeth Elden was to inherit all the assets, the house, everything."

The lawyer laid down the paper as my mother fumed. I slunk further into my chair as she sputtered.

"That's *not* how it's supposed to be."

The lawyer shrugged. "Well, it is, and she can tell me what she wants, not you."

They both stared at me. I rose from my fatigued slouch, leaving the office. "I'll give her enough to pay off the debts. That's it."

She started to stutter, jerking to her feet to follow me out. It didn't matter, though. I could feel him out there, a tugging deep inside, urging me back to the house. Back to him. I couldn't ignore him; the way I knew I couldn't escape. And I didn't want to.

Mom grabbed my arm, and whirled me around. "You can't ignore me."

"I can, and I will." I removed her hand from me, truths revealed in the days I'd spent in his arms. "You all knew something was in that house, and you led me like a lamb to the slaughter. It was supposed to be you, wasn't it?"

She took a step back, cheeks scarlet as though I'd slapped her.

"You think I didn't know?" I pressed her back, saw her fear, and she wasn't my mother anymore. "I saw all the photographs; he never came to you. Did you send me to that house to take on something you could never face?"

She paled, her hands shaking. "We never speak of Aunt May's affliction—"

I laughed. "He's not a disease. He's a promise, one you failed to keep, and now I have to pay for it."

I left her behind, driven to be at the house, his call ringing inside me, and I didn't know what he wanted.

"I'm here." I trembled, saying the words and waiting for him, afraid and wanting all at once. I knew nothing of the bond, only that I needed him as much as he needed me. It left my hands clammy, my heart palpitating, and his voice drifting through my mind.

A yearning in my soul kept me in the house until the lawyer's meetings. I'd explained to an empty hall how I had to leave for only a few hours, and the tightness around my chest eased until I could drive away. The need came back at the lawyer's office. Drove me to be done with my mother. But for the first time, I wanted to be home. Home was wherever he called me.

"Please, don't be silent," I begged, trying to forget the tormented night of the storm, the sheer anger, the dark, the grief and lust all tangled as one. The way I'd cried, but I'd never enjoyed sex so much. And I wanted more. Couldn't stand the desperation in my own voice as I clutched my keys, waiting for him.

"I'm sorry." He stood at the far end of the hall, surrounded by the light of a fading sun. "I should not have pressed upon you while you grieved. I wanted you, but I was mourning too."

The sun shone through his form. But I knew it was real. Just like he'd possessed me, that grief and sadness took him, and while I'd remained unhurt, it was because I belonged to him. But that didn't mean we had to stay with Aunt May's memories.

"We don't have to stay here... unless you can't leave."

His eyes widened. "We don't?"

I shook my head. "Aunt May wanted to, but now... with her money, we could go anywhere, if you wanted." I swallowed, fear rising not just of him but being stuck among these houses. This dead town wasn't mine. "I can take you everywhere. We can see the world, just you and me. Because you won't ever let me feel alone." The confession left my heart raw but comforted by his presence.

He stared at the house, a glimmer of tears in his lashes. "I miss her. But the longer I stay, the more I hate what took her from me. Time and god and things neither of us can control. We should go. While we still have time. While you have time."

I let go of my held breath. "You'd do that... for me?"

He smiled and held out a hand, and when I took it, it was warm, hot as I remembered his body on mine. "I promised."

About the Author

EJ started her author career in 2014 self-publishing a steampunk series called the Last Prophecy. In 2019 she wrote *Behind the Veil*, signing a contract with Literary Wanderlust, released on the October 1st 2021. Her second novel with Literary Wanderlust, *Echo of the Evercry*, will be out on July 1st 2023. She also released scifi series, *Queen of Spades*, now an award-winning series. Studying a Graduate Certificate in Creative Writing at Deakin University, she is also a mentor for Write Hive, and a Futurescapes Alumni.

In July 2023 she will be reading submissions for a neurodivergent anthology for Deadset Press. She has a short non-fiction story called *I Can't Hear the Sea* with Gothic Seaside, and fiction stories *The Promise* with Grendel Press, and *Moth Dust* with Savage Planets.

She's a judge for SPSFC, volunteer for Flights of Foundry 2022, panelist for Weekend Writers, member of RWA (Aus) and Sisters in Crime (Aus), and avid earl grey tea drinker, whose muse is a real pain.

When not writing, reading, or drowning in stories, she walks on the beach with her two rescue dogs and supportive spouse in southern NSW, Australia.

ANY
COMICS

MOVE FAST AND BREAK THINGS

BY KIT WALKER

The charming little deli just off Palm Springs's main strip was transplanted directly from the 1960s: white stucco embellished in shades of mint and candyfloss. Not at all the kind of place one would expect to hire a mercenary. Even under the shade of the patio awning, the air was so hot it seared Victor Keane's lungs.

"Is the idea to lay low and blend in?" Corinne dropped into a plastic patio chair across from him. "Because I'm pretty sure you're the only guy within ten miles under the age of a hundred."

"This is where people go to retire," Victor replied. "I'm retired."

"You're thirty-four. Men your age don't retire. They're just unemployed."

Corinne didn't order anything; after years of observation, Victor had determined she subsisted entirely on mineral water, air, and spite. She drew a tablet from her shoulder bag and stabbed at its screen with fingers like spiders' legs. "What do you know about Cameron Spalding?"

"Not much."

Corinne slid the tablet across the table. She'd always possessed a sense of the theatric that lent itself well to manila folders and grainy photo printouts, severely undercut by the relentless march of technology. On the screen was a photo of a middle-aged man with an air of carefully cultivated dishevelment: Cameron Spalding, American citizen, forty-seven years old. Net worth somewhere in the billions.

"Tech guy?" Victor guessed.

"On the financial side. Brought his trust fund in on a few ventures that paid off big." Corinne propped her elbows on the table and leaned forward. "Spalding's getting weird. Last year, he bought an acreage out in the Rockies and started hiring armed guards. Stayed pretty quiet until recently."

She was waiting for Victor to ask what happened. He didn't, just to annoy her.

Corinne huffed, and continued: "A van full of civilians on a camping trip went missing a few weeks ago. Once someone got around to tracking the GPS, it turned up at the edge of Spalding's little mountain fortress."

"Why are you talking to me about it?"

"Spalding has friends in DC," Corinne said. "Those friends are pretty reluctant to call the cops on their nice, wealthy, all-American pal Cameron Spalding. Meanwhile, it turns out one of the missing civilians is Skylar Cantrell."

"As in Cantrell Energy?"

"Yep. Emmett Cantrell is *very* motivated to get his granddaughter back."

Victor shoved the tablet back across the table. "I'm not getting involved in a fight between rich lunatics."

"Of course not. You have a functioning brain. Which is why Cantrell is offering an absurd amount of money to change your mind." Corinne settled back in her seat, too relaxed for Victor's liking. "Phaedra Hill is onboard."

Victor glared at her.

Corinne's face was the picture of innocence. "You've worked with her before, right?"

"That's cheap," Victor said. "Even for you, that's cheap."

Corinne shrugged.

"Fine," Victor said.

"Good." The tablet went back into Corinne's bag.

As she stood, Victor asked, "Why me?"

Corinne shrugged again. "This is a messy job. Home ground, civilian opponent. Situations like that, soldiers get confused. They hesitate. You won't."

As instructed, Victor reported to the airfield at 0800. There was a tilt-rotor waiting: an overpriced consumer model of a VTOL aircraft originally designed for the military, which had a long and distinguished record of crashing at every available opportunity.

Corinne waited in the shelter of the hangar, with three other mercenaries.

"You already know Hill," she said. "She'll be your medic."

Phaedra Hill had the build of a rugby player and the general demeanor of a kindergarten teacher. Phaedra had left the service to transition; when the civilian sector proved nearly as unfriendly as the military, mercenary work had been the only option left.

She wasn't happy about it.

Corinne indicated the other two, equally broad and ripped with a near-identical assortment of questionable tattoos. "This is Mike Lenox and Simon Brandt. Lenox, Brandt, meet Victor Keane."

Brandt grinned. "The crazy one?"

Victor shrugged.

"Heard you were an Army Ranger," Lenox said.

"Got the tab," Victor replied. "Never served with a unit. You?"

"Navy SEALs."

Victor suppressed a grimace. Even among special forces, SEALs had a reputation. Phaedra's look of dismay matched Victor's own.

"Keane is team leader," Corinne said. "You all report to him."

Brandt and Lenox groaned. Phaedra's expression froze into a blank mask.

"No arguments," Corinne snapped. "If you have a problem, back out now."

The groans settled into low grumbles, then silence.

"Rules of engagement?" Phaedra asked.

Lenox snorted a laugh; Brandt rolled his eyes.

"You're cleared for lethal force. Try and stick to self-defense."

"'Try,'" Brandt muttered under his breath. Lenox choked back another laugh.

"One last thing," Corinne said. "You may be tempted to take a shot at Spalding. Don't. There are many things the authorities are willing to ignore about this situation. A dead American billionaire will not be one of them."

Cameron Spalding's alpine mansion was at the far end of a long and heavily patrolled access road, so the tilt-rotor dropped Victor and his team twenty miles into the dense woodland of Spalding's backyard. The forest had lain untouched until the invasion of the luxury home industry; the stuff of postcards and wildlife documentaries.

As the staggering downdraft from the tilt-rotor's takeoff faded, Phaedra said, "Victor. I need a minute."

Lenox let out the quiet "ooh" of a schoolboy whose classmate was in trouble. Victor motioned for him and Brandt to move along. "What's the problem?"

Phaedra wouldn't look at him. "Fucking everything, Vic. Last I heard, you had a psychotic breakdown."

"That was just the defense my dad's lawyers came up with."

"So you were perfectly sane when you shot your best friend in the face?"

Her knuckles were white around the strap of her medical bag.

"I'm fine, Phaedra."

He didn't tell her he took this job to watch her back. She wouldn't thank him.

"You really are fine, aren't you?" Phaedra said. "It doesn't bother you at all. What you did."

"I'm not going to shoot you in the back, if that's what you're worried about. I'm not a sociopath. Or psychopath, or whatever you're supposed to call it."

"I know you're not. So what are you?"

"Hey!" Brandt shouted, startling them both. "You ladies coming?"

Victor aimed a middle finger in Brandt's general direction. To Phaedra, he said, "Are you going to be okay?"

"Probably not."

Unfortunately, Emmett Cantrell had spared no expense. Instead of paper maps, the team had a tablet loaded with satellite maps of the area. Even with its steel frame and rugged rubber case, the thing felt like it was about to snap in Victor's hands.

The maps showed a small, isolated building about halfway between the drop point and Spalding's mansion. Closer observation from a ridge overlooking the site revealed it was an old, two-story cabin—built in the 70s as someone's wilderness getaway, then left intact when developers bought the land. There was a brand-new pickup truck parked next to a partially overgrown dirt track that wound away into the woods; a generator hummed from a shed nearby.

The team's loadout also included a DSLR camera with a telephoto lens so massive it required its own carrying handle. Through the camera's viewfinder, Victor counted two sentries. Movement in the windows suggested at least two more people inside.

"Might be where they're holding the asset," Lenox said.

Phaedra looked dubious. "Wouldn't Spalding keep the hostages close?"

"We're here anyway," Brandt pointed out. "And there must be *something* important in there."

Victor hummed an agreement. They'd need to eliminate the sentries first, and quietly.

He glanced at Phaedra; her eyes were fixed on the house, every muscle wired with tension.

No, not tension. Dread.

"Brandt," Victor said. "You and I will handle the sentries. Lenox, Hill, hold this position."

Phaedra's shoulders slumped in relief.

The sentry paced in a rough square around his post, unaware or uncaring that the noise might cover the footsteps of someone else.

Victor approached from the direction of the house. The sentry clearly expected trouble to come from the outside in; it wouldn't occur to him that something might get past him and double back. Victor's knife came out of its sheath with a bare whisper of sound.

The knife went into the sentry's lower back in one smooth thrust, slipping easily into his kidney. The sentry's body seized in blinding, paralyzing pain; his mouth opened in a silent scream. Victor stood and caught the sentry as he toppled, gently lowering him to the ground.

For a moment, the sentry almost looked betrayed. Then his face went slack.

Victor wiped his knife clean on the body's pant leg and sheathed it again.

From the other side of the house came a panicked shout that cut off into a choked, gurgling noise.

Shit.

As quietly as possible, Victor sprinted toward the source of the noise. His rifle swung up into firing position at the sight of a figure standing there, but it was only Brandt with a dead sentry at his feet.

There were two slashes in the sentry's throat: a shallow aborted slice, and a longer, deeper stroke that had cut off his scream and, shortly afterward, everything else.

Brandt's hand was bleeding, and there was something dazed and brittle in his expression when he said, "My hand slipped."

Victor lowered the rifle. "Should've gone for the kidney."

Brandt blinked. "I don't do that."

"The fuck does that mean?"

Indignation rose up behind the cracked glass of Brandt's eyes. "It means fuck you, I don't do that!"

Hurried footsteps crunched through the undergrowth toward them. Victor spun, raising his rifle again, as Phaedra and Lenox emerged from the woods.

Phaedra froze; her face went white.

Victor lowered his weapon. "You heard it too?"

"The whole fucking county heard it." Phaedra studied the scene, then looked to Victor. "Do we back off?"

"No," Victor replied. "Move in."

They closed on the cabin from both sides; Phaedra and Lenox covered the front door while Victor and Brandt approached from the back.

The locks had been changed recently; there was still a pale void on the back door where the old lock had been. No keyhole—just a chip reader and what was likely a formidable deadbolt.

The door's frame, on the other hand, hadn't been replaced since the cabin was built.

Victor's radio hissed. *"Smart lock on the front door,"* Phaedra reported.

"Same on this side," Victor answered. "They already know we're here. Kick it in."

"Hell yeah," Brandt crowed, and put his boot to the lock. The frame splintered. The door swung open.

The wood-paneled interior of the cabin was empty, with nail holes in the walls where pictures had once hung. The only furniture of note was in the den, where books and papers lay scattered across a cheap folding table next to an open laptop.

Behind the table was a metal folding chair, toppled onto its side.

Victor and Brandt met Phaedra and Lenox in the kitchen—littered with empty plastic bags and frozen dinner trays—and confirmed via signals that the first floor was clear.

From upstairs came low voices, and a muffled *thump.*

Victor signaled for the rest of the team to stay put and made for the stairs.

There were two doors at the top: one hung open, revealing an empty bedroom, while the other was nearly closed. Rifle at the ready, Victor nudged the second door open.

A lone guard stood at the center of the room: young, maybe early twenties, with a pistol trained on the doorway and Victor. His other arm was wrapped around the throat of a civilian roughly Victor's age, with a soft face and large dark eyes.

"Easy," Victor said to both of them at once. "Don't do anything stupid."

"Back off," the guard snarled. The gun shook in his hand.

"It's okay," Victor said. "What's your name?"

"Fuck you." The guard took a shuddering breath. "Casey."

"Casey," Victor repeated. "You're not a soldier, are you?"

"Fuck you."

"It's okay," Victor said. "That's a good thing. You've never killed anyone, have you?"

"... No."

"Tell you what." Victor unslung his rifle. "I'll put my gun down, and you can put yours down, and nobody has to shoot anybody."

Casey didn't reply, but Victor held his rifle out to the side.

Slowly, mirroring Victor's motions, Casey swung his own gun away, then down.

Victor knelt; Casey did too, as far as he was able. Both guns hit the floor with a startling clatter.

Then the hostage dropped to the floor, pure deadweight. Casey swore and stumbled under the sudden burden.

Victor was on him in a second. The back of his hand, loosely curled, came down on the top of Casey's head with a *crack*, right at the seam between three skull plates.

Casey collapsed; the hostage scrambled out of the way. Victor knelt and checked Casey's pulse.

The hostage had put the bed between himself and Victor and now hid behind it. Victor circled around, hands empty and held out at his sides.

"You okay?" he asked.

The hostage shook his head, and an unruly lock of hair fell into his eyes. Victor resisted the urge to brush it away.

"I'm not going to hurt you," he said.

The hostage risked a quick glance at the body, then back at Victor.

"He'd have called his boss the moment we left." Victor crouched until he was eye-to-eye with the hostage. "I'm Victor."

The hostage swallowed. "Adrian." His shirt wasn't buttoned all the way, and sweat had pooled in the hollow of his throat. "I'm Adrian Yates."

Victor held out a hand to him, palm up. "Would you come downstairs with me, Adrian?"

Adrian's hand was soft and gripped Victor's so tightly it hurt.

As Victor helped him to his feet, Adrian's eyes strayed to the body on the floor.

Victor moved to block his view. "Don't look."

On their way out, Victor paused only to pick up his rifle.

"One hostile," Victor reported upon his return to the kitchen, Adrian in tow. "Dead."

Brandt paused in the process of sifting through a pile of empty pill bottles. "That's not Skylar Cantrell."

Adrian took a half-step back. "What do you want with my TA?"

"This is Adrian Yates." To Adrian, Victor said, "We were hired to find Skylar."

"You're not with the military." Adrian's attention darted rapidly between the four of them. "Mercenaries?"

"Yeah." Phaedra offered him a rueful smile. "Sorry."

"Shit." A short laugh, tinged with hysteria, burst from Adrian's mouth. "Goddamn it."

"Do you know where Skylar is?" Lenox asked.

"Probably in the main house," Adrian said. "With the others."

Brandt crossed his arms. "Why aren't you with them?"

"I was planning to escape," Adrian said. "Spalding found out. Took it personally. He couldn't get rid of me, so instead, he banished me out here to do my research."

"Research?" Victor asked. "On what?"

"Entheogens," Adrian said. "Psychedelics used for spiritual or religious—"

Lenox caught on first, and laughed. "Drugs?"

Adrian rolled his eyes. "Yeah. Drugs. I'm an anthropologist. I study ancient divination practices."

"Spalding wanted *you*," Victor realized.

"He read my thesis," Adrian said. "I'm not sure he understood much of it, but now he thinks he can transcend the physical. Ascend to a higher plane of existence."

"With drugs," Victor said. "How's that going?"

"Not good. He's, uh... frustrated." Adrian touched a healing cut over his cheekbone; his eyes went hazy. "He backhanded me once. Not that hard, but his ring caught me on the cheek. I keep waiting for him to do it again." He blinked. "Sorry. I don't know why I said all that."

Upstairs, a phone began to ring.

With Adrian in tow, the team only managed to put a few miles between themselves and the house before they lost too much light to continue. Their loadout included night vision goggles, but Victor preferred not to use them; they rendered the world as an indiscriminate green smear that was barely an improvement over pitch darkness.

They didn't dare risk a fire. Victor took first watch and sat on a fallen log with his back to the camp, methodically cataloging noises and shapes in the darkness.

Nothing changed until the end of his shift, when a faint rustle disturbed the leaf litter behind him. Victor spun at the waist, drawing his sidearm in the same movement.

Adrian stood at the other end of Victor's gun, frozen, hands half-raised. "Sorry."

"Don't sneak up on guys with guns." Victor lowered his sidearm and holstered it again. "You should be sleeping."

"Can't." Adrian had a silver emergency blanket slung over his shoulders. He pulled it tighter around himself, as if to hide inside. "Can I sit here?"

Victor shrugged, and Adrian carefully perched on the log next to Victor, warm all along his side. Adrian had two healed-over piercings in his left ear. Victor found himself wanting to run his thumb over them.

He looked up instead. There were parts of the desert where one could see the sky as it really was: no clouds, no light pollution, just vast shapes in a darkness so endless that staring up at it felt like falling. It wasn't the same, here. But it was close.

"I heard some tech company wants to put billboards up there," Adrian said. "Sell ad space."

Victor's stomach churned. "Are they all as crazy as Spalding?"

"Half the richest guys on Earth are trying to crack immortality. The other half want to go to space. I guess Spalding couldn't decide and split the difference."

"With drugs."

"You keep saying that," Adrian said, annoyed. "Humans have used entheogens since before we were technically human. Priests and shamans all over the world eat magic mushrooms or drink psychedelic teas. The Oracle of Delphi was huffing volcano fumes."

"Why?"

"That's what I've been trying to figure out." Adrian huddled deeper into the blanket. "... I had strict parents. Once I got to college, I tried *everything.* So one night, my roommate offered me some mush-rooms he got from a guy on the Internet. Ended up in the middle of a field, crying. Also naked. I was convinced something was *looking* at me." He paused, then continued, as if reciting something he'd written down: "If there's such a thing as the divine, then only in a state of delirium can the human mind truly reach for it."

Victor was too caught up in his own thoughts to answer.

Adrian noticed. "What are you thinking about?"

"Ranger school."

"That isn't as cute as it sounds, is it?"

"Nope," Victor said. "They drop you into the wilderness to run exercises with minimal rations and four hours of sleep every night. For two weeks at a time."

"Jesus."

"I started hallucinating," Victor said. "Everybody does."

Adrian slid down off the log, rolling up onto his knees in the dirt and shuffling until he and Victor were face-to-face. "What did you see?"

Victor didn't have the words to describe it. How the impact of every raindrop on his skin shattered into mesmerizing fractals. How the world around him flattened into shapes and colors that lost all meaning. How the air in front of him seemed to open, and he understood, all at once and down to every atom of his being, that something so infinitely huge it shouldn't have even been aware of his existence had, for one brief moment, taken notice of him.

"I reached out for something," he said, "and it reached back."

Adrian leaned in until he and Victor were only a few inches apart, gazing into his eyes as if the answer to all his questions lay somewhere behind them.

Victor wanted to kiss him.

His watch started beeping.

Victor stood, so abruptly that Adrian lurched back onto his heels. "Shift change."

Adrian blinked and couldn't seem to move.

"Get some sleep," Victor said, and went to kick Brandt awake.

"What kind of security do they have up at the house?"

They kept Adrian between them as they walked. Spalding's mansion was only a few miles away, but it was slow going through the woods and they didn't dare follow the road.

"A lot of guards," Adrian said. "I think Spalding recruited most of them online."

"How many?"

"I don't know."

A disturbance in the trees drew Victor's attention.

"Great," Brandt groaned. "We should have left him in the—"

"Shut up," Victor hissed.

Brandt's mouth snapped shut.

In the dead silence that followed came the *crack* of a gunshot.

Victor shoved Adrian down behind a tree stump, then ducked to join him. Phaedra, Brandt, and Lenox all dove for cover.

There were silhouettes in the forest—roughly half a dozen, all of them firing as they fanned out to encircle Victor's team. Victor signaled for the others to break cover and fall back, herding Adrian behind him. If Adrian was right, these were automatic weapons in the hands of amateurs—they'd make a lot of noise, fire blindly into the brush, but shy away from direct fire at human targets.

Mostly. From somewhere off to Victor's left, Lenox screamed.

Victor didn't look, his attention fixed on the rifle in his hands and the targets ahead; he dropped one, then another.

The team retreated faster than their opponents could advance. By the time they'd exhausted their rifle ammunition and backed into a rocky overhang, nearly ten minutes later, Victor was fairly sure they were clear.

Lenox slumped against the rock, bleeding from the socket of his right arm, which hung useless at his side.

Phaedra rushed over and began to strap a tourniquet around Lenox's shoulder. At such an awkward angle, it would only slow the bleeding. Once the tourniquet was in place, Phaedra clamped her hands over Lenox's shoulder, front and back.

If Lenox hadn't passed out yet, he wasn't far from it.

"We need a medevac," Brandt said.

"This isn't a government job," Victor fired back. "There's no medevac."

"Extraction point's a few hours away," Phaedra said. "We might make it."

"So let's fucking extract!" Brandt snapped. "Fuck this job!"

Still dazed, Adrian said, "What about the hostages?"

"Vic." Phaedra's forearms flexed as she bore down on Lenox's shoulder. "I don't think I can stop the bleeding."

Victor keyed his radio. "Control, this is Echo One."

Over the radio, Corinne answered: *"Copy, Echo One. Mission status?"*

"Echo Four is critically injured. We need extraction."

"Do you have the asset?"

"Negative."

"Extraction isn't possible until the asset is secured."

Phaedra didn't dare take her hands off Lenox; instead, she shouted, loud enough to be heard over Victor's radio: "Lenox is bleeding out! Get us out of here!"

The only answer was static.

There was a scuffle behind Victor, and a quiet, surprised gasp from Adrian.

Both of Adrian's hands scrabbled at the arm Brandt had across his throat. Brandt stood behind him, pressing a knife into Adrian's side.

"Cantrell is our ticket out," Brandt said. "Spalding wants Yates. We can trade him."

Victor reached for his sidearm.

"Careful," Brandt warned. "You want Spalding's guys to hear a gunshot out here?"

Brandt took a step back; Adrian stumbled along with him.

"Victor," Adrian called, voice trembling.

Victor couldn't follow. Lenox was going nowhere fast, and Phaedra wouldn't leave him.

"I'll find you," Victor called back. "I promise."

Brandt backed away, step by careful step, until the forest swallowed them.

A few minutes past nightfall, Lenox's breathing rattled to a halt.

Phaedra noticed the moment Victor did. He kept his back turned as she gasped and cursed through her attempts to revive him; she wouldn't want him to see her cry.

It was nearly an hour before Phaedra said, in a voice gone hoarse, "He's dead."

Victor sat next to her, shoulders pressed together, as Lenox's body cooled.

Finally, Phaedra took a long, shaky breath and said, "Brandt's not coming back."

The mansion was a monstrosity of glass and marble; a French chateau designed by an American who didn't understand the appeal. The bulk of the house's security had assembled in the central courtyard to inspect the steady procession of expensive cars making their way up the road.

Cameron Spalding was having a party.

The house sat at the top of a rise. Farther down the hill was an access door to the basement, with only a token security presence.

Victor and Phaedra remained under cover of the treeline, studying the guard patrols through the long lens of the camera. As shifts changed and guards came and went, each one paused at the basement door and leaned toward a panel mounted next to it. Moments later, the door would open.

Phaedra handed the camera to Victor and said, with relief, "Facial recognition lock."

Victor swept the camera from one guard to the other until he found one facing the treeline and snapped a photo.

They had to take the case off the tablet to get the camera's memory card into it.

Sneaking past the guard patrols was easy enough, but the real challenge was getting the tablet into the door camera's field of view. Neither of them dared approach it head-on, in case it was programmed to report any unrecognized faces.

Back pressed against the wall next to the door, Victor pulled up the guard's face on the tablet and stretched until it sidled into the camera's line of sight.

The lock beeped, and Phaedra ducked past to yank the door open.

Ahead of them was a long, cinder block hallway lit from above by harsh fluorescent lights. Doors lined both sides, which Victor tested as they went. Most were locked; one opened into a full but untouched wine cellar. Another, near the end, opened to reveal a zippered plastic medical barrier—the kind usually found in disease wards.

"Hold here," he whispered to Phaedra.

She nodded and put her back to him, swiveling to watch both ends of the hall. Victor stepped over the threshold and closed the door behind him.

Beyond the barrier was a makeshift infirmary, the space along the far wall divided into curtained alcoves. From within one recess came the sound of someone struggling against restraints.

Victor twitched the curtain aside to reveal Simon Brandt, strapped to a gurney.

Stark terror swept over Brandt's face. He seized in his bonds, no longer struggling to break free but instead scrambling to get as far away from Victor as possible. "Keane—"

"Easy, Brandt. I'll kick your ass later." Victor holstered his gun and moved to undo Brandt's restraints. "Where's Yates?"

From the next alcove came a hoarse, "Here."

Victor finished freeing one of Brandt's arms and ripped the curtain aside to reveal Adrian, strapped down just as Brandt had been.

"Oh my god." Adrian smiled: a slow, besotted grin. "You're beautiful."

"Thanks."

"I couldn't see it before," Adrian continued, slow and dreamy, as Victor unstrapped him. "I do now. I can see all of you."

Victor pried one of Adrian's eyes open. Fully dilated. "They drugged you."

"Both of us," Adrian said.

Victor sensed movement behind him, a moment too late to stop Brandt from grabbing his sidearm.

Whirling to face him, Victor put himself between the gun and Adrian. Brandt was trembling, the gun's barrel wavering in Victor's face, his pupils blown wide.

"I see you." Brandt had a strange buoyancy to him, as if he'd been laboring under a burden now gone. "What you really are. Like mold, cobwebs, all tangled up inside your head—"

"Brandt." Victor raised his hands to Brandt's line of sight, empty and open. "You're not making any sense."

Adrian said, "Something reached back."

Victor couldn't risk looking at him. "What?"

"Ranger school," Adrian explained. "You said something reached back. You brought it *home* with you."

"Shut *up*!" Brandt screamed. His trigger finger twitched.

Victor slapped the gun down, jamming the web of his thumb under the hammer. Brandt pulled the trigger, but the hammer struck flesh instead of the firing pin. Victor's free hand darted to his belt.

The knife went up under Brandt's jaw, into his brain.

Brandt struggled to speak for several seconds. There were tears in his eyes. Then Victor pulled the knife free, and Brandt fell.

Victor knelt just outside the widening pool of blood, pried his gun out of Brandt's still-twitching hand, and holstered it. Adrian was leaning over the edge of the gurney, watching him.

"Does it make you do it?" he wondered. "Or does it just make it easier?"

"Where's Brandt?" Phaedra asked, when Victor returned with Adrian in tow.

Adrian wobbled; Victor steadied him and said, "KIA."

Phaedra handed Adrian her canteen; he drank in huge, greedy gulps. She said, "Is he gonna be okay?"

"M'fine." Adrian handed the canteen back.

Victor said, "We're not leaving him here."

Phaedra didn't argue any further.

The door at the end of the hall opened into a narrow stairway. The stairway, in turn, led to a massive kitchen that had never been used. The interior of the mansion was like a museum: pristine, monochrome, and cavernously empty. Music and muffled voices echoed distantly from across the house.

Victor and Phaedra started for the door, but Adrian—more lucid than he'd been a few minutes ago—nudged them toward a winding staircase instead.

There was a landing on the second floor that overlooked the mansion's great room; assembled below were easily two dozen of Spalding's guests.

Victor recognized a few of them from television or the news—usually reports on some scandal or another. The rest were, no doubt, friends or colleagues of Spalding's. There was, judging by the guests' behavior, a plethora of drugs on offer.

The man himself held court near the tall picture windows overlooking the courtyard.

"Thank you!" Cameron Spalding shouted, just slightly too loud. "It's so awesome you could all make it here today!"

There was a manic charisma to him; he commanded attention, if only out of concern that he was moments away from biting someone's face off.

"You're all here because you're the best and brightest humanity has to offer," Spalding continued, in the tones of someone high on attention and also several different stimulants. "You've conquered everything this world can throw at you. Aren't you tired? Aren't you *bored*?"

A cheer went up among the guests.

"It's time for the next step! We're meant for something greater! We are *disrupting human evolution*, folks!" Spalding slammed the considerable remainder of his drink. "Let's move fast and break things! Fuck yeah!"

At the edge of the room huddled a small knot of four people. One of them was Skylar Cantrell.

The guard assigned to the hostages was bored and inattentive. As one of the party's guests passed, Skylar darted past the guard to grab her by the wrist.

"Please," she said, just barely audible over the music. "Please, you have to help—"

Disgusted, the woman wrenched her arm out of Skylar's grip.

A bellow of "Skylar!" resounded across the room.

Spalding strode toward the hostages, pausing only to offer a quick apology to the guest who'd been "disturbed."

"This is unacceptable behavior," he snarled, rounding on Skylar. "If you keep harassing my guests, I'll have all of you put downstairs. Do you want that?"

Skylar shook her head, frantic.

Crouched next to Victor behind the landing's banister, Adrian started to shake. Victor found Adrian's hand with his own and squeezed.

"We can't just go in shooting," Phaedra said. "We'll get the hostages killed."

Adrian nudged Victor, then pointed to a wall-mounted touch screen at the base of the stairs below them. "It's a smart home," he said. "Some of the controls don't need a password."

"Which controls?"

"Temperature. Music. Lights. When I was trying to escape, I planned on cutting the lights for cover."

"Already pretty dark in here," Victor noted. "Cutting the lights won't do much."

"Not necessarily," Phaedra said. "Ever open a fridge in the middle of the night?"

Victor moved into position near the edge of the room, watching as Phaedra did the same from the other side.

Adrian waited next to the smart home terminal; at Victor's signal, he nodded, and Victor closed his eyes.

Behind his eyelids, the lights flared, then went dark.

For a moment, the noise in the room rose into a cacophony of confused shouts and complaints, before the party's music ramped up to full, deafening intensity and drowned them out.

Victor opened his eyes to murky but navigable darkness. He'd preserved his night vision; everyone else in the room wasn't so lucky.

He and Phaedra swept in on the hostages' position. A guard loomed up out of the dark, blind and stumbling. Victor punched him in the temple and lowered him to the ground as quietly as possible.

The other guards were scattered throughout the room, just as confused as the guests, except for one that had guessed the source of the problem and begun to wade through the crowd toward the stairs.

Adrian's position.

Fuck it.

Victor drew his sidearm and fired. A bloody hole erupted at the base of the guard's skull, and he crumpled.

The music wasn't enough to cover the gunshot. Somebody screamed, and the ballroom dissolved into chaos as the guests stampeded for any exit they could find.

Phaedra reached the hostages moments before Victor did; she grabbed Skylar by the arm and firmly tugged her away.

"It's okay," she said, nearly shouting in Skylar's ear. "We're here to help you."

Blind and shaken, Skylar could only nod and let Phaedra tow her back to the landing.

Adrian wasn't there. The dead guard's holster was empty.

"Shit," Phaedra said. "Where's Yates?"

"Adrian?" Skylar's eyes swept the darkened room, although she was surely as blind as the rest of the guests. "He's okay?"

There was a burst of gunfire from across the room. The guards were starting to panic.

Phaedra said, "We can't stay here."

"Get the asset to the extraction point," Victor told her. "I'll find Adrian."

As he turned to leave, Phaedra's hand closed around Victor's forearm.

"Vic," she said. "Good luck."

Her hand slipped from his arm, and Victor caught it in his. He squeezed.

"Thank you," he said.

Phaedra nodded with a weary smile.

They parted ways. Phaedra dragged a protesting Skylar back toward the basement exit; Victor moved deeper into the house.

Someone had finally cut the music. Barely audible over the muffled chaos of the house were two voices arguing somewhere on the second floor. Victor followed them to the master bedroom.

It was the bedroom of a man who fantasized that he was above such banal indulgences as sleep: cavernous, spare, and white, with curtains drawn over what was surely a spectacular view. Adrian stood at its center, with the guard's stolen gun pointed at Cameron Spalding.

"Adrian," Spalding was saying, as if scolding a misbehaving pet. "I understand you have concerns about what we're doing here, but if you put the gun down and let me explain—"

"You ran our camper off the road." The gun rattled in Adrian's hand. "You threatened my friends."

"To achieve great things, we all need to make sacrifices—"

Adrian screamed, "I'm not your fucking *employee*!"

Victor moved into the room and immediately drew Spalding's attention.

"Listen," Spalding called to him, "this is all just a misunderstanding. Get the gun away from him, and whatever you're being paid, I'll double it."

Victor said, "Adrian."

The line of Adrian's shoulders went tense. The gun didn't waver.

Victor circled Adrian until he could see his face in profile. Tears marked long tracks down his face, his jaw clenched shut and trembling.

"Adrian," he repeated. "Time to go."

"He won't stop," Adrian replied. "He'll just keep taking whatever he wants and using it up and throwing it away. Anybody who cares can't stop him, and anybody who can stop him doesn't care." His finger twitched on the trigger.

"You don't want to do that," Victor said.

"You do it all the time."

Victor stepped closer and extended his arm along Adrian's, fingers gently wrapping around the gun.

"I'm different," he said. "You know that."

Adrian's only response was a wordless sob. His grip on the gun went slack. Slowly, carefully, Victor tilted it up and out of Adrian's hand.

Victor's other arm went around Adrian's shoulders, pulling him close as Adrian slumped against his chest.

Spalding's demeanor was unchanged, without a hint of gratitude or even relief. At no point had he ever believed he was truly in danger.

Victor pressed a gentle kiss to the top of Adrian's head. "Don't look."

He pointed the gun at Spalding's face and pulled the trigger.

About the Author

Kit Walker is a writer of horror, crime fiction, and dark sci-fi/fantasy. Born and raised in Canada, they've recently been shipped overseas to Newcastle upon Tyne in England. Their other work can be found online at www.inferiorwit.com.

ACKNOWLEDGMENTS

We would like to express our deepest gratitude to our staff editors, **Rachael Swanson** and **Kasey Kubica**, for their tireless efforts in reviewing submissions, proofreading, and overall helping us stay on track throughout the creation of this anthology. Their dedication to this project and attention to detail have been invaluable.

We also want to thank **Dany Rivera** for her beautiful story art, which has added a new layer of meaning to the stories we've collected. Her talent and creativity have truly enhanced this project. You can find her at danycomicsarts.com

We are also grateful to our volunteer submission readers, **Suhas Sridhar, rklep13**, and **Blake Pingleton**, who generously shared their time and expertise to help us sort through the many submissions we received. Their feedback and insights were crucial in helping us identify the most compelling stories for this anthology.

A special thank you to our anthology contributors: **Alex Fox, Brett Venter, Antony Paschos, Roger Landes, Charlotte H. Lee, Melrose Dowdy, Johnathon Heart, Mia Ram, Kevin Folliard, Rajiv Mote, January Bain, Liam Hogan, E.J Dawson, Kit Walker**

Finally, we want to extend our appreciation to all the authors who submitted to this anthology. We recognize the time, effort, and passion that goes into writing and submitting work for consideration, and we were grateful for the opportunity to read and appreciate each submission.

Thank you to everyone who has contributed to this project in any way. **We could not have done it without you!**

If you liked any of our stories, take a moment to stop by our Amazon page and leave a review!

COMING SOON!

Beyond the shadows, discover the untold tales of darkness and redemption—a haunting anthology that proves monsters are more than meet the eye.
Our next anthology, **More Than A Monster**, will begin preorders on August 1st, with the full release scheduled for September 8th.

Visit our website and join our mailing list to get updates on sales, author interviews, and art sneak peeks!